My Wife
&
Master Jake

By PEBBLES LACASSE

Wife and Master Jake © August 2019 Pebbles Lacasse

ISBN 978-0-9920069-6-9

Cover design © 2019 cover artist Pebbles Lacasse
First Edition August 2019
Photographs by Pebbles Lacasse
Cover Model David Mancini

Published by Pebbles Lacasse
www.pebbleslacasse.com

PROLOGUE

I will tell you my story, a story about how I slipped deeper and deeper into the painful pleasures of bondage, discipline, and submission. The most exciting thing about this story is that I couldn't be happier that I allowed myself to let go of my control, giving myself up to his will. He trained me to let go of my fear because it was a weakness that held me back. I discovered power in my submission.

CHAPTER ONE

Henry, my husband, introduces me to a co-worker before scurrying off to talk to someone else. Every year, I beg him not to leave me alone with strangers at his boss's annual work party, and he's good about sticking beside me, but not today. He leaves me standing in front of this well-dressed, gorgeous man whom I know nothing about other than that he works with the ass I married… the ass who is currently walking away, leaving me alone with a hot stranger. I will bring this up with him later.

This man, whose name I've learned to be Jake O'Keeffe, has piercing blue eyes. The way he stares at me with a steadfast expression has my insides quivering. I don't want him to think he intimidates me, even if he does. I lift my chin and return his gaze, also not blinking or looking away. This is beginning to feel rather uncomfortable. I'm becoming uncomfortably warm, and my cheeks are likely flushing a beautiful crimson

The man smiles, lifting only one corner of his mouth. He looks down at his martini glass and swooshes his olive in the liquid. He clears his throat and laughs. Without lifting his face, his eyes shift to meet mine. His expression shifts, becoming quite serious. His glare is even more intense. "Mrs. McDavid, you intrigue me. We should get to know one another better."

I intrigue him? How? We just met, and I haven't said a word to him. This guy has some balls hitting on his friend's wife… if he is hitting on me. I could be reading too much into this situation. It could be an innocent gesture of kindness because he does want to get to know me better like he said, but I'm not that naïve. "And why is that?"

"I'm sure we could benefit one another a great deal." His voice is smooth. He lifts his glass, pausing to lick his lips before sipping his drink. Why did my gaze fall to his mouth? I wonder if his kiss tastes as good as I imagine it does. For fuck sakes, I'm married!

"How do you figure?" Why am I still talking to this man? I should walk away before this goes too far. But he is so damn sexy. The thought of him and I fucking while our bodies glisten with sweat is diminishing my self-control. I shake my head and clear my throat.

"I would very much like to give you incredible pleasure if you'd care to grant me permission. This could be a win-win situation."

I am stunned by how brazen he is. There are people around who could have overheard his proposition. Although he's speaking in a hushed tone, a keen ear could be lurking. What would Henry say about his friend hitting on me directly after he introduced us? Would he punch this presumptuous, backstabbing *friend* right here in front of everyone?

Fine! I'll play along. "Explain to me how this would be a win-win situation. I mean, look at you, I'm sure you can have any woman you want. I'm married, and I get plenty of sex. So, no thank you. I don't need a good fucking from you or anyone, other than the man I married."

It's been a while since I've had another man in my bed. I don't cheat on my husband, but I'll admit that I have fantasized about it. Would it be wrong for me to admit that I am one hundred per cent flattered that this young, hot stud is telling me everything I need to hear to convince me to go ahead with an affair? Fuck, I can't do this with him or anyone. I'm committed to Henry. If I wasn't, we'd be on our way to finding a bed right now. I'm not a slut, not at all, but this man has my panties wet from wondering what his touch would feel like.

To be a good wife and stop this before it goes any further, I turn to walk away. He grabs my arm firmly enough that I can't free it without making a huge scene. He stands close to me, so close I can feel the heat from his chest radiating against my back.

"I'm not talking about fucking you, although that sounds very intriguing. Your pleasure is what I'm referring to."

I scoff, pulling my arm from his grasp, turning to look at him. "And then you'll fuck me, right? That would be your pleasure."

"Did you not understand? Giving you pleasure would be to my benefit. The more excited you become, the greater my reward," he explains, as he moves in even closer, pressing his chest against me.

I try to step back, but people are behind me. He's enjoying that I'm no longer able to hide my intimidation. I swallow hard and brush away the errant tress of hair from my cheek, tucking it behind my ear – the same ear I can feel his hot breath on.

"So, my pleasure is your reward? Only my pleasure? If you get to touch me and fuck me, wouldn't your pleasure would be found in that and not in my reaction? Do you think I'm stupid? I'm not some naïve bimbo who's swayed by the bullshit you're spewing. Why don't you try your moves on a younger, naïve floozy? I'm taken. You must remember my husband, Henry, the man who introduced us?"

I turn to walk away, and again he grabs my arm. This time, he pushes his firm chest against my back. The most seductive voice I've ever heard whispers in my ear. "Oh, trust me, the young floozies have nothing on you. They bore me. You intrigue me. Meet me Monday before noon at Bethel's Café on Jerekson Avenue. What's the worst that can happen in a public cafe? I doubt you'd permit me to fuck you in front of the other patrons."

When he releases my arm, I walk away without looking back. I wonder if he's watching me. My pussy is drenched. My labia are slipping against each other as I make my way toward the unsuspecting Henry. Jake O'Keefe has my body betraying me, but I made a commitment to my husband… one that I plan to keep.

There's no way I will meet that cocky, young buck at a café, public or not. To be honest, he could sway my morals with his good looks and charming demeanour. I've never considered cheating on Henry. What is it about this man that has me questioning everything I believe in? I roll my eyes as I gulp my champagne, hoping to drown my desire for him.

"There you are." I approach Henry and the stunning woman he's conversing with. They both turn to look at me.

He slides his arm around my waist. "Jenna, I'd like you to meet my beautiful wife, Beth." The gorgeous redhead puts her hand out to greet me. She smiles, and her straight, white teeth seem to gleam as they reflect the flickering flames from the Tiki torch behind me.

I'm not jealous of this beauty before me. I know my husband is in love with me and would never stray. At the very least, I can't see his busy schedule allowing the time for an affair. Although, I wouldn't blame my husband if he had dreams of sleeping with this woman. She radiates self-confidence, with a seductive quality about her that can't be taught. The way she carries herself and speaks with a soft voice has me drawn to her. I can imagine how irresistible she is to men. If she were to turn on the charm, my husband would crumble under her spell. Any red-blooded man would.

"It's wonderful to meet you. Henry is always bragging about you. When he talks about you, he paints the picture of a goddess with a mind much sharper than his own. He wasn't wrong, you are astonishingly attractive."

"Thank you, Jenna. It's certainly nice to meet you. My husband has mentioned how valuable you are at your job, but he failed to mention how astonishingly beautiful you are," I say as I study Henry with a curiosity that makes him laugh nervously.

"That's because nobody can hold a candle to your beauty, my love. But I'm sure I must have mentioned it once or twice."

"No, I don't think so. I'm sure I would remember you telling me about the buxom beauty that works alongside you."

Jenna giggles. "Why would he? I don't work with Henry on a regular basis. I work with Richard, Stacey, Jake, and Kevin most of the time."

"Oh, I must have misunderstood. When I was walking up, it seemed like you two knew each other well." I'm trying not to sound jealous or like I'm accusing them of something deeper than a simple friendship.

10

"Beth, trust me, he would never stray from your bed. He's one of the good ones," she says, winking at me before casting a glance at Henry that seems to have meaning behind it.

As she walks away, Henry pulls me in close to him. Our faces are almost touching. "Beth, you are my world. There's no room in that world for another woman. I don't have the time, nor the energy."

"She's dangerous. You'd be wise to keep your distance." Henry rolls his eyes before kissing my forehead. "Are you ready to get out of here?"

"Not yet, Honey. William hasn't made his dreaded yearly speech. We can go right after that."

My dear friend, Amy, has pulled her husband, Lou, away from his boring conversation with William. I've stood patiently by Henry's side many times while William told yet another tedious golf story that neither I nor Henry cared anything about. Neither of us has ever held a club. Even though I couldn't hear the conversation, I know it was about golf. It's always about golf.

William has never married and doesn't seem at all interested in finding someone special to share the rest of his life. I've known him for fifteen years and have yet to see a woman or man on his arm. Perhaps he enjoys having the bed to himself and full control of the television. I can see the benefits of being single, but on the flip side of that coin, I can also imagine how lonely life would be. Still, some people are happiest flying through life solo.

Amy smiles at me before rolling her eyes. We pretend to kiss each other's cheeks as we pucker our lips but never touch. Women are careful not to smear our lipstick. She whispers, "That conversation was one-sided and lasted forever. How long were we standing there? I could sense my hair turning grey."

I laugh. "So, anything new and exciting with you? I haven't talked to you in a while."

She shrugs. "Other than the overdramatic crisis of Richie losing his first tooth? No, nothing new. You?"

I smile, picturing her holding him down, yanking out his loose tooth while he throws an Oscar-worthy tantrum. I love him, and he's an adorable kid, but for a seven-year-old, he's way too whiny. The boy cries too often and over the most non-crucial things. If he considers life to be too hard while he's a kid, he's in for a rude awakening when he gets older.

Amy is a stay-at-home mom who works twenty-four hours a day, every day with no vacation time or sick days. I'd rather go to work than stay home raising whiny, sticky, miniature devils who would rely on me for every single thing in their hyperactive young lives.

They can be so sweet and loving, but I can't let that draw me in. They're a petri dish for every contractible disease known to humans. I always assumed the life of a housewife and mother would be mundane. It's anything but. Amy is always busy tending to others, doing nothing for herself. Everything she does is to benefit the house and family. No, thank you! It's not for me. I own a cat, and that's enough mothering to quiet my ticking biological clock.

"Nothing too exciting. I'm still working on the book. I can't seem to find the right ending. My editor is getting annoyed with me. She's pushing me to get it done. The more she pesters me, the harder it is for me to focus."

Amy interrupts, "The book about the mystery man in the cloak? That will be a bestseller. I know it."

"Yeah, that's the one. I hope you're right." The guys are not listening to us. I'm not sure what they're talking about, but whatever it is, both of them have furrowed brows and unusually serious expressions. They must be talking business.

I lower my voice to ensure nobody can hear me. "Something struck me as odd. There's a guy here who asked me to meet him at a café on Monday. Can you believe that? Henry introduced me to him and suddenly left us to go talk to someone else. He's very brazen."

"Really? Is he hot? Who is it? Point him out; I need something to fantasize about later." Her eyes scan the crowd as if she knows who she's searching for.

"I can't see him."

"Well, what's his name? I might know him."

"I only caught his first name, Jake."

"No shit? Yeah, I met him. He's dreamy! There's just something in his demeanour that screams hot, dirty, disgustingly delicious sex. I'd bet my house he's a wild man in the sack."

I laugh. "Uh, huh! So, you have met him."

"Yeah, I have."

"You wouldn't, would you?"

She shrugs her shoulders and exhales a long sigh. "I would like to have the opportunity. If someone like that asked me to meet him at a café, I'd go in a heartbeat. I wouldn't go to his place for sex, of course. Lou is enough for me. Besides, I don't have the time or stamina to keep up with that young sexual prodigy... not that I haven't masturbated to the notion of his sweaty body on mine."

I take a moment to picture her scenario but with me under his body, not her. A cold, nervous twinge in my belly snaps me back to reality.

"I'm married and truly happy, so it's not like I'd take it outside of that cafe. Starting something with Jake would only cause problems in Henry's career, and our marriage, if we were ever caught. Do you think I should go?"

"Do I think you should go?" she pauses, pondering the idea as she sips her nearly empty glass of champagne. "Hell yeah, I do! Go have lunch with the guy. Hear him out. See what he wants. Think of it as taking a break from your writing. Maybe the time away will help you find your ending. Don't have sex with him... or do! Years ago, I remember you telling me that Henry suggested you two bring a third person into the bedroom. He didn't specify whether that person had to be a male or a female, right?" I nod, so she continues. "Maybe hot-guy-Jake can be that third. Give me every dirty detail if you do; just don't fall in love with him."

"I couldn't anyway. Henry is the love of my life."

William interrupts us by clearing his throat over the loudspeaker. He's ready to start his speech. As a waiter passes by,

Amy and I both swap our empty champagne glasses for full ones. When I thank him, my eyes shift past him to a face looking at me through the crowd of bodies.

Jake's eyes don't leave mine as he lifts his glass to toast me. He nods, only once. My tummy flutters. What is it about that man that has me contemplating a secret meeting? I turn my gaze toward William, trying not to appear taken in by Jake's seductive leer. Why is my body heating, as if his eyes are touching me where I would prefer his big fingers or his hot tongue? *Stop it, Beth!*

When I glance his way to see if he's still looking at me, I see Jenna approaching him. She's smiling and talking to him. The way her hand lightly touches his shoulder and the facial expressions she uses are meant to entice. He leans toward her and says something that she doesn't seem to like, judging by the shift in her demeanour.

She empties her glass and shakes her head at him. She says something before walking away. He turns his face to me, but I look back at William, hoping the man didn't see me watching his interaction with the lovely Jenna.

As usual, William's speech drags on. He doesn't seem to notice that he's losing our attention. He ends the sermon with a toast to the crowd before handing off the microphone to the singer. The band plays as the people scatter in search of good conversation, or an unnoticed escape from the party.

Henry asks, "Do you want to go?"

"Sure. Are you finished here?"

I kiss Lou's cheek, marking him with a red stamp of lips, and air-kiss Amy. She whispers, "Go, have lunch with the hottie. Have a good time but not too good, and call me as soon as you get home."

"I don't know," I reply, scrunching up my face.

"Please, let me live vicariously through you." The desperate expression on her face is one I've seen many times. She wasn't a party girl, so she doesn't have many stories of her own to reflect on.

"I'll consider it."

Amy is my best friend. We've been like two peas in a pod since high school. I was her maid of honour at her wedding, and she was mine. She insisted I be in the delivery room, standing right next to her husband when she birthed all three of her children. I will admit, it was disturbing on so many levels but also miraculously beautiful to see the instant love she had for each one of those slimy, screaming micro-humans.

I can tell Amy anything and trust that, no matter how intriguing the secret, she'll take it to her grave. She has my complete confidence. We know things about each other that we can never tell our husbands. Our life choices differ from one another, and yet, nothing has changed between us.

We made a pact in college that once a month, we would dress up and go out to a bar to blow off steam. We'd get drunk and dance with men we don't know. So far, we haven't broken that promise to one another, except for when she was pregnant. For nine months, she was my designated driver because she drank nothing stronger than apple juice.

We still danced, but when the slow songs came on, we would dance together. Few men will choose a pregnant woman to dance with. The odds of taking her home for a hot fuck are very slim. Flirting with a stranger on a dance floor while my pregnant friend sat alone at a table was ridiculous and just plain selfish.

CHAPTER TWO

I ask Henry, "What do you think of Jake?"

He takes his sights off the road ahead and looks at me with a very curious expression. "Jake? How do you mean?"

"Well, is he a nice guy, a good worker, intelligent? Do you like him, or is he an asshole?"

Henry smiles with a quick chuckle. "Is he an asshole? No, he's a super nice guy. Too nice, sometimes. He's patient and always ready to help if you ask for it. He's very intelligent, and we're lucky to have him on our team. So, yes, I like him. Why do you ask?"

"No real reason." I look out the window and watch the streetlights as our car passes beneath them. I can't hide this from Henry. "He made a pass at me. I think."

Henry looks at me and asks, "You think?"

I sigh. "No, I'm positive he did. He asked me to meet him for lunch on Monday. To me, that sounds like he has greater intentions than just a friendly lunch date. He's supposed to be your friend, but he's hitting on your wife. To me, that doesn't sound like a super nice guy."

Without looking at me, he replies, "Maybe you should go."

My eyes are drawn back to Henry. I try to read his facial expression, but he's blank-faced. "Are you serious? You want me to go on a lunch date with one of your coworkers? A guy who hit on your wife. Really? And, what if he wants to further our *friendly* relationship? Should I go along with that too?"

He shrugs and then says, "Maybe you should go and find out what he's proposing. You'll be in a restaurant, so it's not like he can attack you, even if that were on his agenda. I highly doubt he'd ever attack anyone who didn't wish to be."

That didn't sound right. "Who would wish to be attacked? What, is he a hired rapist or something?"

He shakes his head. "No, not a rapist exactly. He's into rough sex. At least, that's what I've been told."

"Rough sex? And you want me, your wife, to meet this guy for a lunch date? What if he jumps me in the parking lot?"

Henry laughs as if he just heard an inside joke that I'm not privy to. "No, baby, he won't. He is a dominant."

"A dominant?" I ask, hoping he'll elaborate.

"Yeah, he likes to be in complete control when behind closed doors or in his dungeon. I'm not sure if that's what he calls it. Dungeon makes me think it's dirty and cold." Is he serious? He seems to know an awful lot about this guy's sexual preferences. Exactly what do they do all day at work? Talk about their conquests?

Curiously, I ask, "How do you know all of this?"

He shrugs again, telling me, "Sometimes, when things are slow, some of us guys sit around and talk. After a few beers and several shots of whiskey, the guys tend to get a little loose with their information. Jake doesn't usually contribute to much of the boastful conversations. There was this one time when we were alone that I asked him if he was gay. I told him that I didn't care if he was and that I'd keep it to myself if he confided in me, but he denied it outright. He explained that he doesn't bring any ladies to functions because they aren't his love interests -- they're playmates only. So, I asked him to elaborate. That's when he told me about the way he likes to *play*."

"No shit?" Now I'm interested in finding out more about this guy. Picturing him wearing leather clothes with a stone-cold expression, ready to take me at his will is making my body heat up in a very personal way. "So, tell me, what is he into, exactly?"

Henry looks at me and smiles. "Wow! Look at you, suddenly so interested. What? Are you getting all hot and bothered about this guy?"

"No, I just want to know more about it," I reply, feeling somewhat embarrassed about my genuine interest in the man's sexual exploits.

"Do you?" he asks.

"Yeah, kind of. I mean, does he hurt women? Like, are they whipped and bruised?"

"I asked him the same thing. Jake said it isn't as if he's trying to injure the women. They want him to abuse them. He claims to never leave marks in visible areas that won't dissipate within an hour or so. He explained that he likes to render the women immobile. He inflicts pain to awaken their senses before sexually pleasuring them but sometimes continuing the pain during the pleasure if the women are into that." He's explaining it as casually as if he were talking about how Jake ties his running shoes.

"So, what does he get out of it?"

"He said he fucks them very hard, makes them suck him off, or he jerks off on them. He does whatever he feels like doing at the time."

"He fucks them hard, huh?" I take a deep breath, picturing him with a woman bent over in front of him while he hammers his pelvis against her ass cheeks, repeatedly burying his hard cock viciously into her. Oh yes, that image is making my pussy wet.

"You're picturing it, aren't you?" he asks, smiling like a cat that just caught a bird. I look at him and giggle, nodding my head. "Go to lunch with him, Beth. I'd like to know what his intentions are."

"Are you serious? You want me to go on a date alone with a very handsome, self-proclaimed, sexually aggressive man?"

He nods, "Yes, Ma'am. I do."

"Why? What's in it for you?"

He shrugs. "I don't know. Let's just say I'm interested in what he thinks of my wife."

"And if he thinks I'm his type and wants to take me to his sex room? Then what?" I ask, teasingly. "I'm going to call it a sex room. I don't like the term dungeon. You're right; it sounds dirty and cold."

"I guess we'll have to cross that bridge if we come to it." He's looking at me with a crooked grin that I know all too well. He's feeling a bit mischievous.

"Are you getting all hot and bothered from the thoughts of your co-worker hurting and fucking your wife?"

"Not hurting, no. Just knowing that another man wants my wife is very arousing. I have something he wants, and that is the ultimate aphrodisiac. So, yeah, my cock is swelling in my pants." He looks at me and then back through the windshield before pulling onto a dark road.

There are no lights in this section of town and no houses for quite a distance. Henry pulls the car off to the side, shuts the engine off, and gets out. I watch as he walks around the car. He opens my door while I undo my seatbelt. He takes my hand to help me out of the car. I nearly fall because I wasn't expecting him to pull me so forcefully. He shuts the door before pushing me against the front quarter panel.

His lips press to mine, harsher than what I'm used to. His tongue invades my mouth while his warm hands lift my dress. I wrap my hands around his biceps just as his hand slips into my panties. He knows my body so well that his middle finger lands on my clitoris without even having to feel for it.

I close my eyes and pretend that Jake is the one feeling me up and not my husband. My body immediately reacts. My clit stiffens under his touch, and I moan when his lips leave mine. Henry yanks down my panties as he drops to his knees in front of me. His hands grasp my ass, pulling my hips forward. His ferocious tongue juts between my labia, viciously flicking at my swollen clitoris. The sharpness of his teeth ignites a firebolt of pleasurable pain the instant he nips at my clit. He's never done this before, but I like it… a lot. His lips press against me, sucking firmly, while his tongue continues to ravish my swelling, imprisoned button. Holy hell, this feels amazing!

Henry momentarily frees my clit and whispers, "Pretend I'm Jake." He doesn't know it, but I already have been. In the darkness, the only obvious difference between the men is the short, dark hair my husband dons, as opposed to Jake's long, blond locks.

In only a few seconds, I'm climaxing. My clit is swelling huge between his teeth. All the nerves are flaring up with heated tingles, slowly radiating through me until my whole body seizes and jerks against his mouth. My knees weaken as my body seems to melt.

He stands up, spinning me around while pushing me against the car. He's being rougher with me than usual, and I like it. I nearly trip because my panties are at my ankles. I imagine it's Jake who's forcing me to bend over the front fender and pulling my dress up, flipping it onto my back. He pushes his hand on the centre of my back, holding me down as he slides his rock-hard cock deep inside my slick pussy in one quick, smooth thrust.

The first hard thrust takes my breath from me. My thighs are forced against the side of the car each time he abruptly buries his thick prick. He slides his fingers through my hair, clutching a fistful and pulling until my back is arched. My breasts are still pressed against the hood. He's never done this before. He has always been very gentle with me. Even when he fucks me hard and fast, there's a tenderness about him. Not right now, though. Strangely enough, I really like this new side to Henry.

My pussy is pulsing around his shaft. Moans flow from within me with every breath. I'm loud enough that my pleasure is likely heard from across the field when I yell. "Yes, fuck me! Oh, god, I'm coming!"

His hips bash against my ass, ramming so hard that the force has me breathless. I don't know if it's because we're outside where anyone might see us, the way he's being so aggressive, or that he told me to imagine Jake as the man who's violating me, but I'm more turned on right now than I have been in a long time. His grunts are getting louder and coming from deeper within his chest. Soon, he's going to have his own release.

He murmurs, "Oh, fuck!" He shoves his pelvis against me, holding every inch of his cock as deep as he can. His prick inflates. I can feel it throbbing as he spills his seed. His lungs slowly force out a long breath, emptying. He takes in several deep breaths, trying to calm his pounding heart. His deflating prick slips from my twitching pussy.

As I lift my chest off the hood, Henry slowly turns me to face him. His hands cup the sides of my face. "Are you okay, Sweetie? Did I hurt you?"

I smile to assure him. "I am better than okay. Did all the talk about your sexually aggressive friend have anything to do with that?"

He kisses my lips before answering me. "I don't know. I imagined myself as being him, taking you like he would. Perhaps it's the thought of another man wanting my wife so desperately that he's willing to ask her out on a date, even knowing she's married to his friend. Maybe it's both reasons. Whenever I catch a guy checking you out, I get a bit excited… in a good way. Maybe it's an ego thing for me. I have what they want."

"And you couldn't wait until we got home?" I tease, poking my finger into his strong abdomen.

"Hell no! Besides, you look way too sexy in that dress to just let you toss it in the hamper. I had to watch you cum while wearing it." Henry smiles at me.

My lips press to his and hold while we each take a long breath. He opens my door for me, as he always does. I get back in the car. I feel sexy and dirty, like a slut who was used for his satisfaction. It's exciting, not degrading. He gets in on his side and starts driving. Not another word is spoken between us for the rest of the drive home. I think we are both lost in our own thoughts about Jake.

Would I like to fuck him? In a world where I wasn't married, absolutely! Would I let him tie me up and beat me? I don't think so, but if my mood was just right, I might work up the courage.

By the time I've taken off my make-up and had a quick shower, Henry is sound asleep. I was hoping we could make love, but it looks like that isn't going to happen.

I wonder if a picture of Jake is on the company website. My tablet is still on my nightstand, so I turn it on and wait impatiently for it to bring up the search engine. Their website has pictures of its employees, so I might get lucky. I begin flipping through page after page. When his face suddenly fills the screen and those blue eyes seem to be staring deep into mine, I find myself biting my bottom lip.

He is a devilishly handsome man with a body that could make any woman damp. His long, blond hair was messy tonight, but in this photo, it's tucked neatly into a looped ponytail. I don't normally like long hair on men, but it suits him better than a shortcut would. He sports a stubbled beard that looks to be silkier than most facial hair. Overall, his skin is nearly flawless. His lips are what draw my attention, even more than his seductive, sky-blue eyes. They are puffy, like soft, pink pillows. For a moment, I imagine how they would feel pressed against my nipple.

To clear him out of my thoughts, I put my earbuds in and turn up the music. I play a few games of solitaire before shutting my eyes for the night. The distractions didn't make a difference. I dreamed about Jake on top of me, fucking me more aggressively than my husband did last night on that dark road. His face was right in front of me, his champagne-scented breath caressing my lips while his naked, sweaty body slammed against mine. I woke feeling more tired than when I went to sleep. It's going to be a long day.

CHAPTER THREE

It's a lazy Sunday morning, and I'm just fine with that. Henry was up early and off to his parents' house to help them with some yard work. I savour this moment of solitude. After the chaotic business of the week, I need this time alone to rebalance my energies and refocus my attempts at finishing this book. Perhaps this will be the morning my writer's brain will do its job and come up with a suitable ending to wow the reader. This manuscript has been picking away at my self-esteem. Some manuscripts have a way of making you doubt your ability as a professional author. Sometimes, even now, I feel like a fraud.

Thoughts of last night's sex scene on the hood of the car pulls my mood in the wrong direction. Murder, mystery, and drama should be on my mind, not rough sexual romance. I shake my head and push the thought from my mind, at least for now. I take the time to drink my coffee in silence, enjoy a bran muffin, and watch the cardinals eat seed from the birdfeeder I refilled yesterday. Half the seed has spilt onto the ground, where the squirrels often hang out to feast on the easy meal.

Maybe if I escape from anything that might influence my mood to either sex or anger, the perfect story ending will pop into my head. I fill the bathtub with water as hot as I can stand it and ease my body in. My lips lift at the corners in a gentle smile. There's just something heavenly about soaking in hot water. I take in a deep breath of the lilac-scented steam, then slip under the water. This is heavenly. Yes, this is perfect!

After my bath, I slip on a pair of shorts and a t-shirt, comb my shoulder-length hair into its preferred style, and smooth a layer of moisturizer onto my face. I opt to abstain from applying any make-up today.

My cell phone rings, jolting me from the silent thoughts in my mind. The caller ID shows it's one of my parents. It rings twice more in my hand while I debate whether or not I want to answer. I wanted a quiet morning, and I know that if I click the accept button, all solitude will all end.

"Hello," I say into the receiver.

"Oh, h,i baby. I was just about to hang up. I thought you were out somewhere and couldn't pick up," my mom explains.

"You called my cell phone, and I always take it with me when I leave the house. Besides, if I don't answer, you can leave me a message. I will always call you back when I can."

"It's not all that important. Leaving a message is more for emergencies only."

"No, Mom, you can leave a message. It's okay to do that. I prefer that you do. So, why did you call?" Resigned to the fact that I have screwed my day up, I shake my head and pour the rest of the coffee from the pot into my mug.

She whispers something to someone I assume to be my father. "Your dad and I were wondering if you were coming over today."

I debate before deciding to lie. "Yes, I was thinking of it."

"Oh, goodie!" she exclaims, proceeding to tell my father of my impending visit.

"What's up, Mom?"

"You always assume I have a hidden agenda. I was just hoping you were coming over."

"I wasn't born yesterday. There's something you're not telling me."

"Fine! Yes, there is something. We picked up some paper for your printer."

"Okay," I say, hoping she'll elaborate further. She hasn't bought paper for me since high school.

"Do I have to spell it out for you?"

I'm nodding my head as though she were standing in front of me. "Yes, I suppose you do."

"I would like you to print out your latest book for me to read. I'm so excited to read it."

"Mom, it's not finished yet."

"I know. You already told me that, but I can't wait. Can you just print out what you have?"

I laugh. "No, it's not finished. When it's done, I will print it off for you, just like all the other books. And you didn't have to buy me paper, Mom."

"I know I don't have to, but I want to replace what you use for my copy. So, what time are you coming over?"

I glance up at the clock. "Um, half an hour?"

"That sounds great. We'll see you then."

I throw in a load of laundry and wash up the breakfast dishes before I leave the house. The traffic around here is minimal on a Sunday, but to be on the safe side, I take all the backroads.

My parents still live in the house where I grew up. They've kept my bedroom how I left it when I went off to college. They say it's because they don't like change, but they've reminded me many times that it's here, should I ever need it. Every once in a while, I lie on the bed and glance around to reminisce. I thought things were so difficult back then. My problems seemed so tragic and earth-shattering when I was a teenager. If I would have known how hard it would be as an adult, handling adult issues and being self-supportive, I would have enjoyed those carefree younger years a lot more.

Mom is energetic as always, never sitting still for more than five minutes at a time. Dad, as usual, is lazily lounging in his recliner with a cup of tea and a newspaper. He's eager to offer his help with any of my home repairs because he knows Henry isn't all that handy at fixing things.

My dad is one of those Mr. Fix-it people. He can repair just about anything, and he loves to do it. Since he retired, he's been itching to get into a major project. My mother won't let him make any alterations to their house, so he's always offering his services to Henry and me. I think he wants to escape my mother for a few hours every day and looks to me to be the excuse.

Our visit lasts well over an hour before I take my leave. I make my way to the grocery store to stock up for the week. Since Henry is most likely still at his parents' house, I stop there after shopping, hoping to help if I can. It turns out that Henry has already left, so I enjoy a quick cup of tea with his Mom and Dad before heading home with my melted frozen yoghurt.

Henry is in the shower when I arrive home. I put the groceries away and toss the clothes from the washer to the dryer. We spend the rest of the day cleaning and enjoying reruns on television, with no further discussion about the proposition I received last night. When day turns to night quicker than we were hoping, we collapse into bed. It's been a busy day. He falls asleep while I lie beside him, thinking about the hot dream I had last night with Jake playing the starring role of the super-stud.

I recall every breath he took, every move of his strong, glistening body and the way his eyes seduced me. I, too, drift off. Once again, I dream of Jake. This time, Henry is watching Jake fuck me. It's exciting, but the anxiety of not coming up with a powerful ending to the manuscript turns a happy dream to one filled with panic, waking me in a cold sweat. The sun is peeking through the gap in the blinds, illuminating the room. I set my alarm to blare ten minutes from now, so I might as well just get up and start the day.

CHAPTER FOUR

Henry wakes not long after I do. I hand him a coffee before he steps into the shower. He takes several sips and sets it on the counter. He showers while I toast a bagel for him. I bring it to him as he's putting on his tie. I've always loved watching him dress in his well-tailored suits. His eyes meet mine through the mirror, and he smiles.

"What's up, Baby?"

I sit on the bed and shrug. "I'm admiring my sexy husband."

"Oh, yeah? So, you like what you see?" He turns to face me, swaying his hips back and forth as he finishes with his tie.

"Need I say that I do?" I reply with a rhetorical question.

Henry crawls up my body until I'm leaning back, his face looking down at mine. He's straddling my thighs and kissing my neck. "Are you going to meet Jake for lunch?"

His question catches me off-guard. "I – um – I don't know. Do you think I should? I don't think I should."

He sits up, looking disappointed. "Give me one good reason why not."

"Well, for starters, I'm married to an ass, but he means well," I reply, giggling.

He chuckles, "Yes, Baby, I'm an ass, but I'm giving you the okay to go. It'll be fun to play his game. Don't you want to go?"

I sit up, pushing him off me. "You want me to play his game? Really? So, what's next? Do you want me to fuck him?"

Henry is now standing and taking a bite of his bagel. He chews slowly while looking me up and down. I don't know why he wears a seductive expression. I'm only wearing an oversized t-shirt for a nightgown. My hair is sticking up where it shouldn't, and I have purple bags under my eyes. I'm not exactly exuding the sexy goddess vibe at the moment.

He swallows his bite before explaining. "Babe, I had a dream last night where you and Jake were..." He pauses while he sips his coffee. "Let me just say that he had you in a bondage chair, and he was fucking you extremely hard. You kept coming and coming. You were having a great time with him. Don't you think that it could be fun to try something, or someone, different?"

I can't believe what I'm hearing. My arms fold across my chest, subconsciously hiding my body from Jake's eyes, even though it was Henry's dream and not mine. Although, I do carry a bit of guilt about all the fantasies and dreams I've had of him. "You want me to fuck him because you had a dream?"

He stands in front of me and takes my hands in his. He kisses them tenderly while looking into my eyes. "Yeah, maybe I do. Not because I had a dream. I've been thinking we should try something new and exciting. This might be what we need to spice up our sex life."

"Are you testing my loyalty right now? Is that what this is? I don't appreciate it at all," I reply, pulling my hands from his.

He rubs the top of his head. "Listen, for a long time now, I have had a fantasy about you and another man getting it on, while I look on. I'm not testing your loyalty. I know you love me and will always come home to me. It's just something I would like you to do."

"Just so we're clear," I pause, thinking of how best to word my thoughts. "You're saying that I should go to lunch with Jake and then go to his house for sex if he asks me to. While I'm there, you want him inside my pussy and my mouth? He might want to stick his hard, throbbing cock into my ass. Is that okay with you, too?"

"Yes," he replies without hesitation.

Mind blown! Seriously? "And if he wants to tie me up and beat me before pleasuring me, is that acceptable?"

Henry is fighting back a smile. "If you'd be interested in experiencing something different than what I have been giving you, yes, I'll be fine with it. It's your choice, of course. Afterwards, if you go through with it, I'd like you to come home and tell me all about it. I want to know how many times he makes you cum, what positions he puts you in, if he bound you, beat you, or made passionate love to you."

"And this will make you horny?" I want to know. I'm ashamed to admit that I'm getting excited about the idea of being skin to hot skin with a young, self-assured man.

Henry takes my hand and places it on his crotch. His prick is thick and hard. "What do you think?"

"Okay, I'll meet him for lunch and see where it goes. Don't you dare hold it against me later when you're jealous that another man fucked me and made me cum. What if he's better than you are? Did you consider that?" I question him with sarcasm in my tone.

"Then I will want you to enjoy him more than once," Henry whispers, while his hand urges mine to rub his cock through his dress pants.

I slink down to my knees, while he undoes his zipper, freeing his stiff prick. With my lips freshly licked, I open wide, taking all of him in one swift head bob. I'm an expert at taking him down my throat. He's moaning and sucking in his breaths between his clenched teeth. I take his hands and place them on my head, pulling them to push my head so he can fuck my face at his will. He clutches wads of my messy hair and humps forward, forcing his dick down my throat. His belly bounces off my nose with each gentle thrust. It isn't more than a minute before he pulls out of my mouth. He grips my hair in one fist and cums on my face while pounding his twitching cock with the other.

Henry takes my hand, helping me to my feet. He wipes my face with a few tissues. I say, "You really are excited about me fucking someone else."

He snickers. "Yeah, Baby, I am but not just any guy. I've been checking out Jake for some time now, and I think he's a good guy. He claims to never let his heart get involved in his sexual liaisons. It's all about the physical and mental pleasure for him. He's attractive, smart, humble, respectful, and best of all, secretive. He'll be perfect."

"So, give me a solid yes or no. If he asks me to go back to his place today, for whatever sexual act he has in mind, no matter what it is, you want me to go, take my clothes off, and let him touch me, kiss me, lick me, fuck me, and even hit me?" I question one final time.

"Absolutely, yes, but only if you want to. The hitting part is completely up to you, of course. If you permit him to spank you or perform whatever other sensual torture he has in mind, then yes, I'm one hundred per cent for it. Afterwards, come home and tell me every single little detail. I want to know everything. Just keep in mind that I will fuck you afterwards, so don't let him tire you out too much. Save a little sugar for me." Henry is smiling at me as if he's the one about to have sex with a near-stranger – a dangerously sexy and intimidating stranger.

"You'd better eat your bagel. Time's ticking, and you will be late," I tell him as I walk away, leaving him to wonder if I'll go through with it. I don't even know if I will. I suppose it'll stay in question until the situation arises. If it arises. Jake might not even be interested in taking me home with him. He may only want to get to know me in a platonic manner because I'm Henry's wife. Perhaps he's read my books and wants to discuss them with me. There are countless reasons for his invitation to lunch.

* * *

I stand in front of the mirror, shaking from the nervous energy rippling through my body. I've decided to wear a lightweight, white summer dress. My bra and panties are flesh-toned so they won't be visible through the dress. I apply my make-up sparingly, so I don't look like I'm trying too hard to be younger than I am. I'm a little older than Jake, but he already knows that, so there's no point in pretending.

When I arrive, I see him already seated in a booth that sits in the far corner of the restaurant. There aren't many people dining this late in the morning. The lunch hour hasn't yet arrived which will likely fill this quaint little diner. He doesn't need to sit at that table unless he doesn't want anyone to hear our conversation. I take a slow, deep breath to calm the acrobats tumbling in my tummy.

The waitress asked me a question, but I didn't hear what she said. I'm too lost in my own anxious thoughts, as my eyes lock on the handsome face of a mere stranger who has the potential to be my new sexual partner. This is someone I might be naked with in another hour. Do I run away like a coward or bravely stay to see what happens next? Should I refuse to leave with him, or throw caution to the wind and follow him to his place? Should I experience something new, as Henry suggested? If I go, do we take his car, or should I drive myself? Dammit! There are so many questions!

I'm going to hell for this!

I shake my head at the waitress and then point to Jake. My knees feel weak, but I do my best to calm myself. Appearing relaxed and in control might give me the upper hand. I need him to believe I am strong and not a fearful woman. He is only one man.

A true gentleman, he stands as I approach and puts out his hand to greet me as if this meeting is a business luncheon. I grasp it, and he leans in to press a tender kiss to my cheek. Okay, not so business-like, after all.

Using that same seductive tone from my dreams, he whispers, "You're beautiful."

My immediate nervous response is to say something stupid. "Thank you. You look very handsome, but how could you not? I mean, shit, look at you! Shit! Sorry, that was inappropriate."

He snickers. "Thank you, Beth. May I call you Beth?"

I nod, knowing my embarrassment is rushing into my cheeks. I'm sure they're a lovely shade of red. *Way to remain cool, Beth!* He waits until I am seated before sitting back down. It's rather old-fashioned but respectful of him. Not enough men behave as gentlemen these days.

"I'm glad you came. I wasn't sure you would." His voice is deep but not husky. It's smooth and sedating.

"Well, I'm here."

He nods with a crooked grin and a glint of carnal lust in his eyes. Before he speaks, I cut him off. "Why am I here?"

Jake folds his hands on the table in front of his chest. "First, what would you like to drink?"

"Coffee, I suppose," I reply, startling when I see movement out of the corner of my eye. The waitress is standing right beside me, but I didn't see her there. He must see how nervous I am. I'm a wreck, but I didn't want him to know that. There's no denying that pipe dream failed the moment I first opened my mouth.

She walks away as he watches my face. "You're extremely attractive, Beth. You intrigue me. Having lunch with you is a great way to see if my initial impression of you is correct. I'm rarely wrong."

"I intrigue you?"

Without pause, he replies, "Yes, you do."

"Okay, so what do your instincts tell you about me?" I'm putting him on the spot to see if he's the type of person to sweat when pressured, or if he's always cool and composed.

"My instincts?"

My gaze locks onto his deliciously inviting lips while he sits quietly, making me wonder why he isn't responding. It's beginning to make my acrobats begin their tumbling routine again. When the waitress appears from behind me, I jolt worse this time, yipping like a small puppy. He pretends to not notice.

She sets a coffee mug down in front of me. She tops off his cup and checks the level of creamer in the decanter before asking what we'd like to eat. I ask for a turkey club and a house salad. Jake orders a clubhouse and fries. She scurries away as stealthily as she had appeared.

"Someone should put a bell on her neck," I say, not joking in the slightest.

Jake smiles. "How about I let you know when she's coming?"

"Yes, that would be great. Thank you. So, instincts?"

"My instincts tell me you are a highly sexual woman who isn't bored with her sex life but could benefit from exploring new avenues. You want to do new things, but you're afraid to open up. There's a wild woman sleeping within you, Beth, and I want to awaken her."

He's so blunt! I clear my throat and sarcasm in my voice and ask, "Oh, you do, huh?"

Unlike mine, his expression is serious, "Yes, I do. If you'll permit me. When was the last time you did something that touched your moral boundaries?"

"Friday night, if you must know."

"And, just what did you do that was so immoral?" He asks in a rather clinical manner, like he's my therapist trying to get a better fix on me.

I swallow hard and cast my eyes down at my mug of coffee. I can't look at him while I explain. "I don't know why I'm telling you this. Henry and I had sex on the hood of the car, on a dark side street on the way home from the party. It was incredible, if you must know." I peek up at him without lifting my chin.

He doesn't look away from me at all. His eyes lock onto mine, stirring the anxiety in my belly as he seems to do with ease. I drop my sights to his puffy, pillow-soft lips.

Wearing no discernable expression, he asks, "Did you picture me touching you?" His mouth moves hypnotically as they form the words that caress my ears. "When you closed your eyes, was it me fucking you on the hood of the car? Was I inside of you?"

I'm breathing heavier than I want to be. My pussy is slick with my arousal. The heat rises in my face as it flushes with blood, proving my guilt. I pry my eyes from his lips, glancing behind me to see if the waitress is sneaking up again. If she is, I'll probably scream because I'm wound up like a jack-in-the-box, ready to explode at any moment.

"Henry told me to."

His whisper is so seductive. "But you were already imagining me, weren't you?"

"Yes," I whisper my confession, ashamed of my betrayal to Henry.

"Did you orgasm?" I nod, unable to speak through my parched mouth. "Did he only fuck you, or did he use his mouth as well?"

"Both," I whisper, unable to get my voice to its regular octave.

"Did he make you cum with his mouth or his cock?"

I nearly coo when his tongue slips from between his lips and teasingly slicks them with his saliva.

My clitoris twitches, waking me from the memory of that night's vivid imagination. I glance away, clearing my throat before taking a sip of coffee. Why am I entertaining this man's arrogance? Because he's intoxicating, that's why!

"Yes, I orgasmed both ways. He's quite good with his mouth and his cock."

"I'm sure he is," he says before taking a sip of his own coffee. "The waitress is almost here."

I turn to see her walking up with two plates. This time, I don't startle. She sets them down before asking if we need anything else. We both shake our heads, so she fades away. He sprinkles salt on his fries and inside his sandwich, while I stab my fork into my salad. We eat in silence for several minutes. Our eyes meet often, but I'm always quick to break the contact.

He sets his fork on the table and asks, "Do you like to give oral sex to men?"

"As opposed to what? Women?" I giggle.

"Since you asked, have you ever been with a woman?" he asks me, before picking up his sandwich and biting into it.

I shake my head and furrow my brow. "This seems very clinical, like I'm having lunch with a therapist."

"I'm sorry. I'm trying to get to know you better."

"Oh, I thought maybe your previous career was psychology." I try to sound as if I'm joking, but it doesn't come across that way.

"I will try not to seem so clinical, as you suggested. How should we get to know one another if nobody asks questions?"

"We could just talk like friends do."

"Do friends not ask one another questions?"

"Yes, but not one after the other."

"Am I doing that?"

"Yes, you are."

"You could ask me a question."

I pause as my brain whips through the hundreds of questions I had lined up to ask him, but I get flustered. Not a particular one stands out. I shrug. "No, I have never … been with a woman."

He follows up with, "Would you like to be?"

"Why are you asking me all these personal questions?"

"Because you're letting me," he tells me. "Okay, let's turn the spotlight on me, if you'd prefer. I'm sure you have plenty of questions for me."

I scoff, sarcastically. "No, not even one!" He smiles as if waiting for me to tell him what day of the week it is. "I have too many to get through during one luncheon."

"Then begin with some of the most burdening ones."

I set my fork down and swallow my mouthful of chewed lettuce. He's forward, so I will be too. "My husband tells me you are a cruel man in the bedroom. Is that true?"

His smile is tight as if forcing himself to hold back a belly-shaking laugh. "I am only as vicious as women want me to be. Cruel? Nobody I've been with has ever referred to me as cruel. I haven't hurt anyone in a way they didn't approve of. Often, when I assert pain, it awakens their senses. There's a physical and mental reaction to different stimuli. It's not always about pain. Sometimes a scent, sound, taste, or soft touch will have an equal effect. When I can get someone out of their own mind, they'll get to a place where only the physical exists. Most people keep their walls up during intimate moments, even if they think they aren't. A hit to the senses – pain, for example – helps to break them down. It's then that I can take them to another level of pleasure, a place some had no idea even existed. They simply have to let it happen."

"And the women enjoy this?" I have my doubts.

"Very much so."

"Have you ever hurt anyone?"

"Of course. Are you asking if I've ever injured anyone? I have never severely injured anyone. There have been some bruises that lingered longer than I'd have preferred them to. Skin sometimes pinches from ropes. A person bled once, but no broken bones or any residual marks that weren't coverable with clothing." Jake stares at me while my teeth grind away at the mutilated bite of sandwich being shoved around in my mouth. I cover my mouth with my hand when his eyes leave my own, lowering to ogle my jaw while I gnash my way through my food like a ravenous dog with a raw steak.

"Why did you cover your mouth?"

I swallow before I'm ready. The food sticks in my throat. I swallow twice more to force it down. I gulp the rest of my coffee before meeting his eyes. "Because you were staring at me while I was chewing."

"Were you going to say something, but your mouth was too full?" I shake my head. "Did I make you feel self-conscious?"

"Yes. You're rather intimidating." Dammit! I said it.

"So, intimidate me. You have the power to do so if you choose to. You can stare into my eyes and force yourself not to look away. One of us will break. It doesn't have to be you. You don't realize the level of power you hold over men. You could rule any situation if you learned how to. I can teach you."

"You want to teach me how to intimidate people?" I laugh and shake my head. "I'm not one of those confident people who can take control of a room by walking into it the way you can."

"And that is where you would be wrong." I shake my head. He continues, "Come home with me, and I'll show you how to harness your power."

I take a deep breath and hold it, fearing what I'll say when I let it out. Should I take a risk that could be an amazing, life-altering experience that will bring Henry and I closer together, or will it ruin us? Do I turn him down and walk out of this café, too afraid to try something new? I should, but I don't really want to do the right thing right now. I want to be bad, to sin, to be the slutty wife who fucks her husband's co-worker. This experience could help me write a great novel about my adventures with this young, confident stud.

Sensing my inner dilemma, he presses his hand against his chest and vows, "I won't do anything you don't want me to do. You can leave any time, no questions asked. Take a chance, Beth."

I hear myself say, "Yes." What? Did I say that out loud? Okay, well, here goes nothing! Jake smiles, pleased by my simple response that could change both of our lives for the better, or the worst. The way he forces his lips tightly together makes him look like he's trying to maintain his level of maturity. It's obvious that all he wants to do is jump up and down with excitement because he has a new toy.

He sips his coffee while looking at my eyes with intent. "Should we go now?"

"If we don't, I might change my mind," I confess.

He tilts his head and whispers, "You can change your mind at any point in time."

"You don't have to be back at work?"

He shakes his head. "No, I cleared my schedule and took the afternoon off."

I joke, "That was a little presumptuous, wasn't it?"

"Just hopeful." Jake grins, then tosses a small wad of bills on the table before standing up. He puts his hand out in a gentlemanly fashion. I take it and slide out from the booth. When I stand, he pulls me in so close that his body is almost touching mine. We are face to face. I can feel his breath on my cheek.

I stutter, "Are... are you going to... to kiss me right here in... in the café?"

"Would you like me to?" The way he whispered, asking permission, in such a calm and seductive manner has me wanting to lean in and sample the delicious pair of lips I've been yearning to taste for almost an hour.

I clear my throat and hope my voice doesn't crack. "No, someone we know might see us." I turn on shaking legs and begin making my way toward the door.

"As you wish," he places his hand on the small of my back, allowing me to lead the way out of the café.

I agree to follow him to his house. Since I'm taking my car, I will have every opportunity to change my mind. There's no doubting that I want him. Yes, I desire to have his hot skin against mine. The curiosity of how his cock will feel buried inside keeps me distracted from my driving. I've almost smashed into the back of his car three times.

For crying out loud, I'm not a teenager about to have sex for the first time! I had been with seven men before I met Henry but no one since, until now. I have to stop thinking too deeply into this. Henry suggested I go with him. If Henry is telling me to go be with Jake, and I want to be with him, why am I having so much anxiety? It's not as if I'm about to have an affair. Am I?

We pull into the driveway of a modest home. It's not flashy by any means. I'm not sure what I was expecting, but a middle-class dwelling in a suburban neighbourhood wasn't it. I expected we'd wind up in a mansion or expensive condo on the top floor of his hotel, like where the dominant lived in that famous book series. I sit in the car, fussing with the zipper of my purse. I can't close the damn thing! The universe is giving me a moment. I'm not sure if I want to get out and test my fate or drive away. Jake taps on my window, startling me. I look up at him to see him smiling at me, waving his finger asking me to roll down the window.

Instead, I open the door and attempt to get out, but my seatbelt is still fastened and holding me in my seat. I couldn't be any more embarrassed. While trying to make light of the situation, I laugh at myself as I undo it.

He suggests, "You don't have to come inside if you've changed your mind."

"I haven't," I tell him in a clear and confident voice.

He smiles again, taking my hand and helping me out of the car. As we enter his house, he gives me instructions. "I'm going to begin explaining the rules we both need to obey. Is that okay, or would you like to start off slower, perhaps with small talk?"

"No small talk. A shot of something stronger than coffee would be ideal."

"Alcohol consumption is something I frown upon when we're about to play, but I'll let that rule slide today. What would you like?"

"Anything strong," I reply with a nervous smile. I glance around his open concept living room/kitchen area, enjoying how well-decorated and impeccably clean his home is. He must have a maid and a decorator. Perhaps one day, I'll ask him. Those questions seem too personal for today's situation. Wait! What? Too personal? He's about to ravish my body in ways I've never experienced, and I'm wondering if asking if he has a maid service would be too forward. What is wrong with me?

He hands me a shot of whiskey. He raises his small glass, and we toast before I slug it down as quickly as I can, hoping it will give me the courage I need to get through this.

Jake takes my hand and begins leading me down a flight of stairs. While we walk, he talks. "You need to remember that you can leave at any time. You are not a prisoner. Second, you are the one in control, even if I've immobilized you."

At the bottom of the stairs, I look at him with furrowed brow and ask, "How is that possible?"

"I will give you two safe words. If you say *yellow*, I will continue with what I'm doing but not advance the intensity. If you say *red*, everything stops abruptly. You will be set free, and I will assess you for injury. We will discuss what made you want to stop and how to avoid it the next time. If you choose to leave, you may do so without any explanation. Although, I do hope you will keep the lines of communication open. Without communication, this will not work."

Jake and I stand outside of a closed door. He takes my shaking hands in his steady palms. "This is about physical and mental pleasure, not love. Our hearts must stay out of this relationship. You belong to Henry, and I would never dream of changing that. I will not always take my clothes off because this isn't primarily about me. I want to open you up to new and wonderful things, but you will always go home to Henry."

"What exactly do you get out of this?" I say, sounding much more sarcastic than I had planned.

"Your reactions will excite me, sexually. If you scream from pain or pleasure, I will get aroused. When I think you are ready, I'll fuck you, or I won't. If I do, I will wear a condom," he reassures.

My mouth has a mind of its own. "You'll only fuck my pussy? You don't want my mouth or ass?"

He smiles and asks, "Would you like me to fuck your mouth and ass, too, Beth?"

"Yes, I suppose so... if the mood is right."

He leans in, brushing his cheek against mine. "I suspect we'll get along quite well."

Jake plants his full lips on mine. His mouth is hot and soft, better than I had imagined it would be. His tongue slips between my lips and stiffens in my mouth. I suck it gently, and he moans deep in his throat. He retracts his tongue; his lips part from mine, but his face remains close.

"I will be gentle with you today. It's about your pleasure. I will bind you. You won't be able to move. Remember, you can stop everything at any moment. You hold that power. You are strong enough to endure more than you think you can. Do I have your permission?"

The heat from his lips has my body tingling from where his lips touched mine to the very tip of my clit. His kiss has left me quivering. At this exact moment, I'm likely to agree to anything he suggests.

Yes, you have my permission."

CHAPTER FIVE

Jake pushes open the door. He takes my hand and leads me through it. My eyes scan the dimly lit, red and black room, trying to see everything in here, even if most of it confuses me.

There are metal apparatuses against the wall. I try to picture how to position a human body on some of them. A chair, similar to the one you'd see in a birthing room at the hospital, is among the equipment. Off to the side rests a bed with silky sheets. Across from the bed, cabinets line the dark-stained wooden walls. A heavy-duty metal chain with a ring at the end hangs from the ceiling. It has me wondering if he'll be hanging me from it by my wrists. I'm curious but so scared that my adrenaline is flooding my bloodstream, and I'm shaking. That shot of whiskey did not do me any favours.

While still holding my hand, he turns me until he is my focal point. "Take a deep breath. You know you can stop this at any time. Please don't fear me." I nod. Oddly enough, his words soothe me. Maybe it's not so much what he says but rathe the tone of his seductive voice that has the knots in my stomach easing off. "I will give you orders, and I expect you to obey them. After today, I will punish you if you disobey. Because you aren't familiar with my wishes and because I promised I wouldn't, I won't punish you today. If you are uncomfortable with anything that I ask of you, just say so, and I'll abstain. Afterwards, we can discuss your concern. Do you have questions, or are you ready to begin?"

"I'm ready to begin." I swallow, but my throat feels tight and incredibly dry.

Jake kisses the back of my right hand before whispering his first demand. "Take off your clothes."

I take a deep breath. I peel off my shirt while I watch him choose a rope from a tall cabinet. When I'm down to my bra and panties, it becomes very real and no longer just a sexual fantasy.

He returns to me but stops a few feet away. His eyes scan my body from head to toe. A bit too clinically, he says, "Everything off, please." I do as he orders, swallowing dry again.

He is watching me as I stand before him, totally naked, and nervously fidgeting with my fingers. I'm not sure where to put my hands. When I shuffle my feet, he insists, "Look at my eyes and don't look away. This is hard for most people to do in any situation. It's even more difficult because you feel vulnerable right now. Don't let that deter you. Know that you are strong because you are the one who can make it all stop with just a single word."

His words give me courage. After a full minute of our eyes holding each other's gaze, he smiles. "You did well. I will tell you everything I do before doing it but only for today. To start, I will tie your hands over your head, and you will remain standing. Are you all right with that position?"

"Yes," I reply, confident that I'm not making a mistake... that doing this with Jake is the right thing. He ties my hands while I watch his handsome face. His eyes cast up to meet mine but only for a few seconds before looking back down at my newly bound hands.

He yanks the rope just enough to get my attention. "Can you escape?" I begin pulling my hands in all directions to see if I can loosen the ropes but conclude that it's pointless to continue the struggle. He nods before leading me by the rope until I'm standing underneath the chain with the steel loop at its end. He fishes the free end through it and begins pulling until my arms are straight up over my head. If he gives one more pull, my heels will be off the floor, and I'll be on my tiptoes, but he doesn't pull it tight. I'm grateful.

Jake ties the rope to my wrists, so it won't come free from the metal loop. He stands only a few inches in front of me, his eyes seeming to read all the secrets I have ever kept hidden within my mind. His fingers brush down my right cheek, ending when they are tucked under my chin, lifting my face and forcing me to look at his eyes.

His voice is sedating... calm and deep. "Before I begin to touch you, what are the safe words?"

"Red and yellow," I reply with a voice so timid that it's barely audible. I'm not sure why, but I startle and gasp when his fingertips brush my ribs.

"Are you ticklish?" he asks, keeping his hand in place.

I shake my head. "Not so much."

He continues grazing his fingertips along the skin of my abdomen and arms. "Look at my eyes and don't look away, even if I do."

Jake cups both my breasts in the palms of his hands firmly. My nipples pinch between his fingers, sending shocks straight to my heated vagina. He leans in, pausing before his lips touch mine. I can feel his hot, sweet breath on my face. His breathing is calm, while I am panting nervously. How is he so relaxed, like he's doing something as mundane as making a cup of tea? He releases my breasts and steps away. He's behind me, and I can't see him. What is he going to do to me? Is he going to spank me now?

Jake's warm, soft hands glide along my ass cheeks until cradling them comfortably in his palms. With some pressure, he squeezes them. It's not painful, but it feels awkward to me. He rests his forehead against the nape of my neck. His breath flows down my spine, awakening the tiny hairs on my back. His hands continue to explore my lower back as though they've never touched a woman's silky flesh. It's flattering to feel like I am the only thing he's appreciating at this moment, as if nothing in his life matters other than my skin. My nervous anxiety is melting away.

Jake's voice is quiet, yet deep. "You have a beautiful body, Beth. Never be ashamed of your nudity. I could look at you all day and never tire of any part of you. Your skin is soft and silky. Your shape is perfect. Your hips are sexy, leading up to a small waist, ideal for my hands to grip when I fuck you hard from behind. Let's not forget about your breasts. They are magnificent." He stands in front of me, a few feet away. "I'm going to take off my clothes now. Are you comfortable with that?"

"Yes, I am." At least, I think I'm ready. I feel safe, even though he could hurt me if he wanted to. Even though I barely know anything about this man, I trust him.

Jake undoes his tie, sliding it from his collar and laying it on the stool next to him. He's in no hurry to show me his flesh. Teasingly slow, he unbuttons his shirt, pulling it off to reveal a washboard abdomen. My sudden inhale tells him I'm pleased. I was not expecting his body to be so fit. He doesn't appear to be quite this sculpted when he's hidden in a suit. His belt comes off next and then his pants. He's standing before me in just his boxer briefs, but he doesn't remove them yet. Instead, his eyes watch my face. I nod. Maybe it's my approval he's waiting for. He pulls them down, and that's when I get to see his package.

The man has a large penis, but it's not so massive that I am rethinking letting him inside me. He's definitely above average, perhaps a bit thicker than Henry's cock. I'd guess them to be about equal in length. Jake turns slowly enough to give me a chance to admire his entire body. His ass is round and firm; his thighs are strong and well-defined. I can't wait to clutch them when he's between my legs, fucking me *hard* as he suggested. I am taken aback by how deceiving his suit was in making his physique seem rather mediocre. I thought he was an averagely built, slender man, but when nude, it's now obvious that he works out on a regular basis.

Jake seems to glide toward me, his firm prick swinging as he does. He kisses my lips once and then says, "Do you like my body?"

I whisper with merely a sound. "Yes, very much."

He smiles, brushing the back of his hand gingerly down my cheek. "Should we continue?"

"Yes, please," I beg him.

His body comes close to mine but doesn't quite make contact. The heat radiating from his skin is so hot that if he were to touch his flesh against me, I think we might burst into flames. His cheek brushes mine as his words flow soothingly into my ear. "I want you to let yourself feel what I do to you. Don't think about my pleasure and don't worry if you aren't reaching orgasm as quickly as you might hope. Getting you to orgasm isn't the focus. I want you to lose yourself in your senses, let your thoughts go, enjoy the moment for what it is. Completely give yourself up to my touch. Do you understand?" I nod, fearing that if he doesn't touch me soon, I will combust.

The instant his body presses against mine, it's confirmed. His skin is volcanic. Jake's hands glide around my sides until one is in the centre of my upper back, and the other cups my ass cheek. He holds me tightly against him, moulding our bodies into one. His face tilts downward until his lips are almost touching mine, but he maintains the distance, not letting them touch. A tuft of his long hair brushes along the tiny hairs on my cheek, leaving them lifted in its wake. His sky-blue eyes burn into my mind as if to learn my most secret thoughts.

Jake's hand glides down my back until it cups my other ass cheek. He squeezes and then continues to pull the cheeks far apart until I squirm. It feels awkward. His middle finger slips between my cheeks and begins lightly circling my asshole. His other hand releases, pulling back to gain some distance and then returning quickly, spanking me. I jolt and make a bizarre squeaking noise that brings a smile to his face. He continues fondling my asshole, smacking me from time to time. I like the combination of tenderness to my ass, the sting of his palm, and the anxious anticipation for the next swat. Surprising to me, it excites my clitoris the same way a tongue would. My vagina twinges after each whack, and it thrills me.

After a final, hard slap, his hot hand ever-so-faintly glides along my ribs until he has my entire breast clutched in his palm. He squeezes, and I cry out. He holds still, not easing his grip but not tightening either. I continue to grumble with each breath, but he doesn't release my breast. I've completely forgotten that his finger is still teasing my asshole because all I feel is the stress on my boob.

"You said you would not hurt me today," I whisper.

He steps back, breaking all physical contact. "Is it too much?"

"Um, no," I tell him, feeling silly that I said anything. I will try to keep quiet from now on.

Jake presses against me; his hands resume their positions. "Close your eyes. Redirect your concentration to what my finger is doing to your ass. Breathe through the pain of your breast and tell your mind that it doesn't hurt. Think only about my finger. See it in your mind. What would it look like to watch it being done to someone else? Would it excite you?"

My breathing quickens. I can still feel my breast being squeezed, but the nerves around my asshole are so aroused that I want to feel that especially. His finger shifts forward, gliding along my dripping wet vagina and immediately back to my ass.

The tip of his digit presses into my tight hole. I take in a sharp breath, moaning on the exhale. As his finger pulls gently at my butt, I forget about my breast. All I feel is the invasion of my backside, and I like it very much.

He separates from me to walk behind me. My eyes dart around the room. What'll he do next? Although it's most likely only a few seconds, it seems too long before he touches me again. Jake's hard dick slides between my thighs, pressing against my slick pussy, while his hands reach around and grab both breasts, squeezing them until I am struggling to get away.

He tells me, "Breathe." I hadn't noticed that I wasn't.

His fingers roll my nipples between them, sending sensational shocks to my clitoris, causing it to swell. My breaths are loud and broken. My body is vibrating with exhilaration. I squeeze my legs together, wedging his stiff prick tightly against my crotch. My hips buck, essentially jacking him off. My pussy is so wet that he slides effortlessly between my thighs.

Jake steps away. I wonder if I did something wrong. I need him to touch me again, or better yet, be inside of me right now. I whisper, "Fuck me. Please, fuck me."

"Patience. Would you be willing to take more pain first?"

"Would it please you?"

He presses his mouth behind my ear and whispers, "Greatly."

"I can take it," I reply, not at all fearing what he's going to do to me. I want him. I want to please him, so he'll continue to please me.

"You remember the safe words?" he asks, more to remind me to use them if I need to, rather than concerned if I had forgotten them.

"Yes, red and yellow," I quickly reply.

His hand slaps my ass much harder than before. I wasn't expecting that. I jerk forward and squeal. He caresses that cheek with his palm before slapping again. The sting is sharp, but it isn't anything that I need to put a halt on. He swats my other cheek. I gasp only slightly. Now I'm ready for it. I know he's going to do it again, and I welcome it. Jake continues to slap my behind until it's burning hot and my pussy is drenched.

He steps forward until his chest is pressing against my back and whispers in my ear. "You didn't stop me. You did very well."

The fingers on his left hand separate my pussy lips, while the middle finger on his right hand slips between them, tenderly rubbing my clit with small circles. He slips a finger inside of me for only a quick second. I want more, much more.

I open my eyes when he instructs, "Open your mouth and suck your juices from my fingers. Tell me, do you like the way your cunt tastes?"

I open wide, taking two of his fingers into my mouth and wrapping my lips around them, sucking as if they were his cock. He pulls them from me. "Yes, I love how I taste."

"Should I taste you?" he whispers, while his fingers circle my clit once again. His other hand is squeezing my nipple, but I relish the intense pinch. The painful sensation is shooting toward my clitoris, igniting those nerves.

Jake slowly circles me. I watch his tummy muscles expand and contract with each easy breath he takes. I wonder how he can remain so calm, while I am panting like a dog on a hot summer evening.

He bends forward, taking my nipple in his mouth, and something wonderful happens. Something I've never had the pleasure of experiencing. I don't know what he's doing, but it's so intense that my clitoris is twitching all on its own. I don't want him to stop, not ever. Moans are riding each rapid exhale.

I watch him as he kisses down my belly and buries his nose against the folds of my pussy. He breathes in my scent while looking up at my eyes. His lips part and press between my folds, kissing them while skipping over my clitoris entirely, driving me wild with anticipation. I want his mouth on my horny little button.

"Lick me," I demand.

He stands up, disappointing me greatly. He grasps my bottom jaw and says, "You don't get to tell me what to do."

"Please?" I plead with him.

Jake snickers. "From now on, I give the orders. Do you understand?"

"Okay," I reply, hoping I'll remember to keep my requests to myself.

"You will address me as Sir or Master when we're in this room." Referring to him in that way seems strange to me. He's younger than I am, so calling him Sir as if he's my superior just seems out of place. Master? I don't know if I can get used to that, but I'll try.

"Yes, Sir." He grins approvingly and sinks down to his knees. He wraps his lips around my clit and begins sucking and stroking it. I know I'm going to cum if he doesn't stop right now. "Oh, yes, Sir!"

He backs his face up long enough to tell me, "Don't cum unless you ask permission and I tell you to cum."

That is sure to be an impossible rule to comply with. If he continues pleasuring me the way he is, I won't be able to hold it back, no matter how hard I try. He is licking and flicking exactly right, as if he has a pinpoint map of my most sensitive nerves. He knows when to titillate them and when to steer clear. I am on the verge of coming already. Ten more seconds and I'll be at a point of no return. I open my mouth to beg permission, but before I can, he stops and gets to his feet. My body is twisting in protest, my thighs squeezing together in a failed attempt to mimic his tongue.

"Do you want to cum?" I'm looking at him through heavy-lidded, begging eyes. I nod and whimper. He is taking great pleasure in my irritation. "Not yet. I want you to fully enjoy it before you let it go. Think about how every nerve in your body is at a heightened level of sensitivity at this very moment. Can you feel it? Your skin is lined with raised hairs, as though your body is electrified. Do you notice how every muscle is tense? Adrenaline is flooding your veins. Experience it, don't be in such a hurry to get to the next stage. Don't worry, I'll make you cum many times before you leave this room today."

Jake kneels behind me and grips my hips, pulling my ass back until his mouth rests easily between my cheeks. His tongue fondles my asshole, licking and teasing it with the heated softness and strength only that muscle can offer. Nobody has ever licked my behind before. I always thought I would be disgusted, but I was so wrong. It's stupefying. My uncontrollable moans are loud and flow from every breath. When his tongue juts into my tight hole, I cry out from the shot of arousal piercing my clit. My pussy pulses each time he slithers in and out of me.

He swiftly pushes two fingers into my vagina. I'm so wet that they slip right in. He's wiggling and tapping them toward the front of my abdomen while his tongue continues to fuck my butt. The pad of his thumb begins to lightly stroke my swollen clit, each time his fingers press forward. Holy shit, this is fucking awesome! I've never felt so sexually intoxicated.

"May I cum, Sir?" I yell. Somehow, amidst the mental fog, I remembered to ask.

"You may." His fingers and tongue keep the pace, not changing their tempo in the slightest. I am so grateful. Henry tends to get excited, so he speeds up, which ruins it for me, usually making the urge to orgasm fade away.

"Oh, god! Oh, fuck! I'm coming! Ah… yes!" My body tenses while my pussy squeezes his fingers, pulsing through the first climax Jake has ever granted me. I can't think or move under my own power or even remember to breathe. I'm floating, lost in a sea of ecstasy. The world around me is spinning at an impossible rate, but not me; I'm weightless and still.

I would fall to the floor if the bindings weren't tied around my wrists, keeping me upright. My legs are becoming so weak, unable to sustain my weight any longer. My whole being is drowning in physical and mental euphoria. As I'm coming back to reality, my eyes gradually open and struggle to focus. My lungs are burning from holding my breath while I ride through my climax. Before I am completely myself again, he pulls his fingers from my drenched pussy and slips one into my butt. Instinctually, I pull my hips forward, attempting to get it out of me, but quickly moan when I realize how wonderful his invasion feels.

Jake's arm wraps around my chest, gripping his hand on my throat but not squeezing, just holding me in place. His lips press to the back of my neck, his breath feeling cool on my steaming hot skin, raising tiny goosebumps all down my back. He eases another digit in, carefully pulling at the opening to loosen it further. He continues to stretch my ass until he's sure I will be able to take his solid shaft without much resistance.

He whispers, "Open your eyes." I lift my lids to see that Jake is holding a condom package in front of my face. I nod, acknowledging that I've seen it. I hear him tear it open, and then I assume he's rolling the latex sheath over his prick.

He lubricates my ass with a gel he seems to have pulled out of the air. Gingerly, he pushes the head of his dick past the rim of my asshole. He's worked it so well that there's absolutely no resistance. There's usually some level of pain, but not this time, not with Jake's skillfulness. As he pushes deeper and deeper into my body, I rest my head back against his shoulder. When he's buried deep, he wraps his arms around my belly and chest, lifting me slightly and holding me against him.

His lips brush just under my ear. His breath is so hot. "Do you like my cock in your ass?"

"Yes, I do."

"Yes, Sir," he corrects.

"Yes, Sir, I do."

"Good girl."

With very slight movements, he pulls his hips back an inch or two before sliding back in. Yet again, my clitoris is stiffening to the point that it's beginning to ache for his touch. His hand glides down my tummy. Two fingers spread my pussy lips while the middle digit teases my swollen button. With his forearm holding my torso firmly against him, his fingertips roll my nipple. I'm going to explode or erupt into a blazing inferno. He stops all movement, holding so still that he's statue-like. I start jerking my hips forward and back against his cock and fingers. My whimpers are begging him to resume. I could cum at any second if he would just move!

I beg with pure desperation, "Please, don't stop."

"You need to ask my permission to cum. I stopped because you were about to disrespect my wishes," he explains with a steady calmness, while I'm delirious from desire.

"May I cum when you start again? Please? Please, Sir?" My body is writhing in his grip. I will do anything he asks of me. Anything!

He continues fucking and flicking, unrelentingly. "You need to ask me."

"I need to cum." My words are nearly inaudible.

"That's a statement, not a question."

"Please, Sir, may I cum?" I plead, knowing I can't hold it off and will cum whether he permits it or not... if he doesn't stop, that is.

He doesn't reply for what seems like an eternity but is likely only a few seconds. "You may cum." His whisper rings loudly in my ear, as if nothing but my body and his voice exists.

Once again, I'm losing my sanity under his touch. As my head drops forward, my thoughts fall away. My body is all I know. My hips fight to buck against him, urging him to continue fucking and rubbing me just right. My held breath is burning in my lungs, but if I breathe, the intensity of this glorious moment ends, and I don't want that. I want to hold on to these sensations forever. My lungs squeeze, forcing the air out, along with an uncontrollable wail that seems to go on endlessly. I gasp for a quick breath. Every muscle in my body is either jerking or vibrating frenziedly.

His hand abruptly covers my mouth, leaving only my nostrils free to sustain my life. My eyes open wide, and I fight off the instinctual desire to fight. I'm no longer getting the excess of oxygen that I require. A buzzing vibrator is pressed against my clit. It's so super-sensitive in its post-orgasmic state. I fight to get away, but it's useless. Jake turns my face and pulls my head back so it's pressing against his shoulder. He's watching my eyes. I am breathing rapidly through my nose but not getting enough oxygen to keep the flickering, tiny white stars from flooding my vision. I want to scream for him to remove the vibrator and his hand, but I can't.

Jake's hips begin humping against my ass much quicker and with longer strokes, while the vibrator stimulates my clit, arousing it for a third time. I won't survive another orgasm. I'll leave my body and mind forever, never to return. Better still, I want to lose myself with him and disappear into an abyss of pleasure.

He licks my cheek and whispers, "Do you like my cock in your ass?" I barely hear his words, yet they seem so loud.

He knows I can't possibly answer him, but I don't think he's looking for a verbal response. "You have a great ass. Do you want to cum again?" I nod, and he snickers, "Well, you won't because you can't ask for my permission. If you cum, I will punish you for disobeying me."

I'm twisting my hips to get away from the vibrator, but he's just too good at keeping it in place, no matter how much I struggle. The second his hand leaves my mouth to grip my throat, I scream, "I'm coming... please?"

His breath is hot on my ear as he whispers one magical little word that means more to me than any single word ever has or ever could. "Cum."

My body stiffens as the climax builds more and more powerful, the tension in my stomach pulling like a thick, elastic band until a flood of cum pours from my depths, running down my legs. As I'm hurdled over the apex of yet another fierce orgasm, a primitive roar escapes, along with all the strength in my legs. I am weak... so very weak.

Jake slides his prick from my ass, then turns off and drops the vibrator. He scoops me up in his arms while releasing my wrists from the rope binding. They fall heavily to my chest, as I have no strength left in them.

All I can do at this moment is breathe. I'm still completely overcome, shaking and gasping breaths of cool air to calm my burning lungs and slow my pounding heart. He carries me to the mattress, gently laying me on my back before disappearing.

I'm alone in the room as my breathing slows to an almost normal rhythm. Logical thought is beginning to take over my fuzzy afterglow. I open my heavy eyelids to see him standing beside the bed, handing me an open bottle of water. I struggle to sit up so I can take a much-needed gulp. After handing it back to him with a nod of my head, he sets it on the nightstand. It dawns on me that I must look like I've been through hell. Realizing that running my fingers through my hair isn't going to fix anything, I give up and hope he'll accept my dishevelled appearance.

He shows me a condom in a package before tearing it open with his teeth. I shake my head, visibly panicking. His eyes meet mine with a worried curiosity. "What's wrong?"

"I thought you had a condom on. You showed me one before you..." I stop talking, wondering why he's smiling.

"Yes, I did have one on when I fucked your ass, but I took it off because I'd like to fuck your pussy now. I don't often go from back to front because some women get infections from that."

"Oh! I just didn't see you take it off. I thought maybe it came off inside me or you didn't actually wear one." I'm feeling a bit silly for overreacting but also very relieved.

Realizing that I'm embarrassed, he comforts me, "I'd rather you relate your concerns to me so you're not needlessly worrying about something. You don't ever have to fear speaking up about a concern. I tell you not to speak during our session unless I ask you to, but if it's important, speak."

"Okay, I will. I promise. Are we done? I don't want to be done just yet."

"Tell me what you want, Beth."

What does he want me to say? Does he want details like how fast or slow to fuck me? Perhaps just a rough description. "Make love to me."

He frowns. "No, I won't ever do that. Your husband can make love to you. I'm available strictly for sexual pleasure but definitely not lovemaking. If you're hoping for more than what I'm offering, you'll be greatly disappointed."

"Oh, no! That's not what I meant, exactly." How can I not find the right words to describe what I want from him right now? I am a writer, goddammit!

"Beth, in this room, I need you to be specific. What do you want?" I simply shrug, not sure of what to say. "Do you want me to lick or fuck your pussy? Fuck your ass again? Stimulate you another way, perhaps? I don't often ask, so take advantage. I do what I want within her boundaries. Because I don't know you well enough to know what you want, I will ask you this one time. What do you want, Beth?"

"Um, I'd like to take you in my mouth."

"Do you want it to be forced, or should I let you have all the control?"

"A little of both, maybe," I reply with a shyness that's unnecessary at this point.

"I don't ever want you to be coy with me. If you want something and I ask you to speak, answer me precisely; otherwise,

I'll do what I want, and you might not like it." He insists, "Get down on your knees and tell me you want to suck my cock."

"Yes, Sir," I say while sliding my weary body off the bed and onto my knees in front of him. He holds his cock in his fist. I'm looking up at him with my lips parted, ready to take him. He's looking down at my gaping mouth. He puts two fingers in and slides them along my tongue until they are in past his knuckles. I watch him lick his lips. His eyes admire the depth his fingers have reached. He's pleased with my ability to evade gagging. He pulls his fingers out, then slides them back in, but now there are three fingers at the back of my tongue. I open my throat and force my tongue against my bottom jaw to prevent me from gagging. I don't want him to see me as an incapable woman.

"Again, tell me what you want."

With his fingers still deep in my mouth, I do my best to say, "I want to suck your cock."

After sliding his fingers from my mouth, Jake says, "This should be fun." His smile lifts the corner of his mouth as he puts the head of his cock between my lips and tells me, "Suck just that much."

I tighten my lips around the mushroom head and suck gently, teasing his hole with my tongue. I watch his facial twitches as my lips work the tip of his prick. He bites his bottom lip while stroking the back of my head with his hand. He lifts his chin and looks straight ahead as if to distract his thoughts from my actions. I start rocking my head forward and back, taking more of him in my mouth each time.

Suddenly, Jake grabs my hair and yanks my head back. He bends down until his face is nearly touching mine. "You only suck what I offer you. Don't be so fucking greedy."

He stands back up while my heart pounds, my eyes wide open, fighting back nervous tears. Why was he so angry with me? I was sucking his cock. Isn't that what men like? I open my mouth and wait for him to put exactly how much he wants to in my mouth. Why am I so upset about disappointing him? He didn't hit me or anything. *Fucking get it together, Beth!*

He whispers reassuring words. "Don't cry. You're stronger than that. You have the power to make it all stop. Do you want to stop?" I shake my head. "You'll learn to follow instructions. If I tell you to do something, you do it how I say; nothing more, nothing less. When I say that I only want you to suck the tip of my cock, that's all you'll suck until I offer you more. Do you understand?"

I nod, still holding the tip of his cock between my lips. I return to sucking softly and licking the tip, staying conscious of how much I'm taking in. I no longer want to cry because he's right; it's my choice to be here, and I can leave if I want to.

I continue playing with only what I'm allowed for several minutes, until he holds either side of my head with both hands, moving his hips forward, pushing much more dick into my mouth. He doesn't stop until his swollen prick is all the way down my throat. He holds in this position while I remain still, waiting for him to pull back so I can breathe again. After the lecture I received about not complying with his wishes, I will only pull back if I'm gagging or desperately in need of air. I trust him to ensure my wellbeing. Hearing him get upset with me again today is not on my list of fun activities. I want to please him. He has pleased me in ways beyond anything I could have ever imagined he could do the first time he is with me. It usually takes years to get to know someone's body that well.

My eyes are starting to fill with tears. I'm not crying; it's an automatic reaction to something buried deep in my throat. My lungs are aching for oxygen. I begin to fuss, hoping he'll realize I'm nearly desperate. He takes pity on me and releases my head, allowing me to pull back. I inhale as quickly as I can to put out the fire in my lungs as my eyes release the puddles that flooded them. I take this opportunity to wipe the wetness from my cheek, hoping he hasn't noticed.

"You did well. How good are you at getting your face fucked?"

Without waiting for me to reply, he pushes his cock between my open lips and firmly holds a wad of my hair on either side of my head. At first, he fucks slowly, in and out. Soon, he's bucking his prick all the way in and then pulling out, immediately forcing it back in again, not giving me much chance to breathe between thrusts. I try to remain calm and relax, breathing when he gives me the opportunity and trusting that he won't choke me to death. Suddenly, it's one thrust too many, and I start to gag. He pushes into my throat several more times before I shove his thighs while yanking my head back. I cough and wipe the tears from my face. Is he going to do that again?

Jake grabs me under my arms and lifts me, forcefully pushing me onto the bed. I land flat on my back. He manages to slide the condom from the wrapper and roll it over his thick prick with incredible skill, all while he rips my legs open wide and falls between them. After grabbing my wrists and pinning them above my head, he slams his hips between my thighs, completely burying his hard cock deep inside my pussy. A sharp wail bursts from my throat, but that doesn't make him ease off. He lifts his hips and thrusts repeatedly, slamming me against the mattress while pinning my chest with the weight of his upper body.

He shifts, bouncing up onto his knees, clutching my waist with a firm grip and lifting my pelvis off the bed. His strong arms pull me into him as he thrusts forward. Each inward jab assaults my g-spot with thought-whirling repetition. A sudden orgasm is beginning to overtake me, and I can't pull it back, nor remember how to form legible words to beg for permission. There is just no time. I cum hard, squeezing his pumping prick as if begging him not to pull out. He doesn't stop fucking, me even though he's well aware that I broke his rule.

Jake fucks me hard and fast for at least five more minutes before flipping me onto all fours with one swift motion. I'm shocked at the strength of this man. Being able to manoeuvre me so effortlessly takes skill and muscle. He's back inside me, hammering away. Henry is a great lover, but he would have cum a long time ago. This guy just keeps on fucking. Holy shit! I can't remember the last time I was fucked this thoroughly. I hope it never ends.

Jake pulls out of me and weaves his fingers into my hair. He pulls my head toward him while shoving my hips away. My body spins as my ass topples to the mattress. Jake yanks off the condom and then clutches his throbbing prick, fist fucking it with a fury. His teeth are clenched tightly, while his squinted eyes pierce mine. He's sporting an evil glare, and it's hot as hell! Fuck, this is incredible!

He growls from deep in his chest. It sounds primal. Semen shoots from his prick, splatting onto my tits. Wad after hot, gooey wad spirt onto my neck and chest, slowly trickling downward. His body twitches and jerks as he squeezes the last drop of cum from his pulsing shaft.

After taking a deep breath, he releases his grip from my hair, allowing me to fall back on the bed. His spent body slides off the mattress and pulls a towel from an armoire. He returns and sits beside where I'm lying. With a tender touch, he begins to wipe his cum from my body. At first, neither of us speaks, relishing in the serenity of the moment.

He tosses the towel to the floor and then breaks the silence that was filling the room like a thick cloud. "Did you enjoy that, or was I too rough for you?"

I smile and stretch my arms over my head. "Fantastic! I haven't been fucked that hard and for that long in… gosh, I can't even remember."

"You need to tell Henry that you respond well to it. Perhaps he'll try harder. Most men think that after their female partner cums once, she's finished when, in fact, it's quite the opposite. If she's worked up just right, she'll outlast any man."

"Henry pleases me just fine, thank you," I say, feeling like he's being too critical of my husband, which rubs me the wrong way.

Jake must have heard the irritation in my voice. "I wasn't saying that he doesn't give you pleasure. Quite the opposite, in fact. It's obvious that he's a very attentive lover because of how well you respond to my touch. You aren't frigid, nor do you frighten easily. I'm simply saying that you like to get fucked hard and fast. Have you told him what you want?"

"Um, not in so many words. He fucks me very well, but he doesn't last all that long anymore. Maybe you can fuck like a rabbit on speed because you're still young, but you will get older, and that will probably change."

"And I'm hoping to have a very understanding wife if or when that time comes. If it does happen, I hope she finds a man my age who will do to her what I no longer can."

"I'm sure she will thank you for it, too."

He grins. "I think you and I will have lots of fun together. The next time you visit, expect that I won't be as easy on you."

"How so?" I ask, hoping he won't be throwing me headfirst into the deep end of his twisted, erotic imagination.

"Well, did you get a rush of adrenaline when I gave you pain from squeezing and spanking?"

"Yes, I think I did. I wasn't sure if I could take it at first, but, as it turns out, I definitely liked it. It seemed to enhance the good touches. After you told me to concentrate on those, I knew I wouldn't let the pain overwhelm me."

"I'm happy to hear that. Once you were able to look beyond the pain, you seemed to thrive off it. The next time you visit, we'll take it a step further. Pain and pleasure ride a very fine line. A person can weave back and forth over that line until it blurs, making it impossible to distinguish one from the other. Your body will soon accept pain as being pleasure. When I get you there, you'll really know what it is to peak."

"Oh, trust me, I *peaked* more times this afternoon than I have in a long time." I smile shyly, biting my bottom lip. "Are you so sure I'm going to come back to you?"

He studies my face. "Yes, you'll be back. You want to see what comes next. It will haunt you if you don't."

He's right; it will.

CHAPTER SIX

By the time Henry arrives home from work, I'm soaking in a hot bath with a few drops of lavender oil and some Epsom salts. I listen as he makes his way up the stairs. He walks into the bathroom with a blank expression that doesn't give me a hint about what type of mood he's in. Does he know that I went home with Jake? Is he angry about it, or quite the opposite?

"So, how was your lunch date with Jake?" Henry closes the lid on the toilet and sits down. He smiles, letting me know that he's curious for the details and not about to serve me divorce papers.

"Lunch was good. The food was surprisingly delicious for it being a simple café." I don't elaborate any further. I'll wait for more prodding from him. Yes, I'm torturing him, in a small way.

"Mhmm, I wasn't asking about how the food tasted. Did you go home with him or not?" he asks, leaning forward with his elbows resting on his knees, hands clasped together.

I bite my top lip and then sheepishly admit, "I did."

"Okay…" Henry's smile urges me to continue.

He's waiting for me to add more information, but I don't. I want him to ask me. I don't know how detailed he wants me to be when I describe the heavy fucking I got from his friend.

"Does he have a dungeon in his basement or not?" he prods.

"He does, but it isn't grungy like we were imagining a dungeon to be. I'd refer to it as a sex room. It was very clean and calming, but it did contain some furniture that a person could be tied to." I'm still not spilling the beans on what happened between Jake and me.

"Beth, you're driving me crazy," he confesses. A curious gleam brightens his eyes. "Please tell me what happened, from the moment you entered until you got back in your car. Sweetie, give me every detail."

I smirk, my face flushing hotter than my bathwater. For some reason, I feel somewhat shy. "Well, he explained that I could leave at any time and that he wouldn't test my pain threshold today. There were other rules and expectations that he explained, but I won't bore you with those. Jake let me experience some pain but not much. When he saw that I was not getting into it, he explained how to use the pain to increase my level of pleasure. After that, he continued. It was..." My words fade away, along with my thoughts. A long silence fills the room as he waits patiently for me to snap out of it and finish my description, but I'm lost in the memory of my first orgasm from Jake.

"Earth to Beth! What happened next?" He pushes for more details, waking me from my thoughts.

"Um, right... details. He told me to strip down, and then he tied my wrists together. A chain with a steel loop on the end was hanging from the ceiling, and that's where he tied my wrists. I was standing and naked. He surprised me by asking my permission. He asked me if I would be comfortable with him taking off his clothes. I said I was, so he slowly took everything off."

He interrupts me. "What does he look like naked? I mean, is he hung like a horse? Just tell me if I should shower with my underwear on if we ever shower together, like at a gym."

I snicker. No matter how powerful he is at the office, he's like any other man when it comes to penis envy. "No, he's not hung like a horse. He's about your size. What did surprise me is that he's ripped with muscle. His stomach is like a washboard, and he's a lot stronger than I had imagined him to be. His suits hide what's underneath, unfortunately."

"I know he works out at a gym almost every day, so he should be fit," Henry says, leaning back and crossing his arms over his chest.

I tease, "Are you jealous of Jake's body, Henry?"

He huffs, sarcastically, "No!" He rolls his eyes. "Yeah, maybe a little."

"He's not you, Henry. I love you and your body. Don't worry, I'm not going to trade you in." I jokingly console his fake fragile ego.

"I know because my body is awesome. I'm only teasing you. Please, continue your story." Henry leans forward on his forearms, wearing a silly grin.

I nod and begin again. "So, he touched me, talked to me, had me so sexually aroused that I thought I would burst into flames if he didn't let me cum, but he still wouldn't. He explained that he wanted me to enjoy the sensations—to truly experience them. Oh, I have to ask permission to orgasm. That's another rule. When I was about to cum, he stopped me because I was going to break that rule. He considers that to be disrespectful. Anyway, he fucked my asshole with his tongue, while fingering my pussy and clit. That brought on my first orgasm. Needless to say, he brought me to three mind-blowing orgasms while I was standing. My legs finally gave out, so he quickly untied me and carried me to the bed. He got me a bottle of water while I calmed my breathing."

"Three, huh? One right after the other, or were they spaced out?"

"The first one happened, and then there was a bit of a break, I assume. It's hard to remember exactly how it happened. My mind kept slipping into a sort of fogginess similar to that of a dream. Surprisingly, the next two came one right after the other. He put a vibrator on my clit right after the first one. I immediately came for the second time when he started fucking long, fast strokes. I wasn't even finished the second one when I started coming again. I lost my mind." My face flushes again, as I recall how intense that third orgasm was.

"Okay, so you're on the bed with the bottle of water. What happened next?" Henry asks, seeming enthralled by my description of how his work friend fucked my ass.

I bite my lip again. "He asked me to tell him what I wanted. I told him I wanted him in my mouth. He asked if I preferred it to be forced, or not. I wanted a little of both, today. He ordered me onto my knees, and then he put the tip of his cock in my mouth and told me to suck only that. I started to, but I got a little too eager and took more of him in my mouth. He corrected me because I didn't follow his instructions. He said he would punish me if I disobeyed him again. I had to start over, basically. Anyway, to make a long story a little shorter, he fucked my face and later pushed me onto the bed where he proceeded to fuck my pussy hard. He flipped me onto my hands and knees. That's when he transformed from a respectable man who wanted to give pleasure, to a man who was going to take it. He fucked me more viciously than anybody ever has. I'm not saying that to upset you, Honey. After some time, he spun me around and came on my tits."

"How much time?" he questions.

I shrug, "I don't know exactly. I wasn't wearing a watch. I'd estimate ten minutes."

"Of constant, hard fucking?"

"Yeah, it was intense."

"I'm surprised he didn't render you unconscious." Henry shifts to move his penis, which, by the look of the bulge in his pants, is engorged. "So, was he too rough with you?"

"Yes, at times, but he did it respectfully. Does that make any sense? I didn't feel like I was in any danger or that he was trying to belittle me," I explain. "In fact, I felt secure, like I had control over everything he was doing because at any moment, at my whim, it could be over.

"Will you be going back?" I hadn't given much thought to returning to Jake's house. I'm still revelling in the glorious aftermath from this afternoon.

"If you permit it, I will," I reply, assessing the expression on his face. He's deep in thought.

He stands up and unzips his pants. He reaches in and pulls out his rock-hard shaft. I honestly doubted he'd get so turned on from listening to me describe how another man jammed his cock into my body and fucked me harder than he ever has.

He tells me, "Suck my cock like you did his."

As I'm getting up to my knees, I'm looking at his eyes, as I did with Jake. I can't get over how excited he is about my rendezvous with his co-worker. He steps forward, his prick leading the way. I begin to do exactly as I did with Jake, including holding Henry's hands on the sides of my head and forcing him to pull my head forward, shoving his prick deep into my throat. He doesn't last more than two minutes before he cums.

I lay back in the tub to rinse his semen off my tits. He is standing with his sagging pecker poking out of his zipper, wearing an odd grin and staring me.

"I had no idea you'd get so worked up about what I did today."

"Why wouldn't I?" He seems confused.

I shrug. "Most men would be raging mad to know their wife was fucked very well, by another man. To also know that he was rough with her while he did it. That usually enrages most husbands. Wouldn't you think?"

"Yes, but we aren't most people," he replies as he tucks his dick into his pants. "I want you to go back, soon. Next time, ask him for more pain."

"We were just like most people before today," I remind him. "So, why do you want him to give me more pain?"

"You said that it excited you. If you want to have the whole experience, ask him for it." Henry walks out of the bathroom into the bedroom. I hear him say, "I can't wait to talk to Jake when I see him tomorrow."

I yell from the bathroom, so I'm positive he'll hear me. "Wait! Are you going to be mean to him? So, what are you going to talk to him about?" I'm concerned for Jake, but I'm not sure why. I get out of the tub and grab a towel before walking into the bedroom, water still streaming down my body. Henry is sitting on the bed beside his folded dress pants and discarded shirt and slipping on a pair of shorts. "I want him to tell me the scenario from his point of view. You know, from behind a man's eyes. I hope I don't get too excited at work," he starts chuckling.

He wraps his arms around me and kisses the top of my head. "I love you, Beth. Thank you for going through with it. Having you be with a dominant man has always been a fantasy of mine.

Don't try to analyse it; I always hoped it would happen. I'm going to watch some television for a while." He leaves me standing dumbfounded, with water still trickling down my back. I am an exceedingly lucky woman.

While I'm slipping a lightweight, pale green dress over my head, I wonder if I would be so enthralled to hear details on how Henry would fuck another woman. Would he get the same amount of pleasure out of it that I did? I'd want to be there to watch it happen, not because I'm jealous, but because I'm sure it would ignite the smouldering sexual fire within me. Maybe I should talk to Jake to see if he knows of a woman who would want to have sex with Henry. I don't know if he'd be willing to be dominated, or not. That's something I will have to ask him.

CHAPTER SEVEN

I've been flowing with ideas for my book's ending and am deep into writing this final chapter when my cellphone rings, jolting me from my train of thought. After looking up at the clock and realizing that I've been zeroed in on this for three hours, I decide to lift my phone to read the name on the screen. Is it worth answering?

"Hi, Henry. I hope you aren't working too hard today."

"It has been an easy day, no worries," he tells me.

"So, did you talk to Jake?" I ask before he has a chance to set the subject of our conversation. I'm curious to know if he got as aroused from hearing the sordid events through Jake's words, as he did from mine. In a way, I hope not. Getting an erection at work might get him into a whole heap of trouble with Human Resources.

"We had a conference that took a few hours. I didn't get a chance to talk to Jake alone. There have been people near us all day."

"Has he been acting strangely around you?"

"No, not at all. So, yeah, I suppose that is strange. I don't know what I was expecting, but I thought he'd act differently. He's the same calm and focused man he's always been. It's kind of weird, don't you think?" he asks.

I lean back in my chair and spin around. From this position, I can look out the window at the birds zipping from tree to tree. "No, not really. You said that he's a very private guy. He probably doesn't want to draw any attention to the fact that the two of you have changed the dynamic of your relationship."

"You make it sound like he and I are fucking," he laughs. "Oh, hang on a second." I can hear someone talking, but I don't know who it is. "Yeah, beer and chicken wings sound great right about now. As soon as I hang up with Beth, I'll be free to leave. Sure, okay. Ten minutes, yeah."

"Who was that?"

"I bet you won't need more than one guess," he teases. "Jake just poked his head in my office and asked me to go for some chicken wings and beer. Why is my cock getting hard? This is going to be interesting."

I start laughing. "Maybe you want him to tie you up and fuck your ass."

"No, no! I can't see myself letting a guy stick his prick in my ass." He means what he says, but he's chuckling, nonetheless.

"So, I gather that you won't be home for dinner. I'll be anxiously waiting for you to tell me his side of it. Maybe I'll masturbate while imagining myself sitting between you two in a booth at a dimly-lit restaurant." That would certainly be a sizzling hot adventure. Hmm, I have a new masturbation fantasy.

"Stop it! Don't do that," he whispers.

"You don't want me to masturbate?"

He replies, "No, by all means, go ahead. Just don't tell me about it right now. I'm already fashioning a semi-hard dick, and you describing a naughty situation like that will have me sporting a full-sized, raging dick. If you keep talking like that, I'll have to jack off before I go for wings with your lover."

"Wait a minute! He's not my lover. He's my..." I ponder the terminology. "I suppose you could say he's my Master. He did insist I call him Sir or Master when we're in the playroom."

He teases, "Okay, your *Master* and your husband are going for chicken wings and beer. That just sounds so bizarre. I have to hang up if I'm going to meet him on time. I'll be home in a few hours. You should expect that I'm going to want to fuck the hell out of you when I get there."

"I'll be waiting," I tell him and then hang up, hugging my phone to my chest. I watch a bird fly from one tree to another and then back to the first one. I can't help but see myself as being that little bird, going from Henry to Jake and back to Henry. If all goes well with their conversation, I'll be repeating the process many times over.

No matter how hard I try to sink my thoughts back into this book, I just can't. All I can think about is Henry and Jake, sitting in a bar, eating wings and drinking beer, discussing how Jake dominated me sexually last night. My clit keeps twitching, letting me know I need a release. Off to the bedroom I go to vibrate myself to orgasm.

What will I picture in my head? Perhaps I will imagine myself sitting in the bar in the middle of both of them, like I teased Henry with earlier. I can picture my hand stroking both their raging hard-ons with unsuspecting diners all around us. Yes, that would be wet-panty erotic.

CHAPTER EIGHT

Henry doesn't come home until nearly ten o'clock. I hear a car door shut and drive off. He's probably very drunk and will be stumbling through the front door. Come tomorrow morning, I'll be driving him to either work or the bar where he left his car. We are both adamant that driving after even only one drink, is grounds for divorce. We have both lost family members due to intoxicated drivers who were adamant that they were sober enough to operate their three-thousand-kilogram vehicle, but after killing someone, suddenly realized that was a grievous mistake.

As I'm coming down the stairs, he begins walking up, with a smile on his face. His dress shirt is untucked and the tie he was wearing is hanging from the pocket of his dress pants. He is definitely a happy drunk, but he isn't nearly as intoxicated as I figured he would be.

"Well, hello there, my sexy little vixen."

"Vixen?" I wrap my arms around his neck when he is a step below me. I like that we are the same height right now. "Did he say I was a vixen?"

"No, he didn't, but he sure does like you." Henry kisses me before ushering me back up the stairs. "He wants to play with you again, if you think you can handle it."

"And you're okay with this, even after you and he talked?" I ask, hinting that I want to know more about their conversation.

He smirks, "Oh yes, quite okay, indeed!"

I slip back onto the bed, closing my laptop and setting it on my nightstand. Henry is taking off his suit and flopping it over the back of the chair while I watch him, comparing how similarly he and Jake undress. "So, what did he say? The curiosity is killing me."

He laughs then walks into the bathroom and shuts the door. He is purposely making me wait, to drive me crazy, just as I had made him wait when describing what it was like to be with Jake. Waiting for something has never been easy for me. I'm very impatient. When I want something, I want it right now and he is playing on that trait.

"Henry," I yell out, hoping he'll open the door and talk to me, but I hear the shower start up, further annoying me.

Several minutes pass before he finally comes out of the bathroom. "Sorry, sweetie, I wanted to brush my teeth and take a quick shower to freshen up. I want to entertain you."

"Oh, really? You think it's that easy, right? You want it, so I have to give it to you." I tease him as he crawls up the bed while looking at me with a dirty grin and sexy eyes. "Tell me, or I won't let you have me."

"Oh, you're going to use sex as a bargaining chip, are you?" he teases.

I push him away with my feet while he playfully wrestles with them, trying to pull my legs apart. "Fucking tell me what he said!" I yell between clenched teeth, laughing the entire time, despite my effort to seem angry.

He grabs my ankles and yanks my legs wide apart, dropping his body between them until his face is directly above my breasts. He's trying to grab my nipples with his lips through my silky nightgown, but I shift back and forth so he can't snag one. He finally rests his chin between my breasts.

"Jake is a very honest man. I like him, but then again, I liked him before he fucked you; otherwise, it wouldn't have happened. Anyway, he asked me if I had any questions about what went on between you and him. I told him to tell me exactly what happened with great detail. So, he did. His story matches yours but with different perspectives. Please don't think I was doubting you were telling the truth. I wasn't." His face has no expression, which I find to be odd.

"I don't think that. Please continue," I urge him.

"He said that you are a quick learner and very respectful of his authority within that scenario. Um, what else do you want to know?" he asks me.

I roll my eyes, "Jeez, I don't know. You were there for hours, and you expect me to think that's all that was said? Tell me more. Start with, did he enjoy me?"

"Sweetie, did he cum?" He returns my question with a question. I nod. "Okay, I'll tell you what you want to hear. Jake said that you have an incredible body. He also said something that you didn't tell me. He told me that you wanted more pain, that you were getting off from it. Is that true?"

I bite my bottom lip, pondering his words. I hadn't thought I was asking for more pain as much as asking for him to continue the sex. After clearing my throat, I whisper, "Yeah. I really do think he's right because there was pain, and I didn't mind it that much. The type of pleasure he was giving me seemed to be so much more intense than it normally would. It's hard to explain."

"He also said you like to be touched softly as well. This I already know," he says while gliding his hands up my thighs and under my nightie, lifting it to expose my pussy. His hot lips kiss down my tummy, coming to rest on my clitoris. Slowly, they part, forming a tight seal around my little button so he can suck and flick it as he has a thousand times before.

I have been waiting all night for his touch and I am not disappointed. My clit is swelling under the caress of his hot breath. His touch is fanning the flames of my already fired up sex. I cup my breasts, squeezing my nipples very hard, just like Jake did. It sends shocks of pain straight down my body. By the time it reaches my clit, the ache is no longer painful. It's like adding dry timber to a raging fire.

My hips tilt up toward his pillow-soft lips, begging him not to stop. My heart is pounding in my chest, trying to beat its way through my ribs. As my orgasm nears, my clit stiffens. He sucks it as if it were a tiny dick while he rapidly strokes it with his tongue. I'm losing my ability to control my own body and I cry out as the exhilaration lifts me, higher and higher, with growing

75

intensity, until finally, I'm tossed over the peak of the climax. The frenzy of twitches, spasms and jolts ripple through every muscle in my body. Slowly, my brain-fog begins to clear while my body continues to vibrate.

"Jake wants you tomorrow afternoon. I told him I'd ask you to call him in the morning," Henry whispers as he flops onto his back. With a flirtatious giggle, he demands. "Now, suck my cock, woman!"

I look at him with a shocked expression. Henry has never been crude with me, but I like it. Having him be more assertive in the bedroom can't hurt, as long as I can set the limits.

While pulling my nightie over my head, I straddle his thighs. I twist the nightie and then tell him to give me his wrists. He looks at me with a furrowed brow, but I urge him to do what I said. Reluctantly, he complies, putting his wrists together. Using my twisted nightie, I fashion a tight binding and tie a knot, pulling on it to ensure he won't get free.

"Where would you like my hands to be, Mistress Beth?" he asks, teasingly.

I smile and reply, "Over your head. Careful, I could get used to you calling me Mistress."

He laughs but instantly stops when my mouth engulfs his cock, taking him completely down my throat and holding perfectly still. I wait until his moan eases before slowly pulling back, sliding him out of my mouth.

"Jake was impressed with how well you suck cock. He said that not many people can take as much as you do, without gagging."

"But I did gag. He held my head a bit too long, and I gagged when I couldn't pull my head away."

"Yes, he said that too. Did you know he was testing you?" I shake my head with his dick down my throat. "Yeah, he wanted you to gag. If you hadn't gagged when you did, he would have continued to hold your head like that until you started fighting him for air. He explained that it's a way to show you that he has control over what happens to you, even though it's actually you who can stop him at any time. But like I said, he is truly impressed with your cock-sucking ability. See, I've been telling you for years that you know how to suck a mean cock."

"So, he was showing me that he was the boss? I just thought he enjoyed how my throat squeezed his prick when I gagged."

"I'm sure it's a little of both," Henry says, showing me that he slipped his hands out of the binding. He reaches down for my shoulders, pulling me up his body. He rolls me onto my back. I open my legs, invitingly. He slides into me slowly, allowing both of us to enjoy how tight this feels. I will loosen after he's in, so we like to savour this first gentle thrust.

His eyes look into mine. His whisper is soft. "I love you so much, Sweetie."

"Henry, I love you, too," I assure him as our lips press together and his body begins to wave over mine. He fills me so perfectly. My calves make their way over his thighs and my hands grasp his flexed ass cheeks, pulling him into me, hard with each deep thrust.

I've cum twice, but he's still fucking me. Why hasn't he given himself over to his own orgasm yet? Henry can never hold out past two of my climaxes. He once told me that by watching my face and body react to his touch, always pushes him over the edge. But he's still fucking me.

Henry flips me onto my hands and knees in much the same way Jake did. That's a new move for him. He shoves his stiff cock deep into my dripping pussy. With his hands holding my hips, he slams against me, over and over until I'm climaxing for a third time. I'm expecting him to erupt half-way through my orgasm, but he keeps pounding away. Just as I'm about to reach my fourth climax, he cries out a high-pitched wail. I'm used to hearing him holler during these moments, but his pitch is slightly higher this time. His body collapses to the bed beside me. He slowly rolls onto his back.

I let my body drop face down. We lie there quietly, with only our heavy breathing to break the silence in the room. As soon as I feel like I can form a full sentence without having to inhale, I say, "Wow! Where did that come from?"

He smiles, replying, "Jake gave me a few pointers."

"Pointers?" My interest is piqued, "Oh, do tell."

Henry turns his head to look at me and explains, "Yeah. I told him that I get off on watching you cum, so he suggested a few tips to prevent me from getting overly excited and blowing my wad too soon."

I start to giggle. "He did? Like what?"

"That's between men. You don't need to know," he teases.

"Oh, come on!" I want to pry the information from him, but I can sense he won't budge. "Fine! Don't tell me, just keep doing it. That was fucking hot! I loved it!"

He smiles boastfully, literally patting himself on the shoulder. "Yeah, you did!"

"Careful, your ego is beginning to fill this entire room."

"There might not be any space in here for you, my sweetness." He's still smiling like a fool.

As I'm getting off the bed to go to the bathroom and clean up, I ask, "So, do you know of his plans for me tomorrow?"

"Yup, but I'm not telling you," he replies, smirking like an idiot with a secret that could change the world.

I shake my head and roll my eyes. "So, you really don't mind that another man is touching and fucking me?"

He looks at me with a serious expression. "Beth, every time I think about it, about him taking control of your body, I get a hard-on. It's bizarre, I know. Most men would be fuming mad to know that some other guy is sticking his filthy cock into his woman, but not me, oddly enough. Does it bother you that it doesn't make me angry?"

"Why would it?"

He leans up on his elbows, "I just don't want you to think that I don't love you with every piece of me. You are my whole world and that will never change. Just because I give my permission for Jake to have you physically, doesn't mean that I love you any less. It makes me want you even more. I know it sounds strange." Henry tilts his head and asks, "How do you think you'd feel if I were with another woman, in the same situation?"

"Like you dominating her? I don't think I'd like that because I'd be wondering why you aren't doing it to me."

He shakes his head. "No, that's not what I mean. What if she were dominating me?"

"I don't know, to be honest. I would hope that it would turn me on, but I can't be sure until the situation actually played out. You couldn't have known how you'd feel after I was with Jake until I was actually with him, right? I mean, you might assume you'd know, but you couldn't really be sure."

Very surely, he replies, "No, I knew. Let me tell you a secret that's a bit embarrassing for me. For about a year now, I've been jerking off nearly every morning in the shower while thinking about you with Jake. Just imagining him inside of you, pleasuring you, works me up. There's no way I could go through a whole day at work if I knew he was going to be in the meetings. And a few weeks ago, there was a stressful day when you were in the bathroom talking to me while I showered. I couldn't jerk off, and I knew the day was scheduled for a long meeting, and he would most certainly be there. During one of the more boring speakers, I began imagining you bent over the big conference table, with your hands tied behind your back. Jake was fucking you so hard that the heavy table began to slide. Needless to say, I couldn't leave the room when everyone else did. My cock just wouldn't soften. Had I not thought up an excuse to remain seated, I would have been humiliated. So, to answer your question... yes, I knew."

"What was the excuse?"

Henry is looking at me with a guilty smirk. "Someone asked why I wasn't leaving for the break, so I told them I just needed a minute to take down some notes from the speech I'd just enjoyed listening to. Jake overheard me and knew something was wrong. The speaker was about as exciting as a root canal. He stayed behind with me. He asked if I was all right and wouldn't leave it alone. I finally told him. That's when he shook my hand and said that we should talk about this another time."

"So, you set me up? You fuckers! Now it makes sense why you insisted I go to lunch with him. You two had this planned all along," I say, pointing my finger accusingly. "And here I thought I'd caught his eye. Oh, my god! He was only doing you a favour by entertaining me. How humiliating! I'm so embarrassed!"

"You did catch his eye. A few years before that day in the conference room, he made a confession to me. He said he had seen you in my office when he was walking past and immediately had a burning desire to have you at his mercy. Sorry, Sweetie, I should have told you the truth, but I wanted to play it out this way for my own thrill. I guess I wanted the suspense of wondering if you'd do it. If I came right out and asked you to have sex with my fellow colleague, would you have?"

"No, probably not. I suppose this was a more exciting way to go about it. I forgive you."

"Let's go to sleep. You have a busy day tomorrow, and you'll need your rest," he says, flicking off the light while he grins cunningly.

"Should I be leery of his plans? I am not going to be able to sleep tonight. You know that, right?"

Henry simply chuckles before rolling onto his side.

CHAPTER NINE

Henry had left before I woke up. There's a note on the kitchen counter stating that he has an appointment and won't be home in time to see me before I am expected to meet Jake. On the note is a phone number. Beside it is Jake's name with a caption that reads, '*call him*'.

I make a mug of coffee while my stomach flutters nervously each time my eyes catch a glimpse of the small piece of paper. What am I supposed to say to Jake when I call? After some self-convincing, basically calling myself out as a coward, I dial the number.

For a quick moment, I debate hanging up. Before I can, he answers. In a lascivious voice, he says, "Hello, Beth."

"Jake! Hi, umm... yeah, it's Beth. Henry left a note for me to call you." I'm relieved my words flowed so easily because my throat has suddenly gone dry. I sip my coffee to help moisten it.

He breathes in deeply and lets it out slowly. "Beth, it's nice to hear your voice. Did Henry talk to you about being my subject today?"

I clear my throat. "He did. Um, so you want me back?"

"Absolutely! Beth, we've only just chipped at the iceberg. Can you handle more? I won't be as gentle this time."

I try to swallow away the imaginary cotton ball that's redeveloped in my throat despite the sip of coffee. "Yes, I expect that I can. What do you have planned?"

I can hear his amusement in his breathy laugh. "What I have planned for you is something you'll have to experience for yourself. Are you willing to step into my playroom again?"

"Yes," I whisper.

"Perfect. I will expect you at my home at four o'clock. Do you remember how to get here?"

"Yes, I do," I say louder than I had intended. My voice is very unreliable at the moment.

"Henry put some clothes in your closet that I insist you wear. You will wear only what is supplied when you enter my playroom. Everything should fit you perfectly. Do you have an issue with my request?"

I shake my head and then realize that he can't see me. "Um, no. No problem."

"Each time you visit me, the intensity of our play will increase. I will be starting with you as soon as you enter the room. The front door will be unlocked, so enter and lock it behind you. Come downstairs, use the washroom if you need, and enter the playroom when you're ready to begin. Please don't take too long; I don't think I can stand it if you do. I'll punish you if you're more than a few minutes late."

"I will do as you ask. Is there anything else?"

"Remember your safe words," he replies. "I will see you at four."

My heart is thumping with either nervous energy or sexual anxiousness. Either way, my adrenaline is pumping. I eat a quick breakfast muffin before taking a shower. I apply some make-up but not a lot. If he's going to be putting a blindfold on me, my make-up will smear heavily, so I'd like to avoid looking like a racoon when I leave his house.

I spend the morning and afternoon writing the ending to the book that I've been struggling to finish in a way that will tie up the storyline and pull the whole thing together. I hadn't been able to until today. Perhaps being slightly distracted has taken me out of my head so the words could flow through me a bit easier.

When the phone rings, I answer it quickly without seeing who it is. "Hello?"

"Hi, lady!" Amy sounds happy.

"Oh, hey. How are you?" I ask, realizing that I failed to call her after my luncheon with Jake.

"So, I haven't heard from you. I just assumed you had chickened out and didn't go for lunch."

I confess, "I went." Silence.

"What the fuck? You went? No shit!"

"Yes, I did," I tell her.

"So?" she waits for me to give her all the sordid details.

"We talked a lot over lunch. I can't give you all the details over the phone." This will not please her.

Amy shows her irritation with a loud growl. "Wait! No fucking way! You'd better tell me something dirty before you hang up that phone." I giggle again but say nothing. She jokes, "You whore! You fucked him! That's fucking awesome! Tell me more immediately."

"We ate lunch while we talked. He invited me back to his place. I went. Amy, you are right in your initial assessment about him being a sexual dynamo in the sack," I confess.

Amy yells, "I knew it!" She's making bizarre sexual grunts that don't seem as inappropriate as they are funny. I can picture her humping the air with her hand slapping the imaginary ass in front of her because I've seen her do that exact same dance many times.

"Describe his body with great detail. Don't be telling me about his blue eyes or big hands; I can see those for myself. I want to know what he's hiding under those fashionable suits."

I announce, "We should meet for lunch."

She huffs, "I wish I could, but I have to take the baby for her doctor's appointment. It's shot time. I hate when they get pokes. So, since we can't meet up, tell me everything immediately!"

"Believe me when I say the suits do him no justice. He is ripped. That man works out hard at the gym. Henry said he goes almost every day." I stop there, hoping not to give her too much information all at once.

"Tell me, is he hung? Wait, no… don't tell me. If he has a pinky finger-sized prick, I will totally die inside," she says, as though her life will seem desolate if I ruin her fantasy of him having a massive penis.

I laugh. "Well, liven up, lady; he's hung well."

She yells, "Yes! I knew it!" I can hear the baby in the background, whining. "So, tell me something weird that he likes to do. You know, something kinky that I can fantasize about while I'm sitting in the waiting room at the doctor's office."

"Something kinky, huh?" I wonder how far I should take this conversation. "He's into..." my words drop off mid-sentence.

"Into what?" she quickly demands.

"Kink," I tell her. "Um, bondage to start with. Giving pain with pleasure. Um, he gets off on being in complete control of me."

"Huh?" she mutters as if she's confused.

I begin to explain and speak slowly and clearly. I close my eyes so I can picture his sexy blues looking deeply into mine as I tell our story. "He tied me up, spanked me, used his mouth on my vagina and asshole, fucked me in the ass. He made me cum several times before untying me and carrying me to the mattress. Then, I opened my mouth, and he fucked my face. He fucked my pussy, making me cum a few more times, and then he came on my chest. There was a vibrator used on me at one point. It was hot, steamy, and erotic on so many perverted levels. I have never cum that hard and that many times during a sexual rendezvous. He got excitement from giving me pain and pleasure, which excited me. The more I screamed, the more aroused he became. He made it all about me. He was teaching me how my body worked. He knew exactly what to do and when to do it and when not to touch me. He took me right to the edge of orgasm and held me there until I thought I would literally explode in a ball of flames if he just blew on me."

"Wow," Amy whispers, captivated by my rambling. "I want him. I want that. I've never had that. I didn't know I was missing it. Great, now you've ruined my sex life forever."

"Sorry, Amy. No, I'm not sorry. You told me to tell you about it. So, it's all your fault in a way."

"Wait, no! Don't blame me for your steamy sexual encounter. If you recall, I said NOT to go home with him."

"I know. Do you want to know something else that's even more nitty-gritty?" I ask her, knowing full well she does.

"Duh!"

I clear my throat, knowing she's going to flip over this little tidbit of information. "Henry set it up."

"Are you fucking kidding me right now?"

"Nope! The two of them conspired on getting me to his house, so I would fuck him."

She asks with sarcasm in her voice, "Why would Henry want Jake to fuck you?"

"He said the idea of it happening has been getting his dick hard for about a year now. So, they set it up."

"Did it work? Is Henry pleased?"

I chortle. "Well, his dick's been hard as steel since it happened. Also, he arranged for me to visit Jake later this afternoon. He actually put a sexy outfit in my closet at Jake's request. I haven't looked at it yet, but I'd bet money it's something sexy."

She busts out laughing. "You said he's kinky, right?"

"Oh, yeah!"

"What if he has a prehistoric fantasy about fucking a dinosaur, and that's the costume in your closet?" She's laughing so hard that I hear her snort.

I picture myself trying to get down the basement stairs in his house wearing a giant dinosaur costume with huge feet, and then I see myself rolling down them. I wouldn't get hurt because of the puffy costume, but the whole concept is very disturbing.

"Why would you put that image into my head?"

"After you put it on, take a picture and send it to me," she demands with a hint of laughter lingering in her voice.

"Okay, I'll do that. Just make sure you don't have your phone face up in the doctor's office. I don't want everyone in the waiting room to get a view of my dinosaur costume."

More snickering from her. "Yeah, I'll be careful. Okay, I have to go. I want the picture, and you'd better call to tell me all about your visit with Mr. Hottie. I want every disgusting detail. Like, take notes if you can. Oh, pictures! Take pictures of him naked, pretty please!" she barks.

I laugh and say, "No pictures or note-taking, but I'll try to remember the details as best I can. Love you."

"Love you, too," she says before we hang up.

* * *

At about two-thirty, I find myself hesitating in front of the double doors that hide the waiting outfit. Not opening them is like teasing myself, but I'm afraid of what I'll discover if I pull on those handles. Ever since he told me the clothes were in there, I've wanted to peek but managed to hold off until now. I pull open the left door but see nothing unusual. It isn't until I open the one on the right that I see a red corset hanging on a black, fabric-covered hanger. It is silky and beautiful, with long shoestring ropes weaved up the front and back. I will use them to cinch in my waist. It is gorgeous, nothing like what I would bother spending money on. I've never worn anything this sexy. These things were for women in catalogues, not for every day women like me.

Attached to the hanger is a matching satin bag containing stockings and a thong to match the corset. I lay them on the bed after removing the hanger. I loosen the shoestring on the front and slip it over my head. Completely undoing the strings and re-fishing them through each of the holes sounds like an unnecessary chore. I secure it tightly and put on the thong and stockings, fastening them to the garters. When I turn to look in the mirror, I'm shocked at how well it fits me. I turn left and then right, admiring how incredibly sexy I am with my waist cinched in, my breasts shoved up, my pussy barely covered by any material at all, and my legs donning silky smooth, thigh-high stockings.

Okay, I look incredible, but I can't leave the house like this obviously. I'll have to wear a dress over this and take it off once I get there. Shoes! I don't own anything that will go with this outfit. My heels aren't all that high, and they're definitely not what I would call sexy. They are efficient, not glamorous.

On the floor of my closet is a box I don't recognize. I open it to find a pair of shiny, red high-heels. They have thick soles which make them seem even higher than they actually are. These will add five inches to my height and make my legs appear even longer. After slipping them on my feet, I'm absolutely shocked to realize they fit perfectly and are quite comfortable despite their intimidating height. How the hell did he know my size when I usually have to try shoes on to determine if I need a half size bigger or smaller? I walk over to the mirror for another peek. Damn! I look like a fucking sex goddess!

Remembering that Amy wants a picture, I search the web for a picture of a dinosaur and text it to her. She responds with a laughing smiley icon. I snap one of me and send it to her and then to Henry. She replies immediately with a shocked emoticon. She then writes, *'fucking hot!'* I send her a happy face icon. Henry doesn't respond to the text right away. He's probably in a meeting and he'll get the message later. I really hope his phone isn't face up on a conference table where uninvited onlookers will catch a glance.

A quick glance at the clock on the wall has me hurrying to finish dressing. After picking out a long, flowing, white summer dress that has tiny red flowers on the skirt, I slip it over my head. I take another glimpse to see if everything that needs to be hidden is just that. If someone were paying attention, they'd know I was wearing a very sexy outfit under my common dress, but I have no plans on stopping anywhere. I say a quick prayer that I won't have an accident on my way to Jake's that lands me in a hospital. I don't want that to happen on any day but especially while wearing this.

* * *

At his house, I enter slowly, looking around to see if he's waiting for me near the door. I don't see him, but then again, he did say he'd be downstairs. I go down each step with care, holding the railing so I can catch myself if I trip. Surprisingly, these heels are much easier to walk in than they appear to be.

Once I've slipped off the dress and set down my purse, I take a deep breath and reach out to grab the handle of the door that separates me from whatever kinky adventure I'm about to experience. My hands are shaking. I clench my fists several times and grasp the handle and twist, pushing it wide open.

I step inside, closing the door behind me. My heart is pounding. My mouth feels dry, and my whole body is shaking uncontrollably from excited anticipation. I have yet to turn around to look for him. I take another breath and turn, finding him waiting patiently for me to ready myself.

Jake is wearing black leather pants, a wide leather band around each of his forearms, a chest harness that rests just above his nipples, and black work boots loosely tied on his feet. He's standing perfectly still, watching me with his hands folded over his chest. I step toward him, but he puts his hand up to stop me.

"I'm ready to start whenever you are," I tell him to break the uncomfortable silence.

He steps forward slowly and says, "No talking unless I ask you to or you're asking my permission to cum."

Jake walks around me. I think he's admiring his purchase. His boots clomp with each step, scuffing the floor as he's coming to a stop. I'm shaking even harder now, and it's cold in here. My adrenaline is surging.

The very second his fingertips graze my arm, I startle and bark out a high-pitched squeak. It felt like his initial touch was laced with electricity as if he'd dragged his feet on a shag carpet. He's standing in front of me, eyes locked in a stare with mine. I'm shaking so violently that my legs just might give out. I'm regretting the shoes now.

His knuckles caress my cheek in an attempt to soothe my anxieties. He assures me, "You are stronger than you think you are. Prove that I am right. Let's begin."

CHAPTER TEN

Jake takes my hand in his. With his right hand on my lower back, he escorts me over to what looks like a metal, spindle-style, footboard of a bed, but it's not attached to the rest of the frame. It's secured to the floor with large bolts and standing solely on its own.

He turns me away from him so that I'm facing the frame. "Lace your fingers together behind your back."

I do as he says without hesitation while scanning the dimly lit room. Today, I'm not quite as overwhelmed as the first time I walked through that door. With fear not overwhelming me, I'm able to take in my surroundings. On the wall to my left are seven ropes, all wrapped neatly and hung according to size. They vary in colours: red, white, black, purple, pink, and beige. The beige rope looks to be the roughest and would likely feel scratchy on my skin. In front of me are several hooks on the wall and the floor, all in various locations. I wonder why he has so many. To my right is a chair that is a cross between a gynaecologist's chair and one from a dentist's office. It's all black with cushioned sections bearing straps with buckles. I might like to be in that chair one day.

Jake has tied my hands behind my back with one of the ropes, but I wasn't paying attention to which one he chose. He left the excess to drape to the floor. Why didn't he just use a shorter rope?

He squats down, wrapping my ankles with two different ropes and then has me spread my legs a bit wider than my shoulders. He secures each ankle to the outer posts of the bed frame. I can't pull them together. Jake rises to his feet behind me. The air in the room falls silent for several seconds, causing my heart to pound from wondering what he's waiting for or what he's about to do. Is he about to spank me? Will he do something just as painful, or worse?

I startle when his smooth-spoken words ring through the stillness. "I could look at you all day. You are stunningly beautiful and sexy, and I can't wait to watch you lose yourself."

He takes the rope that's binding my hands and gently pulls it toward him. I fight to keep from losing my balance. If he continues to pull, I will fall to the floor. He doesn't stop. Struggling is of no use. I'm going to fall! My back slaps against his chest, and I gasp. I can feel the firmness of his leather harness through the silkiness of my corset. His lips kiss my neck with a tenderness that instantly calms my fears and sends shivers down my spine. My skin is lifting with tiny bumps as a sudden heat radiates through my core.

Jake steps forward until I'm standing under my own power. He takes up the slack in the rope as he walks around the frame, forcing me to bend forward at my hips as my arms raise up and over my head. He continues to pull until I am bent over the cool metal rail with my face nearly touching the spindles. My legs are pressing firmly against the frame, straining the muscles on the back of my legs. I hear him tie his end of the rope to one of the steel hoops mounted on the floor. This is not a comfortable position. The backs of my legs are going to ache all day tomorrow.

As he's walking around me, his fingertips glide along my chilly skin, starting at my fingertips and brushing up my stretched arm, all the way down my corset until both of his hands are testing the firmness of my ass cheeks with light squeezes. His soft, hot lips press onto my right ass cheek. His hands slide quickly down my ass and outer thighs, slowing once they reach my stockings. He must have a thing for their silkiness because he is caressing my legs from my ankles all the way up to my garters.

His fingers slip under the gusset of my thong and pull it away from my dampness, while the other fingers explore, spreading my pussy lips. He tucks the gusset of my panties between them before grabbing my ass cheeks again.

He's nibbling the skin on my butt, his teeth taking tiny nips at my flesh. It pinches, but it's not terribly painful by any means. It's more like a friendly nip from a puppy.

Suddenly, his lips press against my asshole, and I squeal. Chills spread all over my body. What is it about a hot, wet tongue applied there that has me instantly willing to do just about anything he asks of me? No matter how nervous I am, this very act is taking me out of my head.

Jake pulls harder on my panties, increasing the pressure on my clitoris. It hurts, but it's thrilling, especially with his tongue toying my ass. His mouth leaves me for a mere second. The wide palm of his hand claps down sharp against my buttock. I gasp, biting my lips so I don't cry out. More is coming, I'm sure of it. I anxiously wait, expecting the next shot of pain, but it doesn't come, further heightening my anticipation of his next touch.

I can see his legs move about from between mine. He walks away but returns with something black in one hand; the other contains a whip with many long tassels hanging from it. I watch as he swings it effortlessly using a gentle spin of his wrist.

Again, I'm starting to shake. This game we're playing is advancing quickly. I thought he would break me in more gradually than he is, but I was mistaken. He's about to whip me! I'm not sure I am ready for this.

His fingertip circles my asshole as cold liquid drips onto it, allowing his finger to push beyond the tight outer rim of my backside with ease. My ass does enjoy a good reaming now and then; it hasn't worn the badge of virginity since I was nineteen. Henry has fucked it many times throughout the years.

I breathe slowly, allowing my body to relax so it can accept the stretching he is about to put upon my sphincter. Soon, two fingers are inside me, stretching and spinning. It isn't long before he has me relaxed enough that he can ease a butt plug into me. The plug is being manoeuvred into my resisting hole with slight spins and constant pressure. It isn't long before my ass gives itself up, allowing the sex toy to pop in and then swallowing it as my rim grips the narrowed base, holding it inside my rectum.

Jake must realize that I'm intimidated by the whip. I yelp when he swings it, slapping the tassels over his palm with a *thwap*. Perhaps I was expecting that he was about to whack me with it.

He squats down behind my legs enough that I can see his face and the whip as he explains, "This is called a flogger. I am going to use it on you. I'm sure you'll enjoy it once you get over the fear of the unknown. What are the safe words, Beth?"

"Red and Yellow," I reply swiftly, proving my nervousness.

Jake's hand reaches through the spindles, cupping my cheek. "You'll feel the weight of the leather and the sting of the strands. I want you to lose yourself in the combination of the sensations. Use your words if it becomes too much."

As he stands up, his hand glides up my stocking as if he's favouring the sensation. Yes, I'm sure he has a fetish for nylon. The tassels flop down on my back, but it doesn't hurt at all. In fact, the chill of the leather gives me goosebumps as the tassels spill over each side of my waist.

He lifts them off and then takes a step back. I observe his legs, hoping to see his body shift so I know when he's about to swing. I watch as the tassels spin through the air as if he's winding up. The tassels slap down on my ass, but again, it doesn't hurt. He's being gentle with me. Several times the leather contacts my flesh, not causing me any distress whatsoever. This feels quite nice actually, like a bizarre massage.

"Prepare yourself," he tells me, but before I can tense my muscles, the tassels crack down on my ass. The ends of the leather strands sting my skin. It stings, but it's not as uncomfortable as I thought it would be. The worst part is that it covers so much area all at once, but the sting is only from the tips of the leather strips.

I follow his feet as they shuffle back and forth as he slaps at me from all angles. My skin must be pink by now because it feels hot to me. The whip falls to the floor as his hand yanks my panties to the side, pinching my clitoris even worse.

It isn't until two of his fingers slip into me without resistance that I realize just how wet I am. My body must have enjoyed the flogging more than I imagined it would have. To be honest, my mind didn't hate it either. I quite enjoyed the sensation.

His fingers reach deep into me, fluttering wildly. I want to cum, but before I can, he pulls them out for a split second, resuming with yet another finger. I'm sure there are three inside of me, sloshing noisily.

"May I cum, please, Sir?" I frantically mutter. He cracks my sensitive ass cheek with his open palm, and I holler, "Please!"

"Cum," he orders with a whisper so faint that I almost don't hear.

My arms and legs pull at the ropes, fighting to get free but to no avail. My core muscles tighten. My cunt pushes at his fingers before spasms clutch at them, trying to pull them in deeper.

I whimper when my climax begins to wind down all too quickly. I'm still huffing, partly from anger that it's over and partly because the muscles all over my body are beginning to ache.

I open my eyes to see him slipping a condom on his rock-hard cock that is poking through the open zipper of his leather pants. He rushes up behind me and slides his prick deep into me. There's no hesitation whatsoever. He's hammering in and out of me without mercy. The head of his stiff dick assaults my cervix with each powerful thrust. Fuck, this feels so good!

I never thought that by giving up my control, I could lose myself so completely simply from the false idea that anything happening is his will. I can forego any stress of performance anxiety. Maybe I like the ease from the guilt of cheating on my husband, even though I have his permission.

Although I feel like I'm yelling, my voice is a mere whisper, "I'm coming." He continues fucking me with incredible force as my cunt throbs around his prick, desperate to hold him inside me.

A long, deep-winded cry erupts from within me until no breath remains in my lungs. I gasp, and that's when another body-quivering orgasm rocks me to my core. He continues to slam hard into me. My mind is spinning wildly out of control and my muscles lock in a soul-quaking climax.

As soon as he's sure I've ridden through the last twitch of physical euphoria, Jake pulls out of me and unties me with incredible speed. Once free, he leads me toward two tall pillars that reside approximately two metres apart from one another. Near the top of each one is a dangling rope with a leather handcuff hanging at its end. At the bottoms are more cuffs, for the ankles I would assume.

He has me stand with my arms stretched out to my sides while he slips each one securely into the cuffs. Using care not to hurt me, with the tips of his boots, he kicks my feet apart one at a time. As my feet spread, he stares into my eyes. His blue eyes show no fear or insecurity in what he's doing. It's obvious that he's been in this situation enough times that it doesn't cause him any anxiety. For me, I'm nervous as fuck but in a curious way.

He kisses my lips so lovingly that for a moment, my thoughts drift to an idea where heartfelt affection exists. Jake is not a person with whom I want to plant that seed. When he grabs my throat during our kiss, there is no doubt in my mind that this is no place for my heart to soften. His grip is so tight that I can barely breathe, and I can feel the blood reddening my swelling face. The only thing I can do is stand here and hope he lets go. I could flutter my hands or try to kick him, but I'll hold off on that unless the situation becomes dire. I trust him – at least, I think I do.

Jake's grip eases. His lips continue to kiss mine while that hand makes its way behind my head. He grips my hair, yanking my head back. His nose glides along my neck as he breathes in my scent. He exhales with a low growl that vibrates my throat. I become putty in his hands. His manly call makes me feel very feminine because I could never make a sound that deep and primal.

Jake ducks under my arm to get behind me, scuffing his heavy shoes on the floor as he moves. He wraps my ankle in a cuff. His hands lightly stroke my legs as he makes his way to the other ankle, fastening it as well. His hands glide up the back of my stockings until two fingers slip beneath the back of my thong. I swear I hear scissors cutting the material. He gives a swift, hard yank, ripping the gusset of panties and freeing my undercarriage completely. My clit is thankful that the material isn't shoved between my labia any longer.

Using the waistband of my panties, he pulls my ass back toward him. His prick slips into my pussy like a guided missile. It's as if his cock just knows where to aim. Jake fucks me with an easy tempo that allows me to feel every vein on his manhood as my lips glide around the shaft. His right hand reaches around me, pulling at my stiff nipple before making its way to my even stiffer clitoris. He massages my little button until it's swelling beneath his two fingers and I'm breathing with long deep breaths. If he continues, he'll have me coming again, but he steps away from me, leaving me teetering on that edge.

I open my eyes and watch as he pulls open a drawer, reaching inside. In the dimness, my eyes can't make out what he picks up, but it makes a clinking sound like a chain. He stands in front of me, holding three metal clips with rubber on the tips. They are connected together by thin metal chains that don't look much thicker than a necklace would be.

"These are clamps. I will put them on sensitive areas of your body, which will feel awkward or a bit painful at first but will be very arousing once the initial sensation eases. Do you trust me?"

"I trust you," I assure him. Yes, I am still concerned about having these clamped onto me.

His eyes stare into mine as his fingers roll my nipples, pulling and pinching them until they are fully erect. I continue to watch his face even when his eyes cast downward. He applies the first clamp. My chest curls forward trying to escape the pain overwhelming my tender nipple. I'm sure it's not as bad as my mind is making it out to be.

He whispers, "Just breathe, Beth. It's not as painful as you think it is." I'm not quite believing what he's saying because it does not feel at all good.

I begin to inhale through my nose and exhale from my mouth to mimic his breathing. He wasn't lying when he said that I would get aroused from the pinching pain. My clit has twitched half a dozen times since he applied it only a few seconds ago. Without meaning to, I smile at him while my breathing slows. His smile is wicked as he clips the other nipple in the equally tight, little pincher. The same initial pain rips through my other breast but soon after, my clit begins to twitch again. In no time at all, I don't even notice the pain, just arousal each time the chain moves.

He holds one up in front of my face while grinning devilishly. "Guess where this one goes?"

"No... No! That's going to hurt too much!" I beg him not to, but he seems to be enjoying my pleas.

Jake's expression doesn't change as his fingers pull and fiddle with the sensitive bundle of nerves between my legs. I'm whining, wanting to scream out *Yellow,* but I'm hesitating because I am curious to know whether it will be as painful as I expect or if I am going to become increasingly aroused from the pressure it brings, thus mimicking my body's reaction to the clips on my nipples.

It isn't long until the clamp bites at the base of my clit. The instant agony it brings has me thrusting my head back with my mouth wide as whimpers fill the air. It's shockingly painful but not like cutting a finger or stubbing a toe. This hurt is strangely wonderful. I have never felt anything like this before. It's as if an elastic band is running inside my body from my clitoris all the way to my belly button and the tension is deliciously straining.

My head flops forward, needing to look down at the chains that connect my nipples to my clit, much like the ignited nerves inside my body seem to span directly from nipple to nipple to clit. I lift my eyes to see him admiring my face. He wears no expression as he stands silently with his arms crossed over his chest.

Jake is a sexy man, no doubt. Most heterosexual women that meet him would crave to see him standing before them as I am right now. Many men would as well. He could easily be a model on the cover photo of a domination novel. I am so lucky that he chose me to be his sex toy.

Jake pulls the chain toward him, and I gasp, crying out sharply. It's wonderful but horrible, too. I'm confused whether I'm supposed to like this or quite the opposite. Either way, I want to experience more of whatever this is. When he lifts the chain up, my clit is being stretched upward, and it's incredible. He pulls down on the chain, stretching my nipples toward the floor. But when the tension is equal between all three clamps and he jerks the chain, my eyes lose their focus. I fucking love this!

He lets the chain dangle while he goes back to that drawer, collecting something else. Could it be more clamps? Where would he put them? He returns, attaching something to the chain while he grins. His eyes meet mine just before he lets the weight hang, pulling down on my nipples. The clamps are not as enjoyable with the weight as they were without it. I don't feel the heaviness on my clit, which is probably a good thing.

Jake walks behind me, pulling back on the waistband of my panties once again. The more my ass juts toward him, the shorter the chain feels, adding more tension on my clit. He slaps my ass with the palm of his hand, jolting my body as a result. The weight jerks, yanking my clitoris and nipples in the process. Holy shit that's fucking incredible! I am moaning so loudly. I truly doubt I could remain quiet even if he told me I had to.

He grips the butt plug, pulling at it but not enough to make it pop out. My asshole is being stretched outward as it attempts to widen enough to allow the plug its freedom. If he pulls harder, it will come out, but he isn't trying to remove it. He waits until my asshole almost lets it go before releasing it so it will get sucked back into me. This, along with the swinging weight, is enough to have me moaning with each breath. My head hangs limply. All of my focus is on my asshole and clit as they are tugged at and teased so wonderfully.

The butt plug pops out, immediately replaced with Jake's slippery, thick cock. His hips press against my butt cheeks, his prick buried deep inside my anal canal. I love the feeling of fullness that ass sex provides. He gives pause to my tensing body until I begin to breathe again. He humps forward, at the same time pulling back on the waistband of my panties. This time, as the

97

weight sways and bounces, my clit and nipples jerk and tug. He hangs onto me, motionless while still inside me, giving me a moment to experience the multitude of sensations.

My moans are deep and throaty the instant he bucks again, repeating the same patience as I revel in the glory of it all. Jake is in no hurry to bring either of us to orgasm. He thrusts, then holds over and over. I can feel my clit swelling without him even touching it. I can't say I have ever been this close to orgasm for this length of time without erupting. In a mad attempt to rub my clit on my inner thigh, I'm twisting my body as much as the ropes will allow. I want to cum so desperately that I'll risk bruising my wrists and ankles to do so.

"Please, Sir, let me cum," I beg. "Jake! Please!"

Jake pulls his thick prick from my ass to go retrieve something from a different drawer than the one that held the clamps. He pulls something out that has a red ball on it. He stands behind me again. I'm a bit concerned as to what he will be doing with that ball. I'm soon made aware when his arms come up over my head, holding straps that are attached to the red ball.

When I don't do what he seems to expect me to do, he orders me, "Open your fucking mouth." I do as he demands. "You will not speak out of turn. When we are in this room, you will only refer to me as either Sir or Master. Today, I will only take away your ability to use your words. The next time you break this rule, you will be punished." The ball sits between my jaws. He buckles it around the back of my head. "Since you can't say the safe words, if you are in distress, scream as best you can while waving your hands frantically. I will stop and remove the ball so you can tell me what troubles you. Do you understand?"

"Yes, Sir, I do," I try to say but, for obvious reasons, can't. He seems to understand, though.

His prick slides back into my asshole with one smooth, slow thrust. The weight barely swings. He doesn't pause between humps. His hips slam off my ass cheeks at a steady pace, his cock fucking deep into my ass. The constant violent tugging of my clit and nipples is fantastic and horrible. I can no longer think a legitimate thought. I'm lost in the joyous abuse that my body is experiencing.

This is all new to me, the physical and mental stimulation have surpassed all of my expectations of what Jake could do to me. I had no idea what our playing would teach me. I've already learned that a continued euphoria before an orgasm has even reached its peak can be achieved. What more can he teach me?

When his two fingers glide between my pussy lips, pinching either side of my clamped clitoris, it launches me into a wild orgasm. I stay at the peak of climax for quite a bit longer than my usual few seconds. Instead, it drags on and on while my entire body quivers. He doesn't change his rhythm. He simply hangs onto me, humping normally. I am silent, lost in the glory of this moment, unable to have a clear thought. I'm lost in a wondrous daze from which I never want to recover.

The tip of his middle finger touches just below the clip and begins gently stroking under the hood of my clitoris. He's barely touching it. It's enough to add an extra wave of heat to wash over the little nib, causing it to further swell. I can't move now; my body is frozen still, unbelieving that this can get any more incredible. Three more thrusts of his hard cock and I've stopped breathing.

My clit burns as if it's being rubbed with a hot poker fresh from the coals of an inferno. So much pain is involved in this orgasm because it seems to be playing out in slow-motion. I can feel every nerve as it ignites, seeming to get stuck in explosive twinges of angry nerves. The ripple effect is felt from my clit, travelling up that imaginary rubber band in my belly, and flaring outward until it's felt over every cell that makes up my being.

I've faded far from my thoughts. I am completely void of all conscious effort at movement and mindfulness. The world has disappeared around me; only my body exists. I don't breathe until he backs away from me, no longer swinging the weight, fucking my ass, or applying pressure to my clit. This orgasm is subsiding, leaving me drooling from around the ball in my mouth. My eyes are barely able to focus, and my lungs burn as I fight to take in more oxygen than the ball gives allowance for. I hang almost completely limp as my weak-muscled legs battle to sustain my weight.

When the world around becomes clear, I see him standing in front of me with something in his hand. I hear a click and see a bright flash of light. That's when I realize he's holding a camera. I am no longer in the sexually gratified, *nothing can irritate me* mindset. I'm instantly enraged. I didn't expect he'd be taking photographic proof of our fling. I did not permit this! What if he uses it to blackmail me? He could destroy my writing career. I start yelling and waving my hands while shaking my head.

He looks up from the device in his hand and says, "If you are worried that I will use this photo for anything other than to send to Henry, I guarantee you I will not. I respect you and Henry enough that I would never risk hurting either one of you."

I am still worried but no longer flapping my hands. It isn't audible as being any particular language, but I'm asking him how I can be sure of that. He simply watches my face as I spew muffled words at him. He steps toward me to show me the picture which stops me in mid-mumbled sentence. The woman in the picture looks like she's been through a war, but her expression is sexy as hell. She looks exactly like me, but I've never seen that expression on my face before. I wonder if Henry ever has. I haven't ever cum like that in my life, so I doubt it. I instantly feel a wave of guilt for having so much fun with Jake. I try to push the awful thought away before it takes over my conscience, making me want to stop this thing we're doing.

"This…" he points to the picture. "This right here is why I do what I do. The woman in this picture has just had the most intense orgasm of her life, and I was the one who gave it to her. Yes, it's a stroke to my overly inflated ego, which I probably don't need." He taps the screen a few times, and that's when I understand that he took the picture with his phone. "I just sent it to Henry."

I start panicking again, mumbling pleas for him to tell me he didn't just send photographic proof of my pleasure to my husband. Jake chuckles while assuring me, "Henry asked me to take pictures and send them to him. He's very excited to see what I've been doing to you."

Jake sets the phone down and struts over to me, swollen dick swaying with each step. He reaches out and unclamps my left nipple. Holy hell! My wail bellows from around the ball gag. The pain is excruciating, especially when his mouth engulfs it and sucks at it feverishly as if he's trying to drink from me. The other nipple is suddenly wracked with pain equal to what the first experienced. His fingers roll the second unclamped nipple between them while I scream and writhe in pain. Soon the ache eases into a luscious hypersensitivity that I quite enjoy.

When his fingers pull at the clip on my clit, I begin whimpering pathetically, anticipating the pain that will burden my sensitive button. The clip is slowly loosened before removing it. It's sheer agony, but I'm relieved when it doesn't hurt for nearly as long as my nipples did. His lips wrap around it while his tongue gently massages. Oh, fuck yeah! I'm moaning with every lengthy exhale. I'd swear that every individual nerve in my clit is being personally tended to. It's remarkable!

Three of his fingers push into my pussy and begin waving like they were before. I'm groaning, holding my hips toward his face as my legs continue to shake. His tongue laps at my clit as his digits fuck and flutter. He's going to make me explode. My clit is so incredibly hyper-sensitive that his tongue feels almost rough like a cat's. I like it very much.

He stops, stands up, and then reaches for something behind me. While looking in my eyes, I hear a buzzing start and soon after feel the wand press against my clit. I'm moaning words of appreciation, but they're just mumbles until he releases the ball gag, pulling it from behind my teeth. I swallow the wad of saliva that had formed in my mouth. Even though I still have drool dripping down my chin, his lips press to mine. When our mouths open, his tongue juts in, rubbing mine softly. I can taste my cunt on his tongue.

When he starts rolling my sore nipple between his thumb and forefinger, an electric pulse tears though me. My body lurches into a screaming clitoral orgasm. His mouth still presses to mine even though I'm crying out and my body is jerking wildly. The peak of this one doesn't last nearly as long as the last, but it's still quite enthralling. He doesn't remove the vibrator which has my clit burning hot.

I'm screaming, "Stop! Sir, please… Fuck!" He doesn't. The pain quickly shifts into pleasure, pushing me into another hard orgasm. My head falls back limply, and my legs turn to jelly. I am hanging by my arms and I don't care that my shoulders are aching. That pain I will gladly suffer through later. Over the next few days, each time I feel it, I'll remember how amazing my body felt at this exact moment.

Jake walks away from me with the vibrator still buzzing in his hand. He comes back with a wide belt that he fastens snuggly around my waist after placing the handle of the vibrator between it and my belly. I'm confused as to how this is going to benefit me since it's not touching my clit but rather just above it. He unfastens my ankles from the posts, which I'm grateful for, not that my legs can be trusted to maintain my weight.

He unwraps a condom as he stands in front of me and rolls it over his ballooned manhood. He squats down and pushes his arms between my knees. In one quick motion, he lifts my legs, cupping my ass with his hands. He lines his prick up to my dripping wet cunt. I watch his face, admiring his perfect bone structure, puffy lips, and sexy eyes that could make me spill my innermost secrets.

He jerks my legs, which shifts my body, not only allowing his cock to fill me but bumping the wand into the perfect position to vibrate the hell out of my clit. I continue to watch his face as he fucks me. His hands tightly grip my ass while my thighs rest over his forearms. My eyes cast downward to admire his abdominal muscles as they flex each time he slams into me. His biceps are beefy from holding my weight in his hands.

When I look back up at his face, I see that he's watching mine. He reaches around my leg so he can touch the settings wheel on the wand. His finger flicks it, immediately revving it into high speed. Shit! Here I go again, bucking my hips and wailing through another overwhelming climactic moment. He doesn't stop until I have orgasmed twice more and cannot possibly survive through another.

He turns off the vibrator and unclips my handcuffs, letting my arms fall limply and painfully to my sides while he holds me against him. I am still wrapped around his body, trying to hang onto him as best as my exhausted muscles will allow. He frees the belt and vibrator from my waist before carrying me over to a chair. Instead of setting me down on it, he sets me on my feet. I stagger on my quivering legs. He grasps my arms to balance me and, once I'm sturdier, sit down in the chair.

While holding both of my hands to keep me balanced on my wobbling legs, he gives me an order. "Suck my cock."

I drop to my knees because my legs simply don't have the strength to lower me gracefully. Without hesitation, I take him into my mouth. He didn't give me specific orders on how he'd prefer me to do it, so I'll suck him the way I want to, the way I'm used to with Henry.

My mouth rides up and down his shaft, taking him completely in until my nose presses to his firm abdomen. My hand massages his testicles when I don't have them sucked into my hot mouth. He's getting close to coming. I can tell because his ass is flexing each time I take his pulsating thickness deep in my throat. Air fills his lungs with long, full breaths and leaves his body with a hushed moan.

His fingers weave into my hair, clutching a large wad of it. When I lean in to take him deep, he pushes my head forward until I have him perfectly down my throat. Instead of letting me back off, he holds me still. I do my best to stay calm, knowing he'll let me breathe soon. If I panic, I'll gag. His hips push forward as he gets closer and closer to his anticipated eruption. He yanks my head back by my hair before standing up and grabbing his cock tightly in his fist. His hand strokes his rigid length above me while he still grips my hair and locks eyes with me.

"You're a good little whore, aren't you?" he hisses with a tensed jaw. His chest curls forward and his muscles flex firmly.

He growls sadistically, just before hot semen bursts from his throbbing cock, shooting onto my neck and chest. He's grunting with each breath until he falls silent, revelling in the sedation of his release.

He frees my hair before sitting back down, his eyes mere slits and his mouth hanging open. He smiles very slightly, no longer looking like the vicious Master that recently had me in his clutches. His face is calm and relaxed. I return the smile before lying back on the floor, enjoying the coolness of it on my overheated skin.

"Thank you for entertaining me today," he says in a sweetness that seems unlike the barbaric man who just came.

I sigh. "Mhmm, thank you. That was... I don't even know how to describe it."

He laughs and replies, "I suppose that's a good thing. You need to know that I thoroughly enjoyed you. I will increase the intensity the next time you visit me. You seem to have handled whatever I've thrown your way thus far with ease. I am not concerned about adding new elements. Here is my phone. You can delete that picture if it'll make you feel better."

"No, it's okay," I tell him. "Keep it to look back on fondly."

"Thank you. I will." Jake stands up and reaches out to me. I take his hand. He helps me to my feet. I walk through the playroom door and he hands me a bottle of water. I gulp down a few mouthfuls and feel the coolness coat my throat on the way down. I make my way to the bathroom to clean myself up before putting my dress back on.

He kisses me once on the forehead before walking me to my car. I drive away, tired but so very happy.

I wonder what Henry will say about the risqué photo.

CHAPTER ELEVEN

"Hi," I say as I walk through the door, kicking off my high heels at the entrance. I wonder if Henry will reply with a happy greeting or if he'll think I allowed Jake to take it too far. Will he be angry about my state of appearance in the photo? I am looking very dishevelled in it.

He's sitting at his desk in his home office. His expression is impossible to read. All he's doing is looking at me blank-faced from behind a stack of papers. I am glad he decided to bring his work home with him instead of staying late at the office like he does way too often. Today, it would drive me crazy anticipating how he'd react when he finally returned home, probably late in the evening.

"Are you tired? Sore?" he inquires, leaning back in his chair. He's still holding his pen, which now taps his lower lip.

My lips curl upward despite my effort to hold it back. I just know my cheeks are flushing; I can feel their heat. "Yes, a little."

"Did you enjoy yourself?" he asks, still seeming stoic.

I tilt my head, lips still curled. "I did."

"The photo Jake sent to me doesn't even look like the woman I'm married to. This woman wears an expression that is unfamiliar to me. He really put one over on you, didn't he?" My lips aren't curled any longer. He looks really upset. What if he's jealous that Jake was able to turn me into a sexually overwhelmed woman as I appear to be in that photo?

"Are you angry?" I question. I need confirmation.

"Come here." He waves his hand for me to walk to him. I stand beside him, looking down into his eyes. His hand slides up the inside of my leg, feeling my stockings. "Take off your dress."

Yes! He isn't angry... quite the opposite, in fact. Without hesitation, I pull it over my head, dropping it to the floor in a heap.

My eyes stay focused on his, awaiting his instruction, much like I do with Jake. Now I can read his face. His devilish grin screams that he wants sex. His eyes scan my body while the tip of his tongue glides along his bottom lip.

"You look hot in that," he whispers. "Kiss me."

I bend down, pressing my lips to his while his hand weaves its way through my hair to the back of my head. As our tongues dance, his becomes increasingly more invasive. He grips my hair in his fist, pulling my head away from his. He looks deeply into my eyes. Henry isn't normally rough with me. I like this new Henry!

"You smell like a combination of his cologne and sex. I can smell the man who fucked you this afternoon."

"All I need is five minutes to shower," I reply, but he doesn't free my hair.

"Fuck no! It's too late, I've already smelled him on your flesh." Henry's eyes focus on my mouth. Soon, two of his fingers are gliding along my lips and finally slipping between them. His digits slowly slide in, rubbing along my soft tongue. He moans softly, his eyelids getting heavy as he watches them disappear into my mouth.

"Feel my cock," he whispers. I reach down, pressing my hand down on the bulge in his pants. I'm surprised to feel him so hard already. "Get on your knees and pleasure me with this very talented mouth of yours."

I wrap my lips around his fingers and suck as they gradually leave my mouth. My hands pull roughly at his belt as I fight to unfasten it. My eyes watch his while I free his prick from the zipper on his suit pants. He is raging hard, thicker than he's been in a long time.

I slip onto my knees between his thighs and hold his hefty erection with both hands, squeezing firmly while I caress the tip, smoothing a blob of pre-cum over its mushroom head. He moans faintly, proof he's enjoying my finger gliding, brushing over the slit now and then.

I take him between my lips and suck gently while the tip of my tongue tenderly teases the slit. I press in, moving my tongue with tiny strokes as though I'm seeking a way inside. Henry's open-mouth breathing is increasingly becoming heavier with each breath. When I look up at him, he's watching my lips through lustful eyes.

"Take all of me," he insists.

I open my mouth wide, allowing his swollen prick easy access to the depths of my throat, should he choose to take advantage of it. His hand gently pushes my head onto his groin. I bump my face against his belly, swallowing his prick into my throat. Each time his mushroom head hits the back of my throat, Henry grunts softly.

"How sore are you?" he asks me. Without pausing, I shrug my shoulders. "Lay over the desk, face down, and spread your legs."

I rise up and follow his instructions exactly. Henry remains in his chair and slips two fingers up and down my slit, playing in my wetness. I so am ready for him to fuck me. I want him! I want to have been fucked by two men on the same day.

His fingers glide into me effortlessly. "Jake had his cock deep inside of you not even an hour ago, didn't he? He fucked you hard, no doubt. Any man would have. How big is his prick?"

"He's big," I reply. "About your size."

"Yeah? Did he fuck you hard, or did he prefer long, rhythmic strokes?" Henry's voice is deep and breathy. Who is this man?

"Both," I reply as his fingers delve deeper into me, searching out the very depths the other man's cock ventured into.

"I'm going to fuck you now." As he stands, his pants fall to the floor, pooling at his ankles. "Reach back and hold your ass cheeks apart for me. I want to see your asshole." With my cheek pressed to the cool desktop, I reach back, placing one hand on each ass cheek. I'm pulling them open, exposing my asshole to the cool air and his awaiting eyes.

Henry's fingers slip from my drenched cunt only to circle the opening of my butt. "Did he fuck you here?"

I whisper, "Yes."

"Should I fuck you here?"

"If it's what you desire, husband." I'm hoping he'll fuck my pussy instead. My ass is a bit sore from the abuse it received earlier from the butt plug and Jake's gorgeous cock.

"No, I'm going to fuck your pussy," he states a mere second before shoving his prick into my hot cunt, burying himself deeply in one quick motion.

I gasp, fighting the urge to cry out. My womanhood is more tender than I thought it was. Soon, though, the pain is overcome with pleasure. Henry has pressed every inch of himself into me and holding. He's groaning softly, his prick twitching inside of me.

"Jake's cock filled your cunt, didn't it? And you liked it, didn't you?" he asks. I simply nod my head, wondering what his fascination is with focusing on the thought of Jake being inside my body. "Do you want me to fuck you hard or make love to you?"

"My body is yours to do with as you please." He let me have sex with another man today, a man that showed me new ways of enjoying my body. As far as I'm concerned, he has the right to fuck me however he wishes. I owe him at least that.

"I don't know what it is, babe, but I am really getting off on knowing he fucked you. You're mine, and he used you for his pleasure." His hips begin to pound against me. He leans over me, gripping the opposite side of the desk for leverage so he can brutally fuck. I am expecting to have bruises on my thighs that I will admire as if they were a well-earned reward.

"Oh. Fuck. Yes!" My words spit from my lips as he hammers into me, each thrust forcing the air from my chest. This is the hottest, nastiest fucking Henry has ever given me. He can be rough sometimes but never this frenzied. Had I known that by allowing another man to fuck me, I would awaken the wildness inside my husband, I would have done it years ago.

"I fucking own you! You're mine!" He growls out a long and deep wail that is much more primitive than I have ever heard Henry make. His hands release the desk, grabbing my wrists instead. As he thrusts forward, he pulls back on my arms. Whatever got into Henry, I fucking love it! The angry, possessiveness of this barbaric fuck is pushing me over the edge of sanity. I'm coming! The room is spinning around me as my breath huffs from my gaping mouth. He's growling like a savage.

"Fucking cum on my cock! I fucking own you!" he yells. "Oh, yeah! Oh, fuck yeah!" He's not usually this verbal, nor this explicit. I like it. His body jerks, his thrusts becoming spastically awkward as he dumps his thick load of hot semen deep inside of me. His prick is ballooning and throbbing against my walls. He remains inside of me as his dick quickly deflates and he gasps for breaths.

Henry's grip eases from my bruised wrists. His long, deep sigh is followed by a hiss of air sucked in through his teeth. His prick slips from my slimy pussy. He lovingly takes my arm to help stand me up, turning me to face him. "Oh, fucking hell! Baby, I hope I didn't hurt you."

I kiss him softly before easing his worry. "No, you definitely didn't hurt me. Where have you been hiding that jealous beast of yours? I really like him."

He steps back with a curious look on his face. "You do?"

I nod, "Oh, hell yes, I do!"

Henry smiles gloatingly, "Well, I guess I'll have to bring him out more often. Sorry about the cruel comments about you and Jake. I know I don't own you."

"So, you're not upset about what happened with Jake?" I ask, knowing full well that he isn't.

He chuckles before reassuring me. "Sweetie, to be honest with you, I was a bit worried that I might regret pushing you to do this after it was all said and done. But I am definitely the farthest from upset. I don't know what it is about knowing that Jake was inside of you. It fires me up to a boiling point but in a good way. I must have some warped psychological shit going on inside my mind that has me all turned around. When I got that picture, I was so excited for you and aroused because you actually went through with it. I could barely contain myself. I knew Jake was touching you at that exact moment, possibly fucking you again. It stoked a firestorm inside of me that was quickly raging out of control. I had to leave the meeting and come home. I told the boss that I wasn't feeling well. It wasn't a complete lie. My cock was so hard that it hurt. I jerked off in the car, in the parking garage at work."

I snicker, "You are a sick, twisted, warped motherfucker, and I love you."

"Hell yeah, baby! You want me all the same," he replies, pulling me close to him so he can kiss me. "Should we call for delivery?"

"Yes! I'm famished. You do that. I'm going to take a bath."

"Yes, relax your bones. I might take another piece out of you later," he says with a wicked smile, riding the comment.

CHAPTER TWELVE

It's been over a week since I was with Jake. I've heard nothing from him, and my husband hasn't suggested another meeting with him. I'm anxious to return to his clutches but don't want to ask. Appearing too enthusiastic doesn't seem like such a great idea. If Henry isn't bringing it up, neither will I. Making Henry jealous isn't my objective. As you can imagine, my thoughts often drift to the memory of that day. I want him again. My body craves his touch.

I've been sitting in front of my computer all morning, trying to start an outline for another novel; each time I do, it starts to get too sexually graphic, and I have to start all over. Maybe I should change my genre. What would my publisher say about that? I doubt it would go over very well. I could write under a pseudonym. Either way, right now, I have to come up with a non-explicit storyline to propose to my publisher. She's already pushing for another book, even though I just sent my recent manuscript to the editors.

I could write about my eye-opening experience with Jake. That would make for one hell of a hot story. Writing from personal experience would be easier than making up the mystery tales I've been writing.

My phone startles me from my erotic thoughts when it rings louder than anyone's cellphone should be allowed to. I cranked up the volume when I was on speakerphone with Amy earlier today and forgot to turn it back down. I won't do that again. The day after I was with Jake, she called, demanding I tell her every juicy detail of my latest adventure. It is harder than I thought it would be to describe over the phone the level of orgasmic euphoria I had peaked to.

Today, she asked to meet for a late lunch after she drops the baby off at her mother's house for the afternoon. Her mom is the typical loving grandmother who always has gum in her purse and hugs-a-plenty. It's nearly two o'clock. I slide in my car and speed off to meet her. She arrives late, same as me, and we meet up in the parking lot. After a quick hug, she punches my arm. I look at her as if she's lost her damn mind.

She confesses, "That's because I'm so jealous of you. Not only is the man tagged as being incredible eye-candy, but you get to have him inside of you. And he's really good at sex to boot! He couldn't be a lousy lay? No, he's fucking fantastic! You're a lucky bitch! I hope you truly know how lucky you are. I would trade places with you in a heartbeat if I could."

I smile and put my arm around her shoulder as we walk to the entrance. "I know you would, and I'd trade with you if I could… but only for one sexual romp. I'll admit, I'm selfish and want him for myself." I snicker while she rolls her eyes.

About halfway through our meals, she asks the one question I wish I had an answer to. "So, when are you going to see him again?"

I shrug and reply, "I don't know. Asking Henry for permission might come across as too eager, and I don't want him to get jealous. I don't necessarily think he would, but just in case, I'm not going to push it."

"Why don't you go see Henry at the office after you leave here? If you accidentally run into Jake in the process, something might light a fire in his pants, and then maybe he'll request a repeat performance," she suggests with the most innocent of expressions, but I'm not buying it.

She has a good point. "Maybe I am *out of sight, out of mind.* Yeah, I think I'll do that."

"I just wish I could be a fly on the wall in his sexy room. Nope, scratch that! I wish I were tied up and sexually abused by him, not some damn fly who only gets to watch it happen to someone else." Amy looks at me with envy in her eyes.

112

"Maybe one day, Lou and Henry will get talking, and something will pique Lou's interest. It could happen."

Amy is shaking her head. "Never happen. Lou is so jealous of any man looking at me with desire in his eyes. He will immediately put his arm around me or hold my hand as if to silently tell the guy to fuck off because he owns me. I used to think it was cute, but it just annoys the shit out of me now. Sadly, no one has recently been overly attentive to me. I suppose with a baby on my arm, two others running rampant around my legs, gum in my hair, and baby vomit on my shoulder, it's not likely to happen. I remember when I was sexy and desirable. I miss that girl. That seems like fifty years ago."

"You are still sexy! You just don't feel all that sexy because you're so damn tired. For a woman who's had three kids, your body is tight, and your skin still fits. That's rare. One suggestion, though; maybe you shouldn't risk it by having another baby," I tease, smirking.

"Can't happen! Lou got fixed right after the last kid. Three is three too many some days, if you can imagine. I love them more than my own life, but damn, some days seem impossible. On those days, I envy your life — motherless and free."

"I don't envy the stress you are under trying to raise three miniature humans so they'll grow to be smart, productive members of society."

I pay the bill today since she paid last time, and then we walk out together. At her car, we hug while she tells me to go to Henry's office and do a little teasing to spark his and Jake's interest. I say that I will try my best.

* * *

When I walk into the lobby, I pass by the beautiful woman I met at the party, Jenna. She's walking out of the lunchroom with a mug filled with something steaming hot. Her skirt is crimson and formfitting to her small waist and curvy hips. The blouse she's wearing is silky and white. As she moves, it snugs up against her breasts, revealing the outline of a lacy camisole. It's not low cut or revealing in any way. Her outfit is office appropriate, but it screams femininity and sexuality. She is absolutely luscious.

I'm sure Henry must fantasize about her often. I do, and I'm not remotely interested in hopping the fence. I can't help but imagine her naked, riding on Henry's rock-hard cock.

Her smile is contagious as she greets me. "Hello, Beth. Are you here to surprise Henry?" We join up and start toward the offices, walking side by side.

"Hello, Jenna. You look lovely. Yes. I was out with a friend for a late lunch and thought I'd stop by to give Henry a kiss."

"Oh, that's nice. You're so lucky. Henry is a really sweet guy and handsome to boot," she leans in to tell me that last part. "But he won the lottery when you said, 'I do.'"

"She's right, he's the luckier one in your relationship." A man's voice seems to come out of nowhere. We both spin our heads quickly to see who's walking behind us. Jake is looking at me with a provocative little smirk.

I just know my cheeks are flushing. Is it obvious to everyone how flustered my mind is and how wet my pussy is?

"Hi, Jake. Where did you come from?" My words sound rushed.

"Yeah, jeez, you came out of nowhere," Jenna adds as we separate enough for him to start walking between us.

"I was just leaving William's office. I saw the two of you walking unescorted and decided it was my manly duty to ensure you both get to your destinations safely." He smiles and then adds, "No, not really. Both of you are incredibly beautiful, and I wanted to be the envy of all my male, and some female, coworkers as I walked between the both of you, one on each arm. Sorry, did I butt into your private conversation?"

Jenna says, "No need to apologize. You're allowed to butt into my conversations at any time." She looks at me, putting me on the spot, whether she realizes it or not. "He's so handsome, isn't he? Look at that face: sexy eyes, full lips, bone structure most men would kill for. I think we're the lucky ones to have you escort us."

He looks at her out of the corner of his eyes with a crooked grin. I wonder if the two of them have ever been intimate together. Maybe I'll ask him one day. Henry said that he doesn't boast about his conquests, but I wonder if he would tell me since he is fucking me... or at least he was. I'd love to know what she's like when she cums; is she a screamer or a breath holder?

We stop walking outside of Jenna's office and turn toward one another. She says, "Well, I should get back to it."

Jake asks, "Are you thinking about working on the idea we were discussing?"

"Hmm, perhaps. Why? Is there something I need to know?" she asks him as if I'm not even standing here.

He smiles and replies, "I just think it will be interesting. You'll have to tell me what comes of it."

She jerks her head in a bragging manner. "Maybe I will, maybe not."

"You are going to take it on, aren't you?" I don't think they're actually discussing a work project anymore.

"Should I leave you two alone, so you don't have to talk in code anymore?" I ask. Now I'm butting into their conversation.

They both look at me and then chuckle. Jenna puts her warm hand on my shoulder. "It was so wonderful to see you today. We should get together for lunch one day soon. I think you and I could be great friends."

I smile at her and then look at Jake while replying to her, "Yes, I would like that very much." My eyes glide back to her, and I add, "I think we could get into some very interesting discussions."

She grins, her eyes shifting quickly to Jake and then back at me. "Stop in and see me before you leave, if you have time."

I reply, "If I have time. If I don't see you before I leave, I'll call you to set up a lunch date."

Jake clears his throat when Jenna walks into her office. His eyes lock onto mine. My tummy flips, making it feel like butterflies are flapping inside of my chest. My clit twitches several times, begging me to open my legs to let him in. I cast my eyes away from him to scan for anyone who might be within earshot. There isn't a soul around us.

"Is there something going on between you two? Something very sexy, perhaps?" I ask.

He snickers and raises his eyebrows, "Would you be jealous if there were?"

"Were or is?" I ask him, definitely more curious than jealous.

We begin walking as he replies, "Nothing between us that you need to know about. She's a very close friend. You could say that we have a lot in common."

I ponder what hidden message is behind his words. "Okay, I'll be more specific, simply for curiosity's sake. Have you ever taken her to your room?"

He smiles as if he has a secret that he's about to fill me in on. "Not in the way you're imagining." I stop walking and look at him with furrowed brow, confused as to why she'd be in his sex room if not to have sex with him. His eyes scan around us before he elaborates. "She has tastes similar to mine."

As if a lightbulb went on above my head, like a cartoon character, I understand what he's saying. "So, she's into dominating women? Really?"

He shakes his head, "No, not women. She's visited my room a few times. Sort of... borrowed it. She and I have never been together."

"Why would she use your sex room?" I ask, wondering why she doesn't have one of her own if she's into it.

"She lives in a one-bedroom apartment. There's just not enough room." I nod, fully understanding their friendship. "Answer me honestly. Were you jealous when you pictured me with her? Don't pretend you didn't. I saw your face."

"I was," I reply as we approach Henry's office door, which is closed.

He smiles and assures me, "I am with you and only you right now. If someone enters my life that sparks my interest, I will be sure to inform you before I take it to another level."

"Why would you? We aren't in an emotional relationship, so I have no right to be jealous or possessive. You don't have to tell me anything."

"First of all, your emotions are legitimate and important. Please don't ever think they aren't. You do not need to hide them from me. Open communication is essential in our relationship. Never hold back anything that might need to be discussed. Second, if I enter another relationship with someone, you will definitely be informed of it before I become intimate with them. I usually only play with one woman at a time. I like to keep things simple."

"But I'm with Henry, and you're young, sexy, and single. If someone better comes along, which they will, I wouldn't expect you to pass up the opportunity."

He tilts his head to the side and sighs. "Why can't you see how incredible you are? Everyone around you is envious of you for one reason or another, but you don't see it. I'm not emotionally invested in you, but mentally and physically, you bewilder me. Just the sight of you has me imagining myself taking you one way or another, right here, right now. Besides, I am not looking to become emotionally invested in a loving, lifelong relationship with anyone, so this thing with us is perfect for me. Why the hell would I pass you over just to play with someone else who will no doubt be less intriguing?"

"How would you take me right now, if you could?" I ask curiously, perhaps as a way to change the subject.

He lifts his chin while his eyes stay focused on mine. As if a switch flipped inside his mind, he suddenly looks like the sexual beast that plays with me in his sex room. "I'd grab your wrist and spin you around, pulling your arms up behind your back so I'll be able to control you physically. Then I'd squeeze each one of your breasts hard enough that you cry out, which will make my cock hard. I'd walk you over to Henry's closed door and push you against it, holding your arm high on your back. At this point, you're completely under my control. I like that. I'd yank down your pants and panties. I'd pull my cock from my zipper and stroke it just a little before taking the condom out of my pocket and ripping the package open with my teeth. After rolling it over my rock-hard cock, I'd reach around you and slide my fingers between your pussy lips. I'd rub your clit while my cock pushes inside of you. I'd fuck you hard and fast, your body smashing against Henry's door. I wouldn't cum until you did, but it would be a very quick and violent fucking." He takes a breath while I continue to stare at his lips, lost in that scenario as it plays out in my mind. "Then I'd pull up your pants, do up mine and walk you into Henry's office like nothing even happened."

I nod for way too long, trying to shake the image from my mind... long enough to regain my senses. "Yup! Yeah! Okay... okay."

"That's just off the top of my head. Give me a few minutes to plan something, and it would be much more interesting, I assure you," he tells me. With his gaze meeting mine, he taps on Henry's door using the knuckle on his left middle finger.

"Come in," we hear Henry speak in a very monotone voice as if he's concentrating on something other than who is knocking.

Jake opens the door as he places his hand on my lower back to usher me ahead of him. "Look who I found roaming the hall."

Henry looks up, surprise washing over his face. "Hello, Sweetie! What brings you in?"

I'm still a little shaken from the sexual escapade that just ran its exciting course in my mind. "I just finished a late lunch with Amy and thought I'd drop in to see how your day is going. Jake happened to stumble upon Jenna and me as we were walking."

"I thought it my duty to ensure she arrived safely," he says, smiling like a sarcastic fool.

"Well, we thank you for that, for sure. I completely trust you with my wife's safety," he replies with the same sarcastic smirk.

"Yeah, this is awkward," I whisper under my breath.

"Why?" Jake asks.

"What?" I reply.

"You said that this is awkward, and I'd like you to elaborate."

I look at Henry and then back at Jake. My face feels hot, flushed with visual proof of my embarrassment. "It's obvious, right? I mean, Henry and you… with me."

"Would you like to have us share you?" Jake asks. Henry is just sitting quietly with his pen in his mouth, witnessing the way Jake is talking to me as if he isn't even in the room.

"Um, where did this conversation go wrong?" I'm avoiding his question as I drop my purse on the leather sofa. I walk over to Henry and give him a quick kiss. "So, how is your day going?"

Jake is leaning on the desk across from Henry while still looking at me as if he's waiting for an answer. I am ignoring him, trying not to meet eyes with him.

Henry looks at Jake and then at me. "Sweetie, you'd better give the man an answer. He is being very patient, but I would imagine his patience is going to run out soon. Besides, I'd like to hear your response as well."

Jake, while very sharply over annunciating every word, asks, "Beth, what do you want?" I look at him and take a very deep breath, letting him know that I'm annoyed that he won't let this conversation die.

"Maybe… I don't know. I'd have to think about it. It would be very awkward having you touching me while you watch," I say, pointing at each man when referencing them.

Jake bluntly asks Henry, "Would you like to watch me take your wife?"

Henry is smiling while chewing on the end of his pen. "Yeah, I'd like that very much." My eyes lock on his, shocked at his quick response. He didn't even have to think about his answer. "What do you think, Sweetie? Would you like to fuck Jake while I watch?"

I can play this game too! "Are you just going to watch or join in?"

"Watch. We'll see where it goes from there," he replies just as quickly.

To seem like I can keep up with their level of play, I reply, patting the desk, "Would you like me to bend over the desk like you had me at home? I could drop my pants and flop face down right here in front of you. Jake could fuck me hard while you watch him make me cum. Maybe I'll cum multiple times. You won't have to imagine his cock inside of me because you'll actually witness it firsthand. You liked knowing that your dick was exactly where Jake's was. What was it you said? Oh, Jake's cock was deep inside of me not an hour before you were. That excited you more than you've been in a long time."

He is wearing a very matter-of-fact expression. "Yes, that turned me on. If he fucked you right here, right now, in front of me, I'd probably have to stroke my cock while I watched. In fact, I have a stiffy just thinking about it."

I'm going to call him out on it. My eyes look at Jake, and I ask, "So, what do you say? Do you want to fuck me?" He simply walks over to the door and slides a heavy chair in front of it. Henry's office doesn't have any interior windows, so nobody can see in with the door shut. My heart starts pounding in my chest so hard that I'd swear it's going to burst free from its captivity. Holy shit! This could really be happening.

I'm standing perfectly frozen, hands still on the edge of the desk. Henry leans back in his chair, licking his bottom lip with a very intrigued expression that I don't recognize him having ever worn.

Jake walks behind me and kisses my neck while his hands reach under my shirt and around to my breasts. He lifts my bra, dropping my tits free from their binding. His fingertips pinch and roll my nipples. My eyes haven't left Henry's face. He's watching Jake's hands move under my shirt. Any second now, he's going to insist we stop. A moan flows from my lips before I can hold it back. Jake shushes me. I nod quicker than the situation calls for. His hands grasp both breasts and squeeze until I'm wincing and biting my top lip to remain quiet. My body arches in its own attempt to escape his fingers.

His hands glide down my belly and undo my button and zipper, letting my pants fall and pool around my ankles. His fingers make their way under the sides of my panties, slowly pulling them down, exposing my most private parts. Henry's eyes are watching every movement Jake makes as if he's trying to burn his actions into his memory. His pen is really taking a beating from the clutches of his teeth.

Jake's fingers slip between my pussy lips, immediately finding my swelling clitoris. As he glides circles over it, I hear his pants drop to his ankles and the tearing open of a condom package. I suppose he wasn't lying when he said he had one in his pocket. Is the man always prepared? As he's rolling it on, his finger hasn't faltered in its choreographed dance over my clit.

With the condom on, he wraps his hand around the back of my neck and pushes me forward. Soon, I'm lying face down on the desk in front of Henry, mimicking the scenario I teased them with. I stare at Henry's dream-like expression, wondering if it's soon going to change to one of jealousy so I can stop this nonsense before it becomes all too realistic for Henry. It's one thing to imagine and know your wife fucked someone; it's another to witness it happen.

Jake's moistened fingers skim up and down my soaked pussy. I hear him suck his fingers to taste me. He pushes the head of his prick into me, pausing for a few seconds and them slamming every inch of his solid prick deep into me until his pelvis is pressing against my ass cheeks. I'm gasping loudly, failing to remember that I need to keep silent.

Jake's hand covers my mouth while he shushes me even more sternly. "Quiet! Not a sound. Do you hear me?"

I nod, unable to speak from behind his palm. Henry is watching Jake's face, not mine. I thought he'd be interested in how I am reacting to being filled by another man's hard cock, but he doesn't seem to be. He looks fascinated by Jake's level of calm control.

"Do you want me to fuck you fast and hard or gentle and easy?" Jake asks me.

"Hard," I whisper the moment his hand lifts from my mouth.

He grabs my hair in his fist, turning my face so his lips can meet mine. His kiss isn't gentle by any means. In fact, it's quite rough and harsh. He releases my hair letting me resume my position of face down on the desk. Using his knees, he pushes my thighs apart until I spread them as wide as I can. His hands find my ass cheeks and pull them apart, squeezing them harshly. It hurts. I have to press my forehead against the desk and bite my lip, so I won't scream.

"Breath easily, Beth," Jake instructs. I nod as best I can, taking a few deliberate breaths but it doesn't help. "I'm going to fuck you hard for two minutes, but you won't cum, and you won't make a sound. Do you understand?"

I nod, even though I'm not sure if I can follow his orders. His hand slides over my shoulder and grips onto me. Without hesitating, he begins slamming me so hard that Henry's desk shifts, squeaking on the floor. Jake grips my waist with both hands, pulling back on my body when he humps violently forward. Within seconds, I'm ready to cum but remember that he instructed me not to. I'll fight to hold off. It's only for two minutes. I think I can handle that. Right?

"Look at your husband." I turn my head and see Henry's eyes watching my face. He's breathing heavily, and his arm is moving as if he's stroking his cock, but I can't see to be sure. Is he jerking off while he watches Jake own my cunt with vicious thrusts? I think he is.

A whimper slips from me, so I immediately pull my lips into my mouth and bite them together with my teeth, but they soon pop open, spilling forth an appreciative moan. Jake's hand is instantly covering my mouth, completely blocking my main airway. My hands grip the sides of the desk to hang on, fearing Jake is going to shove me across the room with this savage assault.

Jake whispers, "Cum, Beth."

Finally! Within the time it takes him to poke my cervix twice, I'm slipping into a body-ceasing orgasm. My eyes blur, and muffled cries are trying to seek freedom from within me. I can feel my wetness streaming down my thighs as my cunt spasms, squeezing his pounding prick with tremendous strength. Holy hell, this is fucking erotic!

As soon as my orgasm ebbs, Jake pulls his prick from my body. His arm slides under my shoulder and lifts until I am standing straight up, his chest pressed against my back. His lips are pecking kisses at the back of my neck and I'm drowning in the heated sensations it carries.

My eyes eventually open when I feel Jake back away from me. Through their haze, I can see Henry leaning back in his chair, focused on his crotch. It takes me a few seconds to realize that he's wiping semen from his belly with a wad of tissues. He came! He enjoyed watching Jake fuck me so much that he came. I feel relieved that he isn't even remotely upset.

Wait! Jake didn't cum yet. I spin around and go to reach for Jake's cock, expecting it to be jutting out from his naked pelvis, but he has his pants already fastened, belted too. My eyes meet his.

"You look disappointed," he states.

"I... you didn't cum," I whisper.

He smiles at me before leaning in to kiss my lips tenderly. He whispers, "Don't stress over it. I am satisfied."

"But how?" I ask, still a bit lost in a daze by the fucking he put me through.

He brushes my cheek with his hand after he lifts my pants up for me to fasten. "Ejaculating is only a small part of it. My goal wasn't my own satisfaction."

"But aren't you still hard?" I ask.

He smiles, "Yes, but it'll ease off in time. Do you want to visit me again?"

"Yes," I reply without hesitation.

He steps away from me and says, "Then my goal has been achieved."

"All you had to do was ask Henry if you could be with me again," I tell him.

"Yes, but this presented itself and seemed like a more interesting way to go about it."

"Interesting isn't the adjective I would use to describe what just occurred here Exciting, breathtaking, provocative, thrilling...

those are just a few more suitable words." I ask in disbelief, "Did you think I had lost interest?"

"Henry had concerns," he replies, looking at my husband when he does.

I follow his gaze to see Henry peeking up at me. "Well, Sweetie, you haven't mentioned Jake at all in over a week. I thought you weren't interested in going back to visit him. I didn't want to ask, so you wouldn't feel like I was pressuring you."

I start laughing. Not a shy giggle but a loud, cackling laughter that fills the room. Both men's expressions are similarly confused. "I didn't want to bring it up in case you got jealous, Henry. I was afraid you would think I was obsessed with having sex with Jake more than I was with having it with you. I figured you'd put a complete stop to this sharing thing if you became jealous. Of course, I want to come back to see you, Jake! Are you kidding me? Sorry, Henry, but I think about the sex I had with him often. Jake, you are smoking hot and, fuck, you're amazing at what you like to do."

Henry says, "Good. You can go see him tomorrow evening."

I lean on the desk and ask, "Henry, what are you getting out of this?"

He looks at me, dumbfounded. "Did you not just watch me clean semen from my pants?"

"Yes, but…" I am cut off when Jake touches my arm.

"Beth, Henry and I have spent a lot of time discussing his investment in this sexual relationship you and I would be entering into, long before it ever began. Reading people is something I am very good at. This," he waves his hand between us, "wouldn't have happened if I weren't absolutely sure Henry was getting exactly what he needed from it."

Henry takes my hand and guides me to sit on his lap. "Sweetie, I love you. Watching Jake demand that you behave while he fucked the hell out of you…" he smiles wickedly. "Beth, the two of you just acted out one of my fantasies better than I had ever imagined it could be. I am getting exactly what I need out of this. I hope you are, too."

I kiss his lips softly. "Just promise that you'll tell me if it goes too far before it becomes more than you can handle."

"And you promise me the same thing," he tells me. We both nod, then kiss once more.

Jake clears his throat. Henry and I both look up to see him standing in front of the desk with a stern expression. "I hope this will bring the two of you closer, strengthening the bond between you, not that I think your marriage isn't already ironclad."

"Hey, I have a question for Henry. Well, maybe both of you." Jake waits patiently for me to continue. I look at Henry to see his brow furrow as he waits to hear what I have to ask them. "Henry, would you ever consider dominating, or being dominated by, a woman other than me?"

He ponders the idea for a long moment. "I might consider it. I really don't think I have it in me to do what Jake does. Maybe that's why watching him with you captivated me the way it did."

"So, you'd consider being *owned* by a woman in the same fashion as Jake *owns* me?"

"Ah," he considers the question once again. "Yes, I would try it. The worse that could happen is I don't like it and it ends."

I look at Jake and grin. His mouth opens as if my motive for this conversation just donned on him. Henry will have experience from someone other than me, and I'm considering Jenna for that task.

"Hold on, Beth. There's more to it than just starting something like this on a whim. Just take a moment to get your feet back under you. This relationship with you and I is brand new, and you are zipping with adrenaline. Think about what will be happening when the two of them are alone together. Consider the intimacy shared between them. It's not something you can just overlook. I want you to take some time to think about how you'll feel when you're sitting at home alone, waiting for him to leave her and come home to you, smelling of her perfume and sex when he does. You have to wonder if you will be as excited as Henry is when you're sitting in his seat, metaphorically speaking. You're either built for it, or you aren't."

Maybe he's right. I should think about it before I bring it up to Jenna or ask Jake to. "Okay, I hear what you're saying. I'll mull it over."

Jake smiles at me and then says, "I'm going to get back to work now. Thank you for the wonderful distraction. I'll call you to let you know what time I'd like you to come over tomorrow. I'll give you instructions if I have any for you." I nod with anxious excitement. Jake nods at Henry before taking his exit, after sliding the heavy chair back in its place. I'm still sitting on Henry's lap. He pulls me closer against him as he cradles me in his arms.

"I love you, Sweetie. Thank you for entertaining my disturbed sexual desires. You must think I'm a horrible husband."

"Why would you say that?"

"Because I got so hot watching you get fucked by someone else. I'm serious, Sweetie, I have never been that turned on in my whole life. Watching his face as he took you... He was lost in the power he had over your body. It was like watching a man fulfil his epic journey. It sounds weird when I say it out loud. I can hear myself speaking the words, but they don't match what I'm thinking and feeling. It seems so much sexier in my mind."

I think I understand. "If I could watch what happened here through your eyes, I think I'd get it. I have opened my eyes to see how lost he gets at the moment just before he teeters me on that invisible ledge between pain and pleasure. It's like he owns the world and it's at his mercy. So yeah, I get it. What I don't understand is why you're okay with him experiencing that with me. You don't feel left out? Don't you want the same thing; to be touched the same way, or to be the one touching? Don't you want to dominate someone or be dominated? I just feel like you're pulling the short straw in this situation. Do you know what I mean?"

"It's not in me to be dominant like him. I want to know that my wife is making *that guy*—who has himself so together and with the world at his feet—become so captivated with her, the way he does. It boosts my ego knowing that he wants you and you're mine. He has everything, but he doesn't have you, not how I have you."

"But he does have me," I whisper.

"No, he doesn't. You leave him and come home to me. Your heart belongs to me. It will never be his. It's the one thing he can't have. Perfect men like him have everything, so when they can't have something, they want it even more. He might understand how the female body works, but he doesn't know you. He will never have the closeness with you that I have. We are one, bonded together forever. He isn't a threat to me at all." Henry has the most loving expression.

My hands hold his face while I look into his doting eyes. "I love you so much."

"I love you." Our lips touch just as a soft knock on the door alerts us.

Jenna is stepping into the office as the door slowly opens wider. "Sorry, I didn't realize you were still here. I don't mean to interrupt. I can come back if this is one of those wonderful, intimate moments and I'm ruining it."

I smile at her as I slip off Henry's lap. "No, please come in, Jenna."

"Are you sure? This can wait."

Henry responds, "Come in. What can I do for you, Jenna?"

She pulls some papers from a beige folder as she walks around his desk to stand beside him. She puts the papers down in front of him, resting her hand on the back of his chair. I sit on the sofa, watching her lean toward him as she points to something on the first page. "Does this seem right to you?"

Henry is quiet for a minute while he scans the sheet of paper she gave him. Jenna looks up at me and takes notice that I'm admiring her. She immediately takes a step away from Henry, removing her hand from his chair. Her quick smile shows her concern that I'll be upset by how close she is to Henry. I nod at her and wink to put her mind at ease. Jenna and I are locked in a silent conversation that belongs only to us. A smile creeps up on my lips, soon to be copied by hers. She puts her hand back on his chair as she takes her place beside him.

"Yup, something doesn't add up here. Take this to William. He needs to see this." He hands it back to her as he shakes his head, obviously distraught. "Good catch. That could have slipped right by us, completely unnoticed."

"It didn't make sense to me. I went over everything twice, but I couldn't get it to line up. All right, I wanted to run it by you first, in case I missed something. I knew it could affect your case with the Bensons."

Jenna is a very smart woman. Henry has boasted about her impeccable work habits, saying that she's invaluable to the company. He has also said that if he needs a case to be tediously picked apart to search for any inconsistencies, she's the one he takes it to. It says a lot about her character that he trusts her the way he does.

Maybe setting him up to be under her rule might not be such a great idea. What if it changes their ability to work well with each other? That is something that would need to be considered before anything started up between them.

Jenna's voice is interrupting my thoughts. I snap out of it to see her waving at me with an infectious smile on her face. "Are you okay?"

I laugh, "Oh... yes. I couldn't be happier."

"You look like you're beaming," she assures me with a wink as she's walking toward the door. "Call me soon."

"I will, for sure," I promise.

Henry looks at me after she leaves and asks, "Call me? What's that about? Are you two best friends now?"

"You wish we were," I say, sarcastically.

He chuckles while nodding, "You know it. I can picture you two curled up together on the couch, sharing a blanket with nothing but a bucket of popcorn between you while watching a chick-flick. Scratch that, no chick-flick... porn," he pauses and then adds, "I'm getting hard again."

I laugh at him and shake my head. "If you think you're going to set me up with her, can you at least give me some notice before you do? She's sexy as hell, but I'm not eating pussy just for your benefit, my dear."

He laughs loudly. "I know, Sweetie. Women aren't your thing."

"But," I say, knowing that I'm about to open a can of worms. "You know, you could fuck her."

"Oh, really? Is that your way of giving me permission to have sex with Jenna?" he asks while standing up and reaching up toward the ceiling with his arms, stretching his body with a loud groan. He wasn't fibbing; he has a bulge in his pants. I'm impressed at the turnaround speed of his erection.

I shrug as I get to my feet. "What if it is?"

"Jenna?" he asks, looking at me as if he's considering it for the first time. "I don't know about that, Sweetie. She's far out of my league. I mean, did you really look at the woman? Beth, that woman is fifteen years younger than me. Why the hell would she want to be with an old guy like me when she could have someone like Jake?"

"She can't have Jake," I state matter-of-factly.

"And why not?"

I clear my throat, not knowing if what Jake told me about her is supposed to be kept in confidence. I can't shut this conversation down at this point; it's gone too far. "She doesn't like to be with guys like Jake."

"Guys like Jake?" he repeats my words with intent to get me to elaborate on what I'm trying to get at.

"Yeah, guys like Jake because she is just like Jake." My words are spoken slowly, nodding with suggestive, wide eyes.

"Oh! She's a dominant? Really?" he questions with a lowered voice.

"Yeah, that's what Jake told me."

For a full minute, I watch Henry stare off into space with his hands in his pants pockets, pulling the material tighter, revealing his ever-growing cock. He's likely picturing her beating on some poor shmuck while she fucks him in the ass with a strap-on. "Does that excite you?" I ask him while shortening the distance between us.

"I'm picturing her dressed in a sexy leather outfit while she has a guy that looks exactly like Jake on his knees on the floor, hands tied behind his back and licking her shoes while she tells him he's not worthy of the privilege," he smiles as if he's enjoying the movie reel that's playing in his imagination. "Yeah, that is a turn-on."

Now I'm picturing it. He's right, that would be a sight to see. "I should get out of your hair. When will you be home?"

"I'm not sure. I have a pile of papers that I need to get at. This past hour has been a bit of a pleasant distraction from my work but still a distraction nonetheless."

Our lips press together, pecking at one another three times before I lightly slap him on his cheek. "I'll just make dinner for myself then."

"I'll order something and have it delivered here. I'm going to aim at wrapping it up by nine if I can get everything done. I should be home around ten. If not, don't wait up. I'll see you in the morning."

"I know you have a deadline to keep, but I do wish you didn't work such long hours. Are you sure you're all right with me going to see him tomorrow?"

He snickers, "Of course I'm okay with it. Just tell me all the yummy details when you get home and don't be too exhausted because I'll want you, too."

"I can't guarantee he won't use me up. I wonder what he wants to do this time?" I try to ponder the possibilities. I'm not sure my imagination is even capable of creating the situation he'll put me in. My legs still ache from being stretched over the bedframe.

"Earth to Beth," Henry calls out.

"Yeah, yeah! Okay, don't work too hard. Love you!" I say as I exit with an arm wave above my head.

Near the elevators, I see Jenna walking out of William's office. She's too far away for us to talk, so she waves at me, and I wave back. A man is passing behind her, his eyes focused on her ass and not the papers in his hand that he had been looking at.

Men are so obvious when they desire a woman. I can read his thoughts so clearly. He wants to bend her over so he can watch his cock slide in and out of her. I jerk my eyes and tilt my head toward the guy after he passes by her, his attention now back on the paperwork. She's too far away for me to comment, but she glances his way then rolls her eyes with an expression of disdain. She mouths the word *asshole*.

I laugh and then step into the open elevator. Jenna seems like a fun, down-to-earth person that I know I'll get along well with. I am going to call her tomorrow to set up a lunch date. Now to get home and jot down some ideas for a new book.

CHAPTER THIRTEEN

Jake called me at nine-thirty this morning to set up a time to visit him this evening. I wonder if I'll ever stop having that heart-pounding, blood pressure rising, dizzying moment when I see his name on my caller I.D.?

I'm tired this morning. Henry didn't get in until midnight. I was still lying awake in bed. Neither of us was interested in being intimate so we cuddled. I was hoping his warmth would put me to sleep, but I tossed and turned most of the night. All I could think about was Jenna and Henry being together. I was doing what Jake had suggested and given more thought to how the two of them together might affect me. The more I mulled over the benefits and deterrents, the hornier I got, but I was too tired to wake him up to pleasure me. Besides, he was so tired when he came to bed that his eyes were closing mid-sentence.

Jake has requested I arrive at his house at six tonight. This time, however, he requires me to be naked when I enter the sex room. He wants me to let myself in and make my way downstairs, like I did the last time. I wonder what he'll be wearing. Maybe nothing at all. I'm not nearly as nervous to see him this time. Now that I've been with Jake a few times, I know he's not going to hurt me without reward, so I'm much more excited than scared.

My thoughts drift into different scenarios he might lead me into. Will he tie me to one of his apparatuses or simply lie me down on the mattress for his pleasure? He seems to enjoy me on the bed but only after he's toyed with me until he's satisfied that I've had enough. Actually, I think he waits until he's sure I am exhausted both mentally and physically before he allows for his own release.

After pouring myself another cup of Columbian extra-strong java, I make my way to my desk and open my laptop. I should write for a while. I spin my chair and flop onto it, turning so I can observe the birds' battle for their spot at the feeder. I debate my options on what else I could be doing today. I'm not creative enough to write this morning. I toss a load of laundry in the washing machine and fire it up and wash Henry's coffee mug from this morning and set it on the dish rack to dry. Hmm, now what?

My phone makes a pinging sound, so I rush to the kitchen to pick it up, hoping it'll be someone interesting who'll keep me occupied until later this afternoon. I'm disappointed to see that it's an email from my editor, informing me that she'll have the book ready for my final approval by mid-week coming.

Instead of setting the phone down, I decide to try calling on Jenna. Maybe she wants to meet for lunch today. Everyone has to eat, so why not eat together? I'd like to get to know her better and check her out as a possible playmate for my husband. I believe Henry would go for it even if he says he's not interested. If she were to make an obvious pass at him, he might be swayed. I'd feel a lot better if he were having sex with someone, too.

Over time, I can see my own guilt eating a hole through my conscience, forcing me to put a stop to this extra-curricular activity. None of us wants that to happen. I shouldn't think this way, and most of the time, I don't, but there are those moments when I feel like I'm cheating on Henry. It would be better if he were playing with someone else as well.

"Jenna Kent's office, please," I request when the main receptionist answers after two rings. I'm not on hold for more than five seconds before she answers.

"Hello. Jenna Kent," she says in her sexy, raspy voice.

"Jenna, it's Beth calling."

"Oh, hey! I'm so happy you called. You are a great distraction for me," she says with a heavy sigh.

"Having a rough go of it today?"

"It's been rather gruelling, to say the least. My brain is fried. This case is never-ending. There's so much paperwork to get through. You know what? I could really use a break. Where should we meet for an early lunch? I suppose I should ask if that's why you're calling?"

My coffee mug slips from my hand and drops to my lap. "Fuck! Fuck, fuck that's hot!"

"Are you okay?" I can barely hear her after I've set the phone down on the coffee table. I tap the speaker icon in time to hear her repeat, "Beth? Are you okay?"

"Shit, shit! Sorry about the language. I dropped a hot cup of coffee all over myself. A whole mug!" I'm still cursing under my breath as I soak up what I can with a wad of tissues.

Jenna asks, "Did you get burned? Like, is it bad? You know what, call me back. You should get in the shower with cool water. You don't want to blister."

"No, I'll be fine. I still had my pyjama pants on, so I ripped them off with lightning speed. My legs are a bit red. It scared me more than anything. I'm fine, really," I explain.

"Do you want me to come over? Should you see a doctor?"

I chuckle. "No, I'm fine, really! There's a big mess to clean up, but I'm okay. My sofa has a lovely brown stain. I've gone through half a box of tissues." I take a breath and toss the stained tissues onto the coffee table. "So, you're interested in meeting for lunch?"

"Now even more than when you first called. It sounds like you're having a worse day than me." She laughs under her breath. "How about we meet at the diner at the corner, by the office? If that's good with you. Or, I can come out your way. We can go anywhere you'd like."

"The diner sounds great. I could eat a greasy burger for lunch." I pause before adding, "and another coffee."

Jenna chuckles and says, "Okay, how about in forty-five minutes? Is that enough time for you?"

I peek at the clock on the wall. "Eleven o'clock. Sure, that works for me. I'll see you there."

"Looking forward to it," she adds before hanging up.

Now to clean this mess quickly and have an even quicker shower so I can get there on time. I don't want to be late. The way my day seems to be going, I'd hate to have a car accident on the way because I'm rushing. Making it through the day with no more injuries is the goal here.

CHAPTER FOURTEEN

I arrive only a few minutes late. Jenna is waving at me from a corner booth at the back of the diner. Only one table is near us, but it's vacant. She chooses tables just like Jake does. When I walk up, she stands and leans in to kiss my cheek. I find that odd because I don't really know her all that well. Maybe she's the touchy-feely, friendly type. Some people are like that.

"Sorry I'm late. I didn't want to speed in case my luck is still on the shitty side," I say, sitting down and dropping my purse on the bench beside me. "Did you order yet?"

She glances down at the menu and shakes her head. "You're not late, and I'm glad you got here safely. And, no, I haven't ordered yet. I got here a few moments before you." The tall, drastically thin waiter walks up with his pad and pen in hand, ready to jot down our orders. Jenna speaks first. "First off, coffee for me and a..." she scans the menu once more before continuing. "I'd like a Cobb salad with Balsamic Vinegar, please."

He looks at me, so I place my order. "I'll have exactly what she's having. Thank you." He takes our oversized, laminated menus before his gangly legs take him to the kitchen. "You sounded like you were having a shitty day at work. What's going on?"

She shakes her head and tells me, "You know what? I'm not at work, so I'm going to take this time away to void my mind of all the bullshit my job entails. This is just you and me for the next hour, or however long you have."

I nod and smile. "That sounds great to me. So, tell me about yourself. I don't know much about you."

She looks up at me with a slightly wicked grin. "We both know that's not true."

"I don't know what you mean," I say, knowing full well what she's referring to.

The waiter sets down our coffees and the condiments. Jenna waits until he walks away before saying, "Yes, you do. Jake mentioned that he told you about my sexual preferences."

"Um, he shouldn't have broken your trust like that. You don't need to worry because I won't tell anyone."

She smiles at me before shaking her head. "I doubt you will. He trusts you enough to introduce you to his lifestyle. I trust his judgement. Therefore, I will trust you as well."

"So, you know... about him and me?"

"Jake and I talk about a lot of things."

"I would never tell anyone about you. If the details of mine and Jake's relationship goes public... We both have much to lose."

"Do you have any questions for me? You can ask me anything." She poses a loaded question. Should I bring up Henry?

"Just how much do you and Jake tell each other?"

She grins before taking a sip of her coffee. "A lot. We are excellent friends and confide in each other often. We can relate to one another better than with anyone else. And, before you ask, no we are not involved sexually. We never have and likely never will. We prefer... submissive volunteers, if you will. Neither of us can comfortably fill that role for the other."

"No matter how hard I try, I cannot picture Jake tied up and getting spanked. Maybe that's because I've only ever seen him in a more commanding sexual role. Then again, I never thought I'd enjoy being on either end of the BDSM spectrum."

"It's not something every person thinks about. We are taught that sex should be basic, perhaps even lovingly romantic each time. Too many people run away from their truest desires, hiding them deep in the closet for fear that their partner, or even society itself, will condemn them for it. I let that go about five years ago when I met a woman by the name of Christy. She introduced me to this lifestyle and took her precious time to teach me her craft. I've felt so much freer ever since, like I've finally woken up."

"Do you still see her?" I ask, sipping my horrendously strong coffee.

"Not anymore, but we touch base on the computer from time to time. I miss her, but she's living on the other side of the country now."

"Well, I'm glad we've both been introduced to this type of playing because you obviously love it, and I am really enjoying myself. I mean, damn! I honestly had no idea that I could cum like that." I scan around the room, ensuring that others aren't listening in. "Jake has a talent like nobody I've ever met. He hurts me, but I don't hate it. The pleasure that follows is like nothing I've ever felt. I'd love to shake the hand of whoever showed him the ropes, pardon the pun." We both laugh.

"I could never see myself in your position, and you would likely be uncomfortable in mine, but you could learn to fake your way through it if you're a good actress. I'm happy that you are pleased with Jake. Don't tell him I said so, but he was nervous to be with you."

I'm shocked! "What? Me? Why?"

"Look at you! You're so beautiful and refined. You must be intimidating to men. How did he put it?" she pauses, tapping her manicured fingernails on the tabletop. "Oh, he said that because you're older than him, you might think of him as not being worthy of your time. He also said that you might not find him to be attractive. Jake looks nothing like Henry, whom you love and adore. Basically, he was worried that you would reject his advances. Just between you and me, I can't see him doing well with rejection. I don't recall a time when he ever has been rejected."

"He was afraid *I* would reject *him*?" This is a surprise to me. "I can't believe he was nervous about approaching me. I mean, he was as calm as someone who's reading the newspaper on a lazy Sunday morning. I was a mess. I could not stop trembling. I was scared but also intrigued, if that makes sense. We sat in the booth over there, and he really sold me on it, and he patiently waited for me to make my own decision whether to go home with him or not.

He was cool and calm the entire time. I'm trying to remember if there was even a moment when he seemed nervous or intimidated, but nothing stands out."

"I'm just repeating what he told me." She shrugs, sipping her coffee as the waiter sets down our plates. "That looks delicious, thank you."

"Thank you," I also say and return my attention back to Jenna when she leans in.

"I have to confess something. After he met you, Jake told me he wanted to go through with introducing you to his playroom. I didn't think it was a good idea. Henry is our superior, and if it turned out badly between you and Jake, it could make for a very uncomfortable workplace. Eventually, one of them might have to move to another company just to ease the strain. I was worried, especially when Jake pushed aside my concerns so easily. I didn't know much about you, so I was worried. It turned out for the better. I hope it stays beneficial for everyone."

"Yes, me too." She nods at me, but I can still see a hint of concern behind her eyes. It's obvious that she's protective of Jake. "Can I ask you when you voiced your concerns? Was it at the yearly barbeque?"

"Yes, how do you know that?"

"I saw you two talking. You looked angry when you walked away from him."

"I wasn't angry so much as worried."

"You said Jake was intimidated by me. I don't intimidate you, do I?"

She shrugs. "Maybe a little."

"Do I send out vibes that I have all my shit together and that I think I'm better than everyone else? I sure hope not."

"You do have your shit together, but I don't find you to be rude or arrogant. You're a strong woman, and I respect that. I like you. We could become great friends," she says while pouring dressing on her salad.

"I don't all of my ducks in a row. My brain is scattered in a million different directions most of the time. It took me two months to come up with the perfect ending to my last book. I haven't anything new and interesting to pitch to my publisher for my next venture. Now Henry, there's a man who has everything running like clockwork. He is someone who absolutely has his shit together."

She nods and swallows the bite that she's been chewing for a full minute now. "You are so right. Henry is like a well-tuned clock. He is never late for anything, prides himself on being well-informed, and manages to do it all while being happily married to a fantastic woman. I enjoy working with Henry. It doesn't happen often enough, but I've learned a lot from him. Many of us have. We look up to him like an older brother. I'd say father, but he is way too sexy for me to put him into that parental box."

Here is my opening. "You think Henry is attractive? How attractive?"

She squints her eyes while she sizes me up. "Let's cut to the chase, shall we? Are you asking if I'd be interested in being intimate with Henry?"

"Please don't take it the wrong way. I'm not accusing you of having had an affair with Henry. If he had been with you, he would have told me. He isn't great at keeping things from me. Although, he did conspire with Jake without me ever suspecting that he was up to something sketchy. He can be such a weasel," I giggle.

"Then what are you asking me, exactly?" she asks.

I set my fork down and cross my hands in front of me. "Can I confide in you?"

"Of course!"

"And it'll be between you and me, never Jake or Henry?"

"Between you and me only," she says while raising her hand as if to vow it.

"I feel guilty that I get to have sex with Jake, but Henry doesn't have anyone. He's explained that he is having a great time knowing that I'm having fun. He says he gets off on hearing the details. Yesterday, Jake took me on the desk in front of Henry. He got off all by himself while watching Jake fuck the hell out of me.

I just wish he would pursue another woman for extracurricular entertainment."

She sets her fork down on her plate. "Henry is the type of man who is in the voyeur category. He likes to watch or hear the details of your sexual exploits, and for people like him, that's enough. We are all wired the way we are and should never apologize for enjoying what excites us. He might not even want to be with someone else. Did you think about that? Have you asked him if he'd even be interested?"

"Well, not really. I talked to Jake about maybe setting you and Henry up. He told me that you are just like him. I had no idea. You are so sexy. If I were considering hopping the fence, I'd land towards you. I'm not, though. I do love penis. Would you be interested in being with Henry?"

"Henry and I have always been very professional, other than simple small talk. From observing Henry, I learned that when I'm at the office, I should keep my conversations on a professional platform. I was with this one guy from the accounting department, and he turned out to be a real jerk. He told a few people that I enjoy having men urinate on me. It isn't true. When it got back to Henry, he defended my honour. He asked me if this was something I wanted people to know about me. I told him the asshole was lying because he felt jilted when I dumped him. He was furious with the guy. Needless to say, Henry humiliated him in front of a bunch of his coworkers by calling him out on spreading a false rumour. So, would I consider risking having that happen again by being with someone from work? No, not with anyone I didn't completely trust. Would I consider being with Henry? Maybe. I trust him and you. I'm not so sure he'd be interested in playing the way I prefer to, however."

"If I casually ask him if he'd like to be with you, and he says he would, are you willing?"

She takes a long, deep breath. "I don't know if we should begin a relationship like that. Let me explain my reasoning. I respect the hell out of Henry. Having him grovelling at my feet and licking my boots while he calls me Mistress could very well alter our dynamic at the office. Although, he is always professional while at work, so maybe it wouldn't. But once that line is crossed, it smears, and you never can go back."

"But like you already told me, you rarely work with Henry, so would it actually change anything?"

"Touché! I can tell you're a writer because you used my words to spin it around on me." Jenna laughs and picks her fork up. She stabs at a pile of lettuce. "Henry's type makes for very good pets."

"Pets?" I am interested.

She snickers. "Yes, I call all my submissives *Pet* because I would hate to either forget their name in the heat of the moment or call them by someone else's. I don't ever want that to happen. Besides, I enjoy belittling them. Henry has a high-stress position."

"What does that have to do with anything?"

"Usually, people who carry a heavy burden and need to be on-point all the time benefit greatly by giving up their control to someone else. It's like taking a mini vacation from their lives. Henry fits that bill perfectly. I'll find out if he would be interested, hopefully without him clueing into my intentions."

"That sounds fair. I'm sure you know how to do it better than I can. I've asked him outright, but he will only tell me how he's happy that I'm with Jake and that he's just fine. I'd like him to try it. He might really enjoy it like I do." I can feel my face flush slightly.

We finish lunch and realize that while getting to know each other well, we had a great time and laughed a lot. She's going to do a little scouting with Henry and get back to me. But for now, I am going home to soak in a hot bath. A little relaxation before giving myself up to Jake will do me some good.

CHAPTER FIFTEEN

I'm standing naked, staring at the open door of Jake's playroom and my heart is pounding. I look down at the soft spot below my rib cage and can see it bouncing in sync with the sound of my heartbeat in my ears. After a deep breath to gain some courage, I walk in, closing it behind me and flipping the lock as I've seen him do.

The room is quiet and darker than the one I just left, so my eyes are trying to adjust. Where is he? I squint as I scan the room, sensing that he's standing behind me. When I hear him take a breath, I jolt, making a strange squealing sound. I knew he was in here, so why am I so tense?

"On your knees, hands on your thighs." His orders are firm and exact. I sink down, assuming the position he described. "I'm going to fuck your mouth and you're going to take it all."

Jake steps directly in front of me, and that's when I notice he's wearing a well-fitting pair of old jeans with rips in the knees and a pair of heavy black boots. His chest is bare, expanding with each breath he takes.

He pops the button on his pants and slowly unzips them. He isn't wearing any underwear. His hand slides into his pants and caresses the bulge still hidden behind the denim material. I want to see it.

"Open your mouth and show me down your throat. I want to see where my cock is going." His voice is titillating in tone.

I tilt my head back and open my mouth as wide as I can. His free hand grabs my hair to hold me steady as he bends over to get a better look. His eyes are heavy and sexy in this lighting, but I can still see the pretty blue that looks like pools of fresh water. I could easily drown in them if he allowed me to stare long enough. He releases my hair and pulls his hand from his pants. He retrieves something from his back pocket that is shiny and black. What is it?

"Keep your mouth open," he tells me as he places metal things in my mouth that look like hooks. The metal sits between my upper and lower molars, holding them open. After he fastens the leather band around my head, he begins doing something on the sides of it that are hoisting my jaw open, wider and wider until it cannot possibly open any more. My mouth is gaping. "Is that too much?"

"Uh-uh," I mutter, shaking my head. This I can handle, but it's uncomfortable for sure.

Jake slides his hand back in his pants, so he can massage his swollen prick. "Now I'm going to fuck your mouth."

He lifts his prick through the open zipper of his snug jeans. His cock is gorgeous, big and thick. I can't wait to have him inside my pussy or ass. My clit twinges and my mouth fills with spit. I can't swallow like this. Drool is dribbling from my bottom lip landing on my thighs. Wiping it with my hand will only get me scolded, so I let it drip. I tilt my head up to look at him, wondering why he isn't fucking my face yet. He's looking at me with lust in his eyes.

Jake smiles before setting the tip of his dick on my bottom lip. He taps it from lip to lip, running the tip of it along the bottom one and spreading my saliva along its shaft with his hand. He takes my hair in both hands and glides his prick so deep into my mouth that it hits the back of my throat. It's an odd vulnerability having something deep in your mouth that it touches your throat when your lips can't wrap around its circumference. It's intimidating. I can't bite if it gets to be too much.

He pulls back and then slides in with little time between insertions. He's holding my head still while his hips do all the work. It isn't long before he pushes his prick down my throat and holding until I gag. As he's pulling back, I start coughing.

"Regain your composure. Do not try to breathe when I'm entering your mouth. That's what you did wrong," he schools me.

My eyes are beginning to water and I'm breathing heavily. A wad of saliva leaks onto my chest and drips all the way to my belly button. It continues to tickle, and I want to wipe my mouth but don't dare move. He pushes deep again, but this time, I follow his instructions and don't immediately gag. I'm waiting for him to pull out but he's holding my head in position. All I can do right now is to concentrate on holding my throat open. I fear I'll vomit if I gag again.

He pulls out, lifting his cock with his hand and tilting it to the side so he can watch himself push his balls into my mouth. "Use your tongue and lick them."

The second I move my tongue, one of his testicles falls out of my mouth. I roll the other over my tongue. He switches them, setting the other just inside my mouth. It's so hard to perform well when my jaw is held open and I can't use my lips. It's nearly impossible to do an impressive job. He pushes his prick into my mouth again, all the way in with no hesitation. He is only holding my hair with one hand while he pulls my head forward and back, so he can hold his body still. It's very hard not to wretch. I fail and start choking. That doesn't stop him from continuing, which is making me gag with more gusto. It takes everything I have to fight my instincts to get away.

He finally releases my hair. Tears are pouring down my cheeks and a small fountain of saliva is streaming down my gaping mouth. I'm sitting with my butt almost touching the floor between my calves while I collect my composure. My jaw is starting to hurt. When my wet eyes meet his sexy blues, his lids appear heavy, like he's lost in deep thought.

"Stand up," he tells me while holding his hand out to aide me. I'm pleased when he removes the mouth spreader. I follow as he leads me to a hip-high, leather-covered bench.

"On your belly."

I lay on it with my legs and arms hanging over the sides and rest my right cheek against the leather. Jake grabs my hips and yanks me along the bench until my pussy is peeking over the edge a smidgeon. He fastens my ankles and forearms with cuffs that are attached high on the wooden frame beneath me. When I'm secured, I look like I'm about to crawl somewhere.

I hear the loud cracking sound before the pain rings true in my brain. Fuck, it hurts! Is that a paddle? He connects again on the same cheek. Shit! Shit! I don't like the paddle at all. He starts in on the other cheek and then alternates until I'm nearly screaming with each wallop. My ass is stinging and feels like it's red hot. His hands span over each cheek and squeeze, pulling them apart. His tongue flattens over my asshole, gliding up and down. It's so hot and slippery. Oh damn, this feels awesome! When his two fingers slip easily into my wet pussy, a loud moan seeps from my body in a lazy and lengthy exhale. He gently fucks me with arched fingers, tapping my g-spot with an easy tempo.

"Thank you, Sir," I whisper, loud enough for him to hear.

The tip of his tongue pokes into my asshole, wiggling frantically. If he keeps this up, he's going to make me cum. I wonder if I have to ask permission today. Maybe I should ask him to clarify that rule for me. No, I will definitely ask because I know how much he likes it when I do. I'm so close to erupting.

Jakes stops touching me, much to my disappointment. I don't hold back my dissatisfied groan, making sure he knows how much I wanted him to continue. His feet shuffle on the floor as he walks away from me, no doubt to pick up some toy he's going to use to inflict me with pain. If I go from experience, the pleasure isn't going to come to a head any time soon. He wants to hear me scream through some pain first.

He drips some cool lube on my asshole and inserts a finger, pulling at the rim to stretch it. He slips two fingers back into my pussy, continuing the same delicious movement as he was before he left me. Another digit enters my ass. He's so experienced at stretching assholes that his fingers feel more like they're massaging me. It is, in fact, quite enjoyable. My pussy is sloppy wet.

Something cold lines up to my butt hole and slowly but forcefully is inserted deep inside. It's a butt plug, but it's very cold, possibly metallic. He sets something on my lower back that has strings attached to it. At least, I think they're strings.

Jake pulls at my breast to free my nipples from between me and the bench. He presses two sticky pads on either side of each nipple. Is he going to use a TENS machine on me? On my breasts? If the strings are, in fact, wires, does that mean whatever he pushed into my bum also streams electricity? Oh, hell! What did I get myself into? I take a deep breath to fight the urge to ask him what he's doing and then beg him not to if, in fact, he is about to electrocute my tits and asshole.

"Tell me when."

I'm about to ask *when what,* but a tickling zap ignites the nerves around my nipples, answering the question for me. It doesn't hurt like I thought it would. This feels tingly and enticing. The tingle is beginning to hurt. It comes in waves.

"Okay, stop there." The zapping makes me whimper and on the edge of crying out when it's at its highest point, but it feels wondrous just before it gets to that point.

A tingle inside my butt immediately directs all of my attention to it. In a matter of seconds, the muscles surrounding the inner wall of my asshole are flexing and relaxing with the same waves of intensity. Each segment lasts for about five seconds before the tension on my muscles begins to ease. There is no pain whatsoever. This is so fucking thrilling! It waves once again, but this time, the muscles hold a bit tighter. Each time it tenses, the rim and inner walls of my ass are forced to squeeze tighter until I cry out and yell, "Okay, okay!"

It eases slightly, enough where I can go back to focusing on enjoying it more than hating it. He cracks my burning ass cheeks with his palms. I scream, mostly from the shock of it, rather than the pain. I was not expecting him to spank me again. The flesh on my cheeks is so sensitive that even when he removes his hands, my skin still feels their heat.

Something sharp is dragging up my calf. It's not really painful at this point, but I can certainly feel its sharpness. It creeps up the back of my thigh. What the fuck is that? It feels like he's cutting my ass cheeks. I know he wouldn't injure me because he said he wouldn't, and so far, he's kept to his word. The pain he grants me hasn't caused injury... yet.

The object slices up my back and I'm crying out. When it rolls over my shoulder, I can see that it looks like a pizza cutter but with sharp spines jutting all the way around the wheel instead of it being a blade. He rolls it down my bicep, walks around the bench, and then begins rolling it up my other arm and over my shoulder. He's heading back toward my super-sensitive ass cheek and I know it's going to hurt so much more.

"This is a pinwheel. Do you like it?" he asks in a very calm, deep voice.

As it nears the abused skin, I reply, "Not particularly."

He rolls it down my calf but doesn't stop there. Soon, he's tracing it along the sole of my foot. I'd swear he's slicing it open because it hurts so much. I'm able to hold back my scream until the pinwheel pushes between my big toe and the second one.

"No! Please stop!" I cry out.

"You know the safe words. Use them if it's too much; otherwise, let me hear you scream," he says while still torturing my foot.

The intensity of the pulses to my nipples and asshole increase to a level I don't want them to be at. I yell a long and drawn out, "Fuck!"

"Oh yeah, scream for me," he whispers, obviously getting off on seeing me in pain.

He stops torturing my foot and walks away. I hear his feet shuffle on the floor as he returns. Something cool presses against my clit. His feet shuffle once again and then the very welcomed vibrations rev up against my swollen little nib, torturing it beautifully.

"Yes! Fuck!" I whisper, not really focusing on the pain as much. The vibrations are more intense and stimulating now than I've ever had the pleasure of experiencing. My clit is incredibly hypersensitive. That must be because of the spasms inside my body from the electrode in my ass. My body is experiencing opposite sides of the pain/pleasure spectrum at the same time. I love it and hate it.

I open my eyes when he weaves his fingers into my hair. "Open your mouth."

When I do what he says, he slides his prick into my mouth but not deeply. Only about half of his cock pushes past my lips. He's fucking my mouth while I scream and moan. Pleasure and pain. Pleasure and pain. I had no idea one could accentuate the other so perfectly.

When he pulls back to let me breathe, I manage to beg, "Please, Sir, may I cum?"

"No, not yet," he tells me while continuing to fuck my mouth. He slips his fingers between my breast and the leather bench until my nipple is pinched in his fingers. He pinches so hard that I wail with his cock in my mouth. "Scream for me."

I'm panting, moaning, and yelling. My mind is beginning to blur far away from reality. I want to cum. The pressure within me is building to monumental levels. It feels like a giant elastic band is stretched taut inside me, ready to snap at any second. I'm fighting the urge to just let go. The nipple squeezing is a helpful distraction from the increasing desire to give into it.

Jake pinches my nose. I can still get air from around his cock but it's a bit of a struggle when he's pushed deep. He tortures my nipple with what feels like a vice-like grip. My face contorts but I can't scream because his cock is too far into my mouth. A muffled grumble vibrates my throat. I have no control over what I say or do at this point. Thinking is simply impossible. My mind is being directed from my tits to my asshole and then to my clit and back but never allowing me a sensible thought.

He strokes my hair with his hand in a gentle, loving way as I'm losing control of myself. He whispers, "Cum, now." That's all it takes for me to let go and release any and all of my remaining sanity. His prick pulls out of my mouth just as my jaw clamps down. Every muscle in my body is pulling, flexing for all they're worth. My arms and legs are straining to free themselves from the straps that burden them.

A gush of cum bursts from my spasmodic pussy, locking tight and then pushing hard as wave after wave of pure ecstasy overwhelms my body and mind. As my climax hurdles to an end, my body starts jerking and quivering. The only recognizable word my brain can manage to form is *yeah* and I keep saying it over and over again in rapid repetition. I was lost in a fog, but it's beginning to clear. The waves of electricity have changed to a thumping sensation. My muscles and nerves are vigorously pulsing around the plug in my ass. Wow!

The over-stimulated nerves in my clitoris are beginning to burn. It feels so hot! His cock pushes into my cum-soaked cunt, and that's when I realize that he's still here. For a moment, I'd completely forgotten about him. How is that possible?

The lovely fullness that's stroking inside my pussy, along with the thumping in my asshole, and the vibration on my clitoris is mind-boggling. A lot is going on in that region. His cock is gliding in and out of me swiftly but not hammering hard into me. I wish he would.

"Fuck me! Fuck me hard! Please!" I yell, pleading with him, desperate for the forceful invasion on my cervix.

"That's right, whore, beg for it," he calmly replies.

I scream, as my clit begins to burn so hot that it's working me into a forced orgasm. "I'm coming!"

Jake cracks my ass with his hand halfway through my climax, ruining it, much to my disappointment. "Beg for my permission!" he yells, slapping me again.

"Please! Please, Master! Fuck me hard!" I call him Master for the first time. He must approve. He's fucking me like the devil himself. The air is being forced from my body with each slam. "Yes! Yes! Yes! Thank you! Thank you!" I can feel myself float away by giving in to the physical sensation and no longer struggling to hold myself in the now. I know nothing but my body. I can't hear, smell, see, or taste anything. Maybe I'm dead. If I am and this is what it means to die, I welcome it.

My body is vibrating, locked in a state of near-constant orgasm. My clit feels like it's as big as a man's cock but most of its length resides inside my body, only about a third of it being revealed. The world around me is lost, shoved out of my existence completely. Only my body remains – my gloriously tensed, over-stimulated body.

Jake grasps a handful of my hair and pulls my head back. I don't even try to resist him. Right now, I don't care what he does to me, as long as he keeps me in this state. Never stop! Please!

I can't even recall how many times I've orgasmed. I lost count after five. There were many more after that. I'm slowly becoming aware that the fucking has stopped and so has the vibration and the thumping. He is carefully extracting the plug from my ass and pulling off the sticky pads. He frees my limp arms and legs. There is no way I can lift my body off this bench. I am just too exhausted.

Jake scoops my near lifeless frame up, carrying me to the mattress. He gently lays me down, slipping between my open thighs while his lips press to mine. Our mouths explore each other's as his prick slips into my swollen pussy. I huff softly as he fills me.

With a quick and steady rhythm, Jake fucks me but only for a minute or two before his muscles tense and his lips part from mine as he pants and grunts escape from his throat. He collapses heavily on top of me. His breath caressing my neck, heating my skin and raising tiny bumps everywhere it brushes upon.

A long, heavy sigh flows from somewhere deep within my soul, taking with it the last bit of my strength. I welcome the weight of his body on mine, so he can hold me down. I feel weightless, like a bird who's been soaring through the air with open wings... sort of floating, but I'm now coming down from the high that has drained and exhausted me. I wish I could be weightless again.

Jake lifts his head and chest, supporting himself on his elbows while his erection wilts within me. His tired blue eyes peer down into mine. He doesn't say anything. Instead, he smiles lazily. The sweat on his forehead and upper lip are proof of the strenuous workout he put himself through. Perhaps, although unlikely, he enjoyed that more than I did.

He sluggishly lifts his body, rolling onto his back. He slowly folds his heavy arms over his chest. I turn my head to look at him and he has his eyes closed. He's taking breaths in through his nose, exhaling through his mouth. When he's calm, he turns his head, meeting eyes with me.

"How was that?" he asks.

I start laughing. "Jake… that was so," I can't find the proper words to express fully how elated I am. I smile at him and shake my head.

"You seemed to enjoy yourself."

"Um, yeah! That was definitely wild. I mean… fuck! At first, I didn't think I was going to like the butt plug and sticky pads on my nipples, but then everything else happened and the fun touches began. I was lost after that. I felt like I left my body. How many times did I cum?"

"I have no idea. I would have kept it going, but you looked like you were about to pass out."

"I thought maybe I was dying. Surprisingly, I didn't care if I did. What a way to go! Oh my god! Who taught you how to do all of this stuff?" I ask, not really expecting him to answer.

He sits up and begins to explain. "I had a few good teachers. Without actually telling her partner, a woman will let them know she's enjoying something by the way her body reacts to a stimulus. You are easy to read and a pleasure to please. You let me push the boundaries and test your limits. I really enjoy that."

He stands up on weak legs and opens the door, slipping into the other room. After a quick moment, he returns with two bottles of water. As he hands me the bottle he just cracked the lid on, I ask, "Do you like it when I'm in pain?"

He chugs nearly half the bottle of water and then replaces the cap before sitting on the bed beside me with one leg curled under his body. "It's not the idea that I'm hurting you that arouses me, so much as watching you experience the pain. By giving me the privilege, you're telling me you believe me to be worthy of using your body how I choose to, even if it's in a way that isn't necessarily pleasurable. That makes me feel powerful. It's very hard to explain it logically. On a physical level, when you scream, my cock twitches. I'm not sure if that answers your question."

Just the act of trying to sit up proves how worn out I am. I take a gulp of the icy water. "I suppose everyone has their strange kinks. I'm happy that you have found a way to enjoy yours and you're not suppressing those urges. I can imagine that wouldn't be good for your psyche."

He nods in agreement. "I'm much happier when I get to play with someone who is willing to play along with my little games. You are doing very well, by the way."

"Doing well?" I question his meaning.

"Yes. I just mean that you seem to be accepting whatever I'm doing to you. This pleases me, and I thank you for it."

"Accepting?" I say the word aloud because it doesn't seem to fit. "I am absolutely flourishing from our time together. It's like I'm waking up, if that makes any sense. It's not that I've been sleeping through sex, but my body is experiencing all these new sensations that I didn't know existed, and I love it! I can't thank you enough."

He suggests, "Now that we have that cleared up, how did you like the electricity?"

I flop back with my arms and legs spread out like a starfish, wearing a huge smile. "Incredible! It felt like my nipples were constantly being sucked while someone was fucking my ass. Not just fucking it. When a man cums, a woman can feel him swell inside of her, and it's a great feeling. That's what it felt like but much more intense and repetitive. It did hurt, but not to the point that I needed it to stop or even wanted it to. So yes, I enjoyed it very much."

"Good. I plan on using that again, maybe more intensely. After what I've seen you do today, I think you can handle it," he says, snickering with a devilish expression. It makes me wonder what he's thinking.

"I accept that challenge. So, what are you going to do with me the next time I visit you?" I push for clues, knowing he won't tell me. He seems to love keeping that a secret.

Jake shakes his head as he takes my hand and helps me to my feet. I cannot believe how rubbery my legs feel. When I wobble, he snickers but grabs my arm to steady me. "You're welcome to use the shower. If you'd like me to help you shower, I'd be very happy to assist." He's wearing a sneaky grin. He can't possibly still be horny. Can he?

"I'll be fine in the shower. Don't avoid the subject. You didn't answer me." I can't help but smile at him.

He laughs. "And I'm not going to. Oh, by the way, when you called me Master, I just about lost control of the situation."

"Oh, really? Master Jake," I whisper seductively as I leave the room. I can hear him clear his throat loudly and then chuckle.

After a quick shower, I dress while finishing the bottle of water. He kisses my forehead before I exit his house, as he always does. I drive home to my patiently awaiting husband with a calmness about me that I can't remember ever feeling. Nothing can irritate me right now, not even the asshole who cut me off and has been weaving in and out of traffic ahead of me.

CHAPTER SIXTEEN

I walk in through the door and see Henry stretched out on the sofa, watching a rerun of a ten-year-old sitcom. He looks up when he realizes I'm home. Immediately, he sits up and shuts off the television. Knowing Henry as I do, I'm sure all of his attention will be devoted to me while I tell him the details. His expression screams curiosity. He pats the sofa beside him with a silly smile on his face.

"Come, sit. Tell me all about it and don't leave anything out. You look tired. Did he wear you out?" he inquires while wearing a curious expression.

I drop my purse on the counter as I pass by it. My legs seem to each weigh one hundred pounds. They are so tired that when I attempt to sit gently beside Henry, they give out, plopping me down with a bounce. I giggle as I sink against the puffy cushion on the back of the sofa. "That man is going to kill me." He knows I'm joking because Jake would never harm me.

Henry leans in to kiss my lips with the tenderness I remember falling in love with, but before he does, he asks, "How many times did he make you cum?"

"I have absolutely no idea. I lost count after five, but there were more," I reply, looking into his wide eyes. "Do you really want the details?"

"Of course," he assures me without hesitation. "You know I do."

"Is it okay if I fill the tub with hot water and sink my exhausted body into it? I've been looking forward to it since I left Jake's."

"How about I get that started for you while you pour yourself a glass of wine?" he asks, already beginning to stand.

I sigh heavily. "That sounds wonderful. Epsom salts and lavender oil, please."

He puts his hand out for me to take, so he can help me to my feet. When I stand, he wraps his arms around me, holding me tightly to his warm body. He kisses the top of my head and then rests his cheek on it, swaying me slowly. I could stay safe in his arms all night. I love my husband so much.

"Okay, get some wine, and I'll meet you in the bathroom," he tells me, swatting my butt lightly as I begin to walk away, causing me to wince. He chuckles, knowingly.

I set my glass on the edge of the tub and begin removing my shirt. Henry steps toward me to assist, removing my bra, jeans, panties, and socks. Gallantly, he lends me his arm to hold so I can step into the tub, but he soon begins to laugh. "What's so funny?"

He slaps my behind and I jolt from the sting. "Your ass is red and puffy. Did he spank you?"

"With a paddle! It really fucking hurt."

"Why didn't you tell him to stop?"

I shrug and roll my eyes. "I suppose on some deeper level, I enjoyed it."

As I gradually sink my weary bones into the steaming hot bath water, I breathe in the calming scent of lavender that lingers in the air. I rest my head against the tub's edge while Henry turns on the jets. The water whips up, pulsing against my back and sore legs. It feels so good. I'm not moving from this heaven any time soon.

"Are you ready to tell me everything or do you want to keep me on the edge of my seat for a few more minutes?" he asks while sitting on the edge of the tub, dangling his hand into the water.

"Okay, I'm ready," I say and then proceed to tell him everything I can remember, hoping I won't forget anything important. Henry listens with great curiosity, not interrupting me even once. After I've told him everything, he pulls his hand from the water and dries it on the towel he has waiting for me. He's quiet as he absorbs the information. No doubt he's running the whole scenario through his imagination as though he were watching it like a movie.

"I'm so happy that you are playing along with my strange perversion. Do you really enjoy going to see Jake? If this is bothering you emotionally, we need to talk about it," he asks while wearing a concerned expression.

I thought he was becoming sexually aroused by my recall of the spicy events, but he seems more concerned with my psyche than his own physical cravings. He looks down at my contorted face and then smiles. "Sorry, Sweetie, I was just making sure you really are good with all of this and that you're not doing it to make me happy."

I take his hand in mine to assure him. "I am thrilled about going to see Jake. It's not Jake himself so much as what he will do *to* me, or *for* me, depending on how you look at it. I'm sure he thinks he's using me, but the way I see it, I'm using him. I do worry about your emotions and whether you're really pleased or pretending to be. Are you sure you're all right with me being with another man? I mean, is there no jealousy, not even a little? He is pleasing my body a lot. Are you sure you won't resent me later?"

He thinks for a moment and then divulges, "Maybe a little of jealousy, but I'm not worried that you're going to leave me for him. You love me, and I love you. We are bonded stronger than any couple that I know. When I picture Jake fucking you, touching your skin, kissing you... it arouses me. If you were to be with anyone else, have an affair with someone, for instance, I'd be furious. I'd feel betrayed by you. I'm sure of it. But Jake, I don't know how to explain it. He's quite respectful of our commitment to each other. He's open and honest about everything. I believe you being with him is exactly what I desire. When you're with him, I wonder what he's doing to you, if you're coming at that very moment, screaming his name... it makes me want you even more. I'm not right in the head, I know."

I feel better now. "Okay, I just wanted to make sure you're all right. If you ever want this to stop, you say so, and it ends immediately. You are the love of my life. I never want to hurt you."

He assures me, "As long as we keep our communication flowing, I'm sure I'll be extremely happy with this arrangement for a long time."

While we're openly communicating, I ask, "So, what about you? I mean, I feel a bit guilty that I'm having sex with someone and you aren't. I'd feel a lot better if you were with another woman, or man if that's what you'd like to try."

"Ah, I'm not sure about being with a man, but thank you for allowing me that option," he says, shaking his head. "Another woman maybe. Do you have someone in mind?"

I bite my top lip wondering if I should ask him about Jenna but decide to throw caution to the wind and just light the fuse. "Maybe. How about Jenna?"

"Jenna? Isn't she into the same things as Jake?"

"Yes, she is a dominant like Jake."

A crease between his brows deepens as he sits quietly, contemplating the possibilities. "First off, she would never be interested in me. She's young and extremely sexy, and I'm not. She could have any man she wants, so why would she lower her standards to be with me? I'm old enough to be her father, if I had knocked someone up in high school, that is."

"And what if she were interested in you?"

He looks at me with doubting eyes. "Is she... really?"

I smirk. "Yes."

"Really?" His interest is piqued. "Okay, but does she want to torture me like Jake does to you, or will she be nice and romantic-like? I have sensitive skin and weak bones," he jokes.

I laugh before answering. "I'm sure she won't do anything you don't want her to do. Just remember, if she's anything like Jake, pained expressions or screams will get her very aroused. The more you cry out, the better the sex will be when it's time for pleasure. It sounds so much worse than it actually is. I lose myself in the sensations. It's as if my mind descends inward. The sex is amazing. I really get off on not thinking about anything but my body and what it's experiencing. I think you should give it a try.

You might like it as much as I do. If you do and decide it's not for you, you'll never have to go back."

"She told you that she wants to play with me? That she wants to have sex with me?" he asks outright.

I shrug. "Not in as many words, but yes, she is interested in dominating you. The only concern she has is that it might change your work dynamic if the authoritative roles are reversed. We can go to lunch with her to discuss it if you'd like. Or, you can go have lunch with her and have a private discussion between the two of you. I trust you completely, and even though I don't know her all too well, I have put my trust in her."

He nods and chews on his index finger. I've known him long enough to know that is a sign of insecurity. "Okay, I'll ask her if we can talk about it. I haven't put the moves on anyone in a very long time, so this should prove to be embarrassing. Has anything changed in the dating scene that I should know about?"

I smile and reply, "How would I know? Besides, you won't be dating her, so don't worry so much. It'll seem clinical when you're discussing the dos and don'ts. At least, it felt cold and unaffectionate when Jake and I set up the boundaries. The only time I would say the sex feels even remotely emotional is when he looks deep into my eyes when I'm coming. But it's fleeting and, therefore, irrelevant. Oh, and he has a thing about hugging me and then kissing the top of my head before I leave his house. It's kind of like telling me that he appreciates me. I do what I can to leave my emotional self in the car. It's physical only. He keeps it completely separate."

"He said he would," Henry tells me, rather matter-of-factly. "All right, if you're sure you won't get jealous, I'll talk to her."

"I can't promise because I won't know until it actually happens, but I don't think I'll get upset about it. She's hot! If I were into women, I'd want her. Go for it, Henry. Take a chance," I say as I pull the plug for the drain.

CHAPTER SEVENTEEN

Henry helps me out of the tub, watches me dry my body, and then follows me into the bedroom. I know his intentions, but I play along, pretending to be naïve. I take my nightie from the hook on the back of the door and flip it, slipping my arms in. Before it can glide down my body, Henry's hands are on my breasts, his chest pressed against my back.

He places soft kisses on my neck. His hot breath tickles the tiny hairs on my skin, teasing until tiny, stiff bumps remain in its wake. His fingers pinch and pull my nipples, awakening my pussy.

"Jake had your body. I have your heart. You are mine. He touches you. He hurts you. He makes you scream. He fucks you hard. I will caress you. I will make you moan from pleasure. I will make love to your heart, mind, and body. He can never have that because you are mine."

Henry spins me around, wrapping his arms around my waist and pulling me against his body. His lips touch to mine, his tongue sensually exploring my mouth. He walks us toward the bed, lifting me to slide me to the middle. His lips never part from mine. My legs spread wide as he kneels between them. His hands glide up my arms, entwining with mine and pressing them to the comforter by my shoulders. Our lips part. He kisses my jaw, neck, collarbone, and down to my breast. He kisses and licks all around my areola, not touching my nipple. I'm needy with a desire for more. His hands leave mine and cradle my breasts, pushing them together so he can suck and bite one nipple, then the other and back again with very little pause. My pussy wants his mouth, wants his tongue teasing my clit, not my nipples.

His tongue glides along my belly. He pauses only to press a gentle kiss to my belly button before continuing on the descent.

My hips tilt toward his mouth the instant his hot breath strokes my clit. I reach down, weaving my fingers into his hair but not forcing his head where I desperately want it to be.

"You are mine. This vagina is mine. He fucked you. He made you cum. I will taste you, knowing he did the same. Tell me you want me. Tell me he made you cum. Tell me…" His mouth opens wide, engulfing my entire pussy and sucking while his tongue explores up and down my folds.

"Oh, yes! I want you, Henry. I need your mouth. I want your body, your heart, your mind. You are mine. He made me cum hard. He fucked me hard. He took my body and used me, and I liked it. I want more of him. His cock was deep inside of me, filling my body completely. You fill me, all of me. I'm yours, Henry. I will always be yours." Henry is moaning, lapping at my clit, sucking and nibbling, bringing me to the edge of orgasm but stopping. I cry out, "Please! Don't stop!" He stands, ripping at his clothes to get them off as quickly as possible. I watch him struggle with his zipper while his eyes watch my face.

My fingers rush to my clit, rubbing it gently to keep myself in a state of near climax but not allowing myself the release. That will be Henry's doing. He will make me cum. I know he will. "I'm yours," I whisper.

"You're mine," he replies as he slides between my legs, pushing his erection against the slick opening of my desperate womanhood. I want him inside of me. My hips jerk upward, forcing the head of his penis past my opening. He grins before pushing all the way into me. His hips lift and fall, slowly at first, as his sensuous, full lips press to mine. Our tongues dance as the pressure builds inside of me. I want to let go, to give myself up to him so completely that it hurts my heart. My hands wrap under his arms and around his strong chest, holding him onto me, never wanting to let him go.

His lips barely part from mine. "I love you!"

"Always," I add.

With enthusiasm, his hips wave against me, gliding his rock-hard penis against my cervix. Over and over, harder and harder.

The surrounding room disappears, and we are floating, our bodies bound together by love. I can only hear his breathing and my heart pounding behind my ribs. My body stiffens, and my heart seems to stop beating.

"Henry!" I cry out.

He pulls out of me, rushing his mouth to my clit. His lips form a seal around my clit and sucks hard, finishing what he has started. My arms stretch out wide, just as my knees are. The closer I get to the most ultimate pleasure a woman can experience, I feel lighter, like I'm about to float away. I grasp the comforter to hang on. The burning hot, tickling tension leading from my clit up to my belly button and beyond is growing. I'm going to explode!

All the muscles in my body painfully tense. Every nerve in my body is on fire. My heart is pounding violently in my chest. My breath holds, locking in my lungs. He pushes two fingers into me at exactly at the right moment. They tap on my g-spot while I cum with so much force that he can barely keep his digits inside me. My pussy spasms, gripping his digits and pulling them into me. His fingers have opened a dam, urging my body to let go. I can hear the sloshing of cum as he prods my g-spot, his mouth still licking and sucking, gloriously abusing my swollen, stiff clitoris.

My body jerks hard, and I'm suddenly hurdled from the euphoric nothingness my existence has disappeared into. My disappointment doesn't last long. Henry flips me over, straddles my ass, pinning my thighs tightly together and pushes his erection between my cheeks and deep inside me. His hands grasp my hipbones and lift my pelvis just slightly. He pounds into me each time he pulls up. My tender, twitching clit is squeezed and stroked by my thighs each time he enters me. He's going to make me cum again!

"Cum for me, Beth," he grunts.

"Don't. Cum. Yet!" Three more times, he rips into me, and I'm thrown into another clit-thumping orgasm. His thickness is filling me as my body quivers beneath him. I gasp for a breath and then another as the fog evaporates from my mind. "I want to taste you."

165

He pulls me up and collapses onto the bed on his back pulling me onto his chest. Our lips meet for a split second before I scoot down his body. My arms stretch along his torso, allowing my fingers to pinch and roll his nipples, sending shots of pleasure to his groin. I open my mouth wide and quickly take all of him. I glide my lips up to the tip of his mushroom head and then back down his shaft, taking him completely. My mouth works its magic, drawing him closer to his own pleasure.

Henry's strong hands grip my forearms, pinning them to his body. They rise and fall on his expanding chest. His prick swells in my mouth as his chest inflates and holds. I work his prick as his climax takes him into a muscle tensing, breathtaking moment of ultimate elation. Like a balloon, he seems to deflate, his body caving in on itself. Hot semen spirts down my throat each time his cock pulses. His body jerks as I suck every drop of spunk from his shaft, my hand helping to squeeze its length.

"Oh, fuck! I fucking love you, Beth."

I slide up his body and whisper, "I fucking love you, too."

I curl up beside him after we pull the comforter over ourselves. His arm rests heavily over my waist. We drift off to sleep in each other's arms.

The way he makes love to me pulls at my heartstrings in ways nobody else could ever do. He owns me, and I own him forever. Although my dreams are mainly about Jake, I can always feel Henry's presence, observing in the background.

CHAPTER EIGHTEEN

I've been writing like a mad genius since I woke up on Saturday. Every morning, I'm excited to get back to it, but that's probably because most nights all I do is dream about my characters. It helps me through my writers block, so I don't mind waking up tired since those dreams help. I've written nearly half the book in only three days. We've had food delivered almost every night. Stopping my flow so I can cook a meal just wasn't in the works this week. Henry doesn't mind since I've been letting him choose the restaurants.

The phone rings, interrupting my writing frenzy. For a moment, I consider letting it go so they'll leave a message. It's usually someone trying to sell me something and I can't be bothered with that right now. Instead, I pick it up to look at the caller ID. It's Henry.

"Hello, my dear," I answer with a soft voice. I spin around in my chair to watch the flock of chirping birds surrounding the feeder just outside the window.

"Hi, Sweetie. Are you still writing?"

I smile as I stand up to go make myself a cup of tea. "Yes, I am so productive lately. The words are pouring out of me. How's your day going?"

"I'm glad to hear it. Really good, actually. That's why I'm calling. I, ah... I went to lunch with Jenna."

"Really?" I am excited to hear more.

"Yes. We went to a place that wasn't close to the office, in case anyone saw us. We don't need people starting rumours. Anyway, at first, it was awkward trying to keep a casual conversation going. I just couldn't bring up what you and I discussed, so everything I was saying sounded ridiculous, dodging the real reason for our luncheon. I was like a nervous high school boy asking a girl out on a date. It was humiliating!"

I want to laugh, picturing him fidgeting nervously, but I fight that urge. I don't want to further injure his ego. This brings me back to the first time he asked me to go to dinner with him. The man was so nervous, I thought he would vomit if I didn't hurry up and interrupt his stuttered proposal to say that I would go on a date with him.

"So, what did she say?"

He clears his throat before replying. "She said that she finds me to be very attractive and that she'd like to get me naked, tie me up, and do fun things to me. Then, she sat there and just looked at me, intimidating the hell out of me. My bottom lip was quivering. It was embarrassing! I couldn't stop it. I finally got up enough courage to ask her if she wants to hurt me. To that, she replied with *only if you want me to*. I shook my head but then shrugged my shoulders like an indecisive teenager."

I have to pull the phone away from my head because I'm giggling, and I don't want him to hear me. I calmly ask, "Did you set up a date?"

"Um, not yet. I told her I wanted to talk to you first. Maybe the next time you go to Jake, I'll go see Jenna. Is it completely ridiculous how I'm so nervous that I fear I'll wake up with a big zit on my nose the day of?"

Now I am laughing and not quietly. "No, I was just as nervous to be with Jake. Henry, you'll be surprised how quickly that anxiety gets shoved to the back burner. If she's good at what she does, you'll forget all about it within the first few minutes."

"You're probably right. I just feel so silly," he confesses. "It's not like I've never had sex before."

"There's no need to feel silly. I think it's normal in this type of situation. I'm happy that you're talking to me about your concerns. So, what day would you like to do this? I'm not free until Thursday, unless Wednesday after seven in the evening works for everyone. By the time we get everything wrapped up and I come home, it'll probably be late. I don't want you to be worried about getting enough sleep for work in the morning. When you get home that first time, you'll be wired, and you won't be able to sleep, no matter how physically tired you are. Mentally, you'll be at high speed. At least, that's how I was the first few times."

"That's true, you were hyped up. Well, I'll suggest Thursday around five. I'll talk to Jake and Jenna. I wonder if she'll want to come to our house or if she would prefer that I go to her place."

"She doesn't have a designated sex room like Jake has, but then again, neither do we. Find out if she'd rather come to our house. I'm fine with that," I tell him.

Henry's quiet for a moment. The phone muffles, so I can't hear what he says. He puts his mouth back to the phone and says, "I have to let you go, Sweetie. Richard just came in with a time-sensitive issue that we need to deal with. Hopefully, I'll get a chance to confer with our two friends to see if Thursday evening is good with them. We can talk when I get home."

"Our *friends*, huh? Richard is still in the room, I gather. Thursday sounds good, Henry."

"Hey, what about pizza for dinner?" he suggests.

"No, I'm going to prepare something tonight," I tell him.

"Okay, I'll see you when I get home tonight. I love you, Beth."

"I love you, too," I say before hanging up. Hmm, now what to make for dinner? I've been too occupied to go for groceries this week. A frozen lasagna is buried near the bottom of the deep freezer, so that's what we will be eating tonight. That was easy!

I spend the rest of the afternoon writing. After plopping the frozen lasagna in the oven at three o'clock, I take a quick trip to the grocery store to pick up a few things that we desperately need. I've been drinking my coffee black for two days, and I'd really like some creamer. Besides, a salad and garlic bread will pair up wonderfully with the lasagna.

CHAPTER NINETEEN

Henry is hopped up all week. I think we've had sex nearly a dozen times since Monday. Today is the day – Thursday, Henry's introduction to the world of bondage, submission, female domination, and possibly pain. He's a bit nervous about receiving punishment, but she promised him that she'd be gentle. He knows he can stop her actions with one simple word, and he trusts her. I have no doubt that everything will work out well, and he will be as fascinated by her as I am with Jake.

As for Jake and myself, he asked me to do as I usually do. Enter the house, make my way to the room, and strip before entering. About an hour before Henry and I are supposed to split-up and meet with our extracurricular sexual partners, Henry steps into the shower with me. I'm washing the conditioner out of my hair.

His hands glide up my back as his body presses to mine, chest to chest. He runs his fingers through my hair to help rinse out the conditioner. Meanwhile, I drop my hands down to his erect penis and begin to stroke his rigid cock, gently and slowly. He breathes deeply, letting it out with a long, soft moan.

The last thing I want to do right now is fuck again. We did last night and again this morning before he left for work. The man is a sex machine lately. He's very eager to be with Jenna. I hope he hasn't built their meeting up in his mind so much that he could be let down when it actually happens. What if it doesn't live up to his expectations? I hope he won't be too disappointed. First times are always a bit awkward. I wonder if Jenna is nervous, too. She told me that Jake was nervous, but I couldn't tell. Maybe she'll seem just as cool around Henry as Jake was with me. That might help ease Henry's anxiety if she is.

I move aside so he can step under the showerhead. He tips his head back, letting the water splash off his face and flow down his body in a steady stream. His prick is so hard in my hands, I know he wants to fuck me. I pick up the shampoo and squirt a little in my hand to slick up his cock for more comfortable stroking. With one hand cupping his testicles and the other working his prick, his lips press onto mine, kissing me with heated passion.

Henry stretches his arms up over his head and presses them onto the walls. His eyes are shut, and he's breathing heavier now. Every time my hand glides down his prick, he humps his hips forward. He's close to coming. With both hands, I grip his prick and hold firmly as I stroke as he likes it. His eyes are now watching the action while his hips buck, fucking his cock into my tight grip. I'm watching his face. Seeing the pleasured expression on his face as he's about to ejaculate has always pleased me.

It isn't long before his body is tensing and jerking. His mouth is open wide. A long exhale escapes his lungs with a deep, satisfied groan. I stroke him a few more times to squeeze out every drop of cum before setting his prick free. When his eyes finally open, they're hooded and glossy. An appreciative smile is quick to grow on his face.

"Thank you, Sweetie. My fear is that she'll just touch my cock and I'll cum. I'm so wound up," he says as we both rinse off.

"Don't worry, it'll work out how it's meant to. You've been so horny lately that I'm sure if it does happen, you'll be hard again in no time. Am I right?"

"I hope you're right," he replies. "Or I'll get so nervous that I'll stay soft like a limp noodle and not get hard at all. Christ, that'll be humiliating!"

"You'll be fine. When is Jenna supposed to arrive?"

Henry looks at the clock in the bedroom as he dries himself off. "She said that she'll get here just before five," he tells me.

"I'll be long gone by then. I'd better hurry!" I say as I rush to put my make-up on and dry my hair.

CHAPTER TWENTY

I walk into the dimly lit sex room and see Jake standing beside a sturdy wooden table. He's wearing a suit, looking like he just got home from work. Fuck, he looks sexy as hell. There's just something about a well-groomed man in a tailored suit that gets me hot. I can't stop shaking. Is it anticipation or fear that has me trembling?

"Come to me, Beth," he whispers in a sexy, calm voice that makes my belly quiver with excitement.

I walk toward him while he admires my naked body. He rounds the table and stands behind me. His fingertips ever so tenderly touch the sides of my neck, gliding down my shoulders and arms until his hands hold my wrists. He pulls them back toward him, holding my hands tightly against his hips. He smells so good.

His hot breath flows over my neck, making my skin tingle. "Beth, you're shaking. I will care for you and keep you safe. You needn't worry. Let go and give your fear to me. Let me hold that burden."

His soft lips press to my skin. A shiver raises goosebumps all over my body. Instantly, my nipples swell and stiffen. His mouth kisses my neck and shoulder delicately, as if I'll break if he presses too firmly. This is very sensual, igniting my female cravings. My mind is calming, my anxiety easing with each graze of his soft lips.

Jake releases my wrists. He turns me around and plants his mouth on mine, kissing me with the same elegance he did my neck. His warm hands grip my wrists with a brutal roughness, contrasting with the gentleness of his lips. He pulls my arms behind me while his lips remain softly on mine, his tongue gently exploring my mouth.

He steps back, releasing my wrists, and says, "Up on the table. Lie on your back." I do as he instructs while he holds my hand to assist me. The wood is cool on my back, and it feels very hard and sturdy beneath me. Jake takes both my hands and lifts them up over my head, securing them in soft leather handcuffs. My elbows are bent over the edge of the table, but it isn't as uncomfortable as it might appear to be. I wonder if he realizes how suave he is in his movements. It's seductive, the way he touches me gently but with a purpose.

Jake's hands skim the length of my body, slipping under my knee and lifting so he can hang my calf over the side edge of the table. He wraps my ankle in a cuff and then pulls the strap snug until I can't move my leg. After securing my other leg in the same position, I'm left with my thighs spread wide. He ever so tenderly tickles his fingertips and hot lips all over my body, being careful not to touch my heated pussy. This is frustrating the hell out of me and he knows it.

He slips a blindfold over my eyes and then kisses my lips just once. I'm disappointed. Watching a handsome man other than Henry seduce me while wearing such a nice suit is a fantasy of mine.

Something that feels like a feather tickles me from my neck to my knee, moves across to my other knee, and begins the journey back up. The soft touch is igniting the sensitivity of my nerves.

I startle when cold liquid drips onto my clitoris, flowing down past my labia and warming as it coats my asshole. His fingers glide up and down my slit, stopping to run circles over my swelling button, making it stiffen under his tender touch. Something cool and hard presses around my entire pussy. What is he doing?

A sensation I have never had the pleasure of feeling engulfs my entire womanhood. All of my lady parts are being sucked into this object. It's as if a huge mouth is creating a seal around everything and sucking all my bits at once. Holy hell, it's amazing! The suction is intense now, pulling my lips and clit until it's nearly too much. I'm moaning, "Yes!"

"Does that feel good?" he asks in a husky whisper.

"Yes, Sir, amazing," I reply. "What are you doing to me?" His only response is a soft snicker, but no explanation follows.

Smaller objects are pressed around my nipples, also sucking them firmly. It hurts but not in a bad way... more sensationally annoying than painful. He continues to graze his fingers along my skin. He has been touching me constantly which helps me to feel safe and comforted. I'm grateful since I can't follow his movements with my eyes.

Jake cautiously presses a finger into my tight asshole. With great patience, he pulls and stretches the outer rim until I am loose enough to slip in another and then another. Moans are slipping from my mouth. If he touches my clit right now, I'll cum in an instant. I am so turned on. I've never had my entire pussy and both nipples sucked at the same time, while my asshole is being manipulated. It's fucking titillating! I can't stop moaning and tossing my head from side to side.

Something cold into my asshole. I'm guessing it's the electrode. I'm instantly thrilled to experience this again but worried that he'll apply the sticky pads beside my nipples, making them tingle painfully like they did the last time.

The device begins to tense slowly in my asshole, gradually increasing the squeeze and then just as gradually eases off until I feel nothing but the plug itself. A few seconds later, it again begins to tense my muscles inside and at the rim of my ass, more intensely this time. When I groan and whimper, I hear Jake set the control box down on the table between my legs.

He taps on the pussy sucking contraption and I nearly cum right then. What stops me is the painful pull of even stronger suction. I didn't think it could get any more intense. Jake stands above my head and presses his mouth to my neck as his hands glide down my chest, cupping my breasts. His thumbs are buried in my cleavage when he squeezes my tits together.

"Sir, please touch my clitoris," I beg in a whisper when his lips part from mine. If he doesn't pleasure it soon, I might start screaming. The desire is almost overwhelming.

Jake's cheek rests against mine. He whispers, "Patience, Beth."

I'm trying to lift my hips and tilt my pelvis just enough so that something will move on my pussy, satisfying my overstimulated little nub. He walks away, separating from me for the first time since he placed the blindfold on my eyes. Right now, although I feel all alone, I'm too sexually aroused to be all that concerned with his absence. I know he's coming back, so I'm not going to panic. Not yet.

When I hear him open the door, that's when a sense of fear starts to build. I am desperately trying to calm my breathing, hoping that I'll be able to hear him and know that he's not far away. I hear the creaks from that one stair in the middle of the staircase. That's when I have to consciously fight to control my level of panic. I am alone down here, tied, blind, and being sexually ravaged by sex toys. It seems like minutes but is most likely only a few seconds before he returns. He places his hands on my tummy to ease my stress, allowing me to get back to truly enjoying this newly achieved intense level of sexual arousal.

Something touches my bellybutton. It's hot... no, cold. I don't know which. My hypersensitive nerves just can't decide. It's a bizarre sensation, not knowing if something is ice cold or burning hot. A trickle of the tempered liquid trails down my waist, and then another. It's an ice cube, and it's melting against my heated skin.

Jake sets something against the pussy sucking object and turns it on. It's a vibrator, a very powerful one. My whole entire vagina is vibrating all at once. I'm barely breathing. My mind begins to slip into delirium. The feeling is wild and intense, but my clitoris feels nothing. It's as if it has gone missing, hidden inside my body, surrounded but untouched by the stimulus.

I scream from disappointment and frustration. It doesn't matter where he puts the vibrator, the joy never reaches the little nib that craves it the most. It's torture! Wonderfully arousing torture!

The vibrator quits; aside from my pathetic whimpers and panting, the room falls silent. The suction on my pussy is alleviated and the object removed, but somehow it feels like it's still on me. When his fingers touch my folds, they feel hypersensitive, as if they have never been touched by anything ever! He pinches them together, wiggling and lightly slapping them. It feels beyond odd, but I love it, and yet, I hate it. I want him to touch my clit before I begin to shriek for mercy. As if he knows my thoughts, his finger slips between my bloated labia until it reaches my hardened, hidden gem.

I exhale loudly as I fight my body's instinctive desire to raise my hips to get closer to the one thing that's bringing me such incredible joy. Just after his finger glides over it, the pleasure-giving digit is gone. I scream, tossing my head back and forth. This is the most gruelling delayed gratification he's done to me yet. It's so torturous, yet it doesn't hurt. I desperately yearn for relief.

One at a time, he pulls the suction from my nipples, stretching my breasts until they let go. Each is swollen, extremely sore and overly sensitive to his breath. The heat of his mouth engulfs each one, as his tongue explores the very awakened nerves. I'm holding my breath, gasping only when my lungs burn. It hurts so bad, but the heat from his tongue shoots to my clitoris through the deeply embedded nerves running down my body, leading straight to my honeypot.

Jake walks around my body, randomly touching me until his fingers pull apart my cunt lips, ever so tenderly. That's when I come to realize just how inflated they are. His mouth slips between the balloons, sucking on my desperate clit. His tongue juts along it three times before I start coming. I try to beg for permission, but it's too late. Words aren't forming. My brain is too distracted by the glory that is taking over me; the satisfaction I have been so desperate for.

My body quivers, muscles tensing with each glorious orgasmic spasm. The electrode in my ass is suddenly throbbing steadily. It seems to be extending the peak of my pleasure. I fear if I breathe, it will come to a devastating conclusion, so I don't dare. My jaw is clenched along with nearly every muscle in my entire body as ripple after ripple of pure elation waves through me, taking my mind to an empty nothingness that exists solely through overwhelming pleasure. There is no other way to describe it and there's nowhere else I'd rather my mind drift to.

Jake's tongue is still making good on my clitoris, sucking and lapping at the now painful bulb. My lungs can no longer hold air and force the breath out of me. A loud scream fills the room, only ceasing long enough to allow for my body to suck in another breath.

All of my existence means nothing right now. The only thing that matters is my clit. He sucks it into his mouth with force, but his tongue glides under its hood with such a gentle caress that it fires me off once more. This time, the orgasm is painful, gloriously so.

I wail loudly, "Yes! Thank you, Master!" My lungs refuse to let air flow, stopping mid breath. When his fingers pinch my hypersensitive nipples, my mind is tossed into an abyss that is so perfect, I never want to return. "Thank you," I whisper with mere a sound.

Clarity gradually returns to me and I open my eyes only to see Jake looking into them. "There you are," he says in a calm voice. I'm upset that he woke me from such a peaceful slumber until he tells me what just happened. "You held your breath for a few seconds too long and passed out. You're okay now."

To my relief, my arms have been freed to move. With Jake's thick forearm under my neck, he helps me to sit up. When he's sure I won't topple over, he walks out of the room, returning with a bottle of cold water. He cracks it open and hands it to me. I'm still wearing the handcuffs. He insists, "Drink."

After gulping down several mouthfuls, I hand it back to him. He recaps it and sets it down on the shelf near the door. His hand brushes down my arm as he smiles seductively, his eyes focused on my vagina. I hadn't realized that it feels even more odd now that I'm sitting up. I look down to see my entire womanhood swollen like I've never seen before. I can't resist touching my labia and slipping my finger deeply between the puffy flaps. My swollen clit is dwarfed in comparison to the two balloons that are supposed to be my labia.

"Holy shit," I whisper.

Jake chuckles as he frees my ankles. He lifts my leg and swings it over the table, to rest alongside the other. I gasp at the arousing sensation caused by my cunt being squeezed between my upper thighs. He wraps his hands around my waist to lift me off the table. I stand with my legs apart, fearing I might damage my pussy if I don't. He's smirking at my discomfort, enjoying my humiliation.

"Stop laughing at me," I beg while chuckling.

"Beth, I'm not laughing at you. I'm simply enjoying how you're reacting to the swelling," he cups my chin, lifting it, so he can press his lips to mine for a mere second. "And I'll laugh at you if it pleases me."

Jake takes my hand and leads me to his red leather loveseat, sitting me in the middle of it. He walks to either side, lifting ropes that are attached to its base. Jake ties them to the metal loops on my hand and ankle cuffs. My arms and legs are spread wide, revealing my swollen cunt to the chilly air. My gaze follows him as he opens a cupboard and takes out a flogger that looks like it has thicker, heavier leather tassels than the one he has used on me before. As I watch him through widened eyes, he swings it gracefully in a figure eight.

The look on his face is undeniably that of a man loving that he is in complete control, dominating the situation. He seems more powerful than ever, but maybe that's because I'm defenceless, and he is anything but.

The flogger slaps my inner thigh and I grumble. It hurts more than the other flogger, much more. Again, he cracks it on my thigh. His eyes are half-closed, and he's licking his bottom lip while wearing a devious grin. It's obvious that he's relishing in my helplessness, and in hearing my pain through my whimpers.

He repeatedly slaps it on my thighs until they are welted and red. I wish he would move onto something else. I instantly regret my wishes when the tassels slap against my bulbous vagina. I cry out, but he doesn't take notice, repeating the punishment several more times before hitting higher up my body. My tender nipples sting on contact. I scream each time a nipple is zinged by a leather strap. The pain shoots through me, turning to twitches of pleasure at my clit.

When Jake finally stops, my chest, legs and pussy are striped with bright pink welts. He flips the flogger's tassels over his shoulder leaving the handle to dangle in plain view. His fingertips follow each welt, while the bulge in his pants grows. I feel a sense of achievement when I see how captivated my Master is, by the welts he so skillfully created in a pattern that could not be made by that of an amateur. I want to please him because he pleases me. Watching his face is the best reward he could ever give me.

He drops to one knee and slips two fingers between my fat labia, sliding into me, without resistance. I am drenched. I didn't think I was all too fond of the punishment, but my body has a mind of its own. His fingers explore my depths, pushing hard before slowly pulling back, only to bury themselves again. His eyes watch mine as I try not to look away, but he's fucking me so well that my lids weigh heavier the closer I come to climax.

Jake stands up, removing his fingers and the pleasure they were bringing me. He takes something from a small drawer in his cabinet. As he returns to me, he unzips his pants, pulling his fat prick free from its confinement. He strokes it several times before slipping something over the end of his manhood, pulling it all the way down to the base. At first, I think it's a condom, but when he pulls a wrapped one from his pocket, I realize it isn't. When I take a closer look, I see that it's a cock ring. His prick is swelling in his grip. He quickly rolls on the condom and then drops to his knees between my legs.

I wiggle, trying to move my pussy closer to him. He leans forward and bites my right nipple too hard. I instantly scream and shift my body, trying to pull away from him, but can only manage to move a few inches in either direction. When I won't stop pulling away, he bites harder. It's nearly impossible to do, but I manage to relax by focusing on my breathing. As soon as I calm down, he sets it free. The point of this lesson is not to move.

Jake's prick slips into me until his pelvis is pressed firmly against my swollen cunt lips. Fuck, it feels so good! I am so damn full! His cock seems bigger, harder, and therefore more enjoyable. It may just be that my labia are so inflated that he seems thicker than he is. Although, with the cock ring on his dick restricting his blood flow, he definitely is engorged.

His hands grip under my thighs and yank, pulling my ass to the very edge of the sofa. When he presses his hips forward, my head swoons, falling back against the cushion. He's so deep inside of me, stretching my cavity, wonderfully. He thrusts his hips, brutally smashing me so hard that he's pushing my hips further into the sofa. He grips my waist, pulling me toward him as he fucks forward. Holy shit!

I mutter, "Yes. Please. Fuck me! Hard!" Much to my dismay, he suddenly pulls out of me and stands up, walking back to his chest of drawers. He opens the third one and pulls out a ball gag. "No! I don't want that. I won't talk anymore. I promise." His response is to smile at me, but he doesn't stop. I know what he's thinking, and I know why he isn't saying it. He's told me several times to use my safe words if it's ever too much. I haven't, so he will continue. After securing it in my mouth and buckling it behind my head, he returns to the violent fucking he was giving me before I so rudely spoke out of turn. I want to cum.

To please him, I beg from behind the ball in my mouth, "Please, may I cum?"

"No," he replies, while still thrusting wildly into me like a dangerous man, solely after his own pleasure. His expression is dark and wicked with evil intention. He keeps his eyes focused on mine. His teeth clenched. He grips the base of my throat with his left hand, pressing down on my collarbone, but not choking me.

"Please, Master," I beg. I'm on the verge of letting my sex explode, but continue to fight it, while anticipating his permission.

"I said no!" he yells and then grabs my throat with both hands. He's using his wrists to press down on my shoulders to help hold me in place. The positioning of his hands allows him the freedom to prevent my blood flow and then release his grip before I get too lightheaded. Over and over he does this, not allowing me to have too much clarity, nor allowing my pleasure to overwhelm me. I just want to cum.

When the fog in my brain clears from its lack of blood, he whispers with panting breath, "Cum," while still hammering into me.

"Thank you, Sir," I reply from around the ball. Just as I'm on the verge of coming, he pulls out of me and releases my throat. My orgasm ceases immediately. I scream like a raging beast, hoping he'll slide back into me and fuck me like he was. I was so close! So close! Pain radiates through my body as it aches for release.

"Please! Why?" I know he hears my muffled cries, but he doesn't answer me in words, he simply laughs with a darkness that tells me how much he's getting off on the control he has. It's up to him whether I cum, or don't. I must be strong. He's testing my strength. I will not show him weakness.

He dribbles lube over his fingers and rubs some up and down my pussy, making it slicker than it already is. Jake slides two fingers into me, easily fucking me with a gentle rhythm. It feels good, but not nearly good enough to bring me the climactic high I so desperately desire. More fingers slip into me until I am stretched painfully, and yet, exquisitely. He pushes into me, widening my entrance even further. The stretch is extraordinarily delicious. I'm crying out with each rapid breath I take. My pussy suddenly lets go with a pop that makes my head spin. He stops pushing and holds perfectly still. I pant with my eyes wide from the fear of wondering what the fuck he's done to me. What the hell is happening?

My mind whirls from pain or is it quite the opposite? I'm not sure anymore. The pain has eased considerably after only a few seconds. With a finger from his other hand, he applies tiny circles on my clitoris, stimulating my most sensitive nerves. A few seconds of this and I have forgotten about the strain on my pussy, and now I welcome it.

"My entire hand is inside of you," he divulges. Disbelieving him, I quickly look down, discovering that his hand is indeed, inside of me, leaving only his wrist exposed. He whispers, "You are so fucking incredible."

He ever so slightly twists his hidden hand a fraction of an inch. My breath holds from the thrilling fullness that is overwhelming me. My head flops back as my brain tries to comprehend how his fist is inside my body, and still able to spin. I've never been so full and at another person's mercy as I am right now. I love this! Oh, please don't stop yet!

He continues to tease my clit. His hand cautiously twists this way and that, easing my mental existence closer to the fine line between reality and fantasy. Will I burst from the agony or drown in the indulgence? My brain can't decide if this is too painful or so fucking wonderful that I might lose myself forever. This feels much like the ice cube from earlier—is it a good pain, or bad?

Jake's mouth suctions around my clit, sucking and releasing in perfect sync with the very slight movements of his hand. I'm so relaxed right now, I have to be. If I tense up, pain rips through me and not enjoyably. My focus is on staying loose and relaxed and not resisting the fist that is entombed inside me.

"Oh my god," I whimper. Am I close to orgasm or has my body simply had enough? The tension is building, my muscles tightening, readying for the glorious eruption. An enormous pressure is building deep inside my belly and becoming more tense than I have ever felt before. My moans are indistinguishable between the agony of defeat and everlasting glory of pure elation.

Over and over, I beg as best I can from behind the red ball, "Please don't stop. Please don't stop…" My head flops back and forth. I can't hold it still. His hand continues its twisting motion while his mouth pulls on my clit, lapping at it with his tongue only twice, before easing the suction. He repeats his actions, not changing anything, surely knowing he's going to make me an orgasm.

My eyes squeeze shut and my jaw clenches around the ball. The imaginary elastic inside of me pulls to its maximum tautness, and then snaps, forcing my body to lurch forward, hold and jolt back against the backrest.

I scream, "I'm coming!"

Before he can say anything, it's already in full swing. He couldn't stop it now even if he stood across the room. I am not breathing, not moving, not thinking. My mind isn't conscious enough to make any of that happen. I can feel every cell that is my body. My vaginal muscles force and squeeze Jake's hand in a valiant attempt to crush it. Whether I push him out or he withdraws on his own, his hand is forced from me, followed by a jet of hot fluid that sprays from my deepest depths. I feel so fucking incredible!

I lift my back off the sofa and try to focus on his eyes. I want to witness his reaction, see if he's pleased with my pleasure. At first, he's blurry, but then again, I haven't taken a breath in a while. Air floods my lungs but quickly rushes back out riding on the back of a long, screeching wail.

I collapse against the leather sofa. My lungs burn, and my throat is raw from screaming. I'm exhausted, unable to fight my restraints even if the house were burning down around me. I couldn't care less if this were when I take my last breath. I wouldn't fight my death.

My eyes slowly open, meeting Jake's beautiful blues. He is looking longingly into mine. He appears calm and completely relaxed. Meanwhile, I'm a dishevelled woman who's shaking so violently that I can't see clearly. My arms and legs are hanging limply, held up only by the restraints. My body is gelatinous. I want to get free.

Jake tells me, "Squeeze your pussy muscles very tightly for a count of three and then let them relax. Do it ten times." As he removes the ball gag, I follow his orders, but find it difficult to do such a task after having my woman parts gaped to such an extreme. When I have completed his demand, I nod. He slowly inserts his swollen prick into me. I fear I may be too stretched out to enjoy him and he certainly won't enjoy it. How could he? To my surprise, his prick feels nice and comfortable, filling me just right.

His eyes watch mine as he begins to move. I'd swear my inner walls are more sensitive now than before he fisted me. I can feel the bulges from his veins as he slowly glides along my inner walls. The likelihood of me orgasming again are slim, my energy completely drained by the last one.

"This feels good," I compliment him before asking, "Will you do that to me again when you're done?" I really do want to cum that hard once more before I go home, but I'm not sure if I can survive it.

"Not tonight," he replies.

"Why not?" I ask, perhaps a little disappointed.

"You'll be very sore tomorrow, as it is. I don't want you to be so sore that you refuse it next time. It would be a pity if you disallowed it." Jake is smiling softly.

I shake my head, "I can't see myself ever saying no to that."

"This is why we're moving on now. Can you feel my cock?"

I nod, "Yes, I can feel your veins."

Jake begins to fuck me at a medium pace and then presses a small vibrator to my clit. I nearly turn inside out. Regardless of the extreme hypersensitivity, the pleasure quickly takes over, speeding me toward the brick wall of another climax.

Suddenly, he drops the vibrator and rushes to untie my arms and legs. He drops back onto his knees but grabs my hips, lifting and flipping me over, so that my upper body is face down on the sofa and my knees are on the floor. He slams his prick into me while reaching around my thigh to hold the vibrator onto my clit. He keeps it in place while revving it up to high speed.

Master is fucking me hard, slamming his pelvis viscously against my ass cheeks. The punishment to my cervix is enough to make me erupt, but the vibration is preventing me from concentrating on his cock. Not until my clit has reached its desired sensitivity. It swells and twitches, sending magnificent shock waves all over my body. My thoughts fall short yet again, and my breath holds in my lungs. Holy fuck! I might not survive this!

I've hurdled over the apex and I'm beginning to breathe again, thankful for another breath. Jake pulls his cock from me, grabs my hair and my arm, quickly tossing me backwards until I'm lying on the floor looking up with a shocked expression, as he kneels over me.

He rips off his condom and jerks his hand over his cock rapidly. Each of his quick breaths whistle through his clenched teeth. His hand is violently assaulting his rock-hard prick, sliding up and down so fast that the skin looks like it might tear. His primitive wails assault my ear canals until a momentary silence and stillness seem to lock him frozen in time, like a beautiful statue. His body lurches forward, his partially closed eyes lock onto my chest as his super-heated semen spurts onto my tits. He jerks once, and then again before releasing a very lengthy, stuttered exhale.

Jake sits on the floor, his back resting against the sofa. He puts out his hand for me to take, so he can help me sit. I assume the same position, beside him. For several minutes, neither of us says anything, we simply bask in our relaxed state of being. Jake is the one to break the silence. "I want you to be honest with me when I ask you questions. If you ask one of me, I vow never to lie to you."

"I haven't lied to you yet and see no need to start. Ask away," I suggest.

"Did you need Henry to go with another woman because you're burdened with overwhelming guilt for what we do and the pleasure you get from it?" Truth be told, that is a question I've been battling to answer for myself.

"Are you trying to psychoanalyze me?" I ask, trying to lead him away from wanting the answer.

"Oh, hell no! I'm way to fucked up to be psychoanalyzing anyone." He chuckles briefly as if he's silently told himself a personal joke. "I'm just worried that you are carrying a lot of guilt around with you and think that Henry, by being with another female, is going to cure that. I promise you, it won't. Guilt is guilt and cannot be solved by making the person you feel guilty toward, also carry guilt."

"What does it matter to you? Honestly, I'm not asking because I don't think it's your business. I just don't see how my guilt should be your concern."

"Your guilt *is* my concern because when you are here with me, I want you here completely and not feeling like you shouldn't be." Jake cups my face and turns it toward his. "My job is to make sure you are physically safe when you are in here with me," He taps his finger on my forehead, "but I want you to always be mentally and emotionally strong, whether you are with me, or not."

"You have nothing to worry about. I am happy and yes, you make me feel safe. My mental strength is pretty good. I mean, I do have some guilt, but I think for me it's normal. Did I set Henry up to ease my guilt? Maybe. Maybe not, but I'm not going to analyze it, right now. I'm happy, he's happy, you're happy, and she's happy. I don't see a problem." I get to my feet and begin walking toward the water bottles but realize just how shaky my legs are. I know I'm wobbling, and dread that I don't look remotely sexy. Oh well, he did this to me. Thank you very much, Sir!

After dressing, he once again hugs me and kisses my forehead before sending me on my way.

* * *

Once I get home, I see Jenna's car parked in the driveway. I quickly realize that they are still upstairs. I can hear them talking. It's muffled, and I can't make out what they're saying, not that I'm trying to. I don't want them to know I'm home. I keep very quiet while pouring a glass of wine and settling in on the sofa. I put my headphones in and crank some classic rock music.

I've been sitting on the loveseat by the bay window in the kitchen for about a half-hour with my headphones in, drinking my wine and reading from a good book.

I notice Henry and Jenna coming down the stairs and hope they don't notice me. Henry is wearing his pyjama pants but no shirt. Jenna has on a black latex corset with a latex thong. She also has latex stockings attacked to the garters on her corset and a pair of very high stiletto heels. Her hair is up in a high ponytail that flows down in waves. To top off her stunning appearance, her make-up is much heavier than I've ever seen her wear. All I can think is how incredibly beautiful she looks. I wonder if Henry was able to hold off on coming… I highly doubt it.

She kisses his lips softly before slapping his cheek and then winking at him with a crooked smile. She slips on her calf-length jacket and takes the large purse Henry carried down the stairs for her. She walks out the door without another glance back.

Henry watches until she drives away, then slowly closes the door. He turns around and leans against it with a huge smile. "Holy shit! That woman is a tyrant, but I can get used to her." He laughs loudly. I don't think he knows I'm home.

"Did you have fun, Henry?" I whisper just loud enough for him to hear me.

He startles, and his knees shake beneath him. His wide eyes scan the room quickly, searching for the source of the whisper.

"I'm on the loveseat," I tell him.

"I didn't know you were home. How long have you been here?" He seems nervous, letting out a strange giggle that I've never heard him make.

"About a half-hour, but I had my headphones in, so I didn't hear anything. She looked hot! Damn, she is a very sexy woman. Did you have fun?"

"Did I have fun? Well, it was different, for sure. Fun… that's not quite the word I would use to describe pain and humiliation, followed by punishment, and then more humiliation. The woman is great at what she does. Her confidence would intimidate even the strongest of men. She bound my genitals with a rope. *A rope!*"

His arms lift and drop from his sides, exaggerating his enthusiasm. "I would have never thought it possible." Henry is shaking his head, and crossing his arms over his chest, as the corners of his lips slowly lift. For a moment, he seems lost in the recent memory.

"She did?" I try to imagine how that would even work, or how it would feel for him. Maybe I should look it up online. "Did you like how it felt?"

"Strangely enough, I did... yes!" he replies enthusiastically. "I can't explain how it felt except that my cock was being wrapped with rope until it was thick with blood and the skin was stretched tight. My balls were so sensitive to her touch, and the head of my dick felt like it was the size of an orange. It wasn't, but it felt like it was." His cheeks flush pink and a shy smile grows wide and toothy. "I really did enjoy myself. I was worried I wouldn't."

"I'm glad. I wanted tonight to go well for you. How do you feel about it?"

His smile is wide. "Tired."

I snicker because I know all too well, how he feels. "No silly, how do you feel emotionally, about what happened tonight? Would you do it again?"

"Oh," he rolls his eyes as if finally understanding what I'm asking him. "Good. I feel good about it. I think it went well. Very well, actually. I'm not going to lie and say it doesn't worry me about how things will be in the office, after tonight. It's going to be different."

"It might be better. Just don't act goofy around her, or extra friendly or coy. If you can act like you normally do, nobody will be the wiser. I'm sure she'd like to keep this hush-hush." I wrap my arms around his naked back and press my face to his chest. He smells just like her perfume. I like it very much. Is it odd that I'm getting sexually aroused from smelling another woman on my husband, much the same way he was excited to smell Jake on me?

"I'm going to try to behave normally. It will be awkward until we find our footing," he assures as his arms pull me in tighter.

"Are you very tired? I mean, do you think you'd like to have sex with me? You're probably worn out, right?" I question.

He takes a deep breath and blows it out slowly, kissing the top of my head before answering. "Babe, I'll do whatever you need me to do, but I'm pretty sure my penis will be a limp noodle for the rest of the night. She made me cum three times. It's been at least ten years since I've cum three times in one night."

I smile and nod with wide eyes. "That's a lot of cum. You'll have to tell me all about it, tomorrow. I'm exhausted, too. I just wondered if maybe you wanted to be with me. You smell like her and I like it. I wish we had the energy to make love while her scent is still on your skin."

"You can smell her pussy?" he asks, looking rather shocked that I would like it.

I shake my head. "No! Her perfume. Yuck!"

"Don't say *yuck*. She smells great... tastes good, too." He's trying to tease me, but it won't work.

"I'll take your word for it. I'm not into women," I remind him.

"But, if the moment were sexually heated and you were wound up, I'm sure you would lick her pussy if she promised to let you cum. And I bet that you'd enjoy it," he is trying to get me to say I would be interested in attempting lesbianism.

"It's not going to happen, Henry. Let's go to bed now," I say while yawning and starting to make my way up the stairs.

"Fine!" he pouts as he turns off the kitchen light, before trailing after me. "You can't blame a husband for trying."

CHAPTER TWENTY-ONE

Ever since Henry was with Jenna, he's been as horny as a sixteen-year-old boy. I don't mind, but fucking two or three times a day is starting to wear on my vagina. This morning, Henry pounced on me seconds after his alarm woke him up. I hadn't even opened my eyes yet before he was sliding up behind me. His prick was already hard. He must have been dreaming something erotic.

This morning, after an intense fucking, Henry told me he'd be working late today, so I should make dinner plans for myself. I called Amy and asked her if she'd like to go out to the bar for our monthly girl's night of drinking and dancing. With great excitement, she jumped at the opportunity to escape her motherly duties, in exchange for a night of fun.

Instead of writing, I decided to clean out the pantry and reorganize it. We've been jamming everything in here, even things that don't belong. I found one of Henry's ties rolled up behind a can of chicken noodle soup. Needless to say, my cupboards really needed some attention.

Amy will be here in an hour. We're going to check out the new bar on Lexington Avenue. Since it's a country music bar, I dress in the faded blue jeans that make my ass look firm and high, like a twenty-year-old's buttocks. I put on a snug-fitting red dress shirt and a pair of black calf-high boots. With just a tickle of make-up to bring out my eyes, I'm ready to go.

Amy pulls up in the driveway, but before she can get out of the car, I'm skipping down the walkway toward her. She glances up and starts laughing at me, probably because I'm skipping rather enthusiastically.

She calls out to me, jokingly, "You seem so down in the dumps. Are you sure you want to go out tonight?"

I wrap my arms around her and pull her in close. "I've missed you!"

"I've missed you too, woman. Get in, let's get out of here before something happens and we have to change our plans," she replies, ducking back into the car.

To avoid traffic, we weave our way through the back roads to while catching up on everything that's been happening lately, in each of our lives. She tells me about the kids and how Lou has been riding on her last nerve. He's so busy at work and putting in so many hours, never seeming to be home until it's nearly time for the kids to go to bed. I think she really needed this time away from the kids and the daily stress that being a mom entails.

She asks, "So, how are things with your Mr. Sexy-man?"

Teasingly, I reply, "Oh, Henry's fine. He's been working long hours, same as Lou."

She shoots me a quick glare. "No asshole, the other sexy man—the blue-eyed, dominant demon."

"Oh, you mean Jake. He is so fine."

She groans. "Girl, you can't leave it at that. Tell me more. You know I need your stories to get me through my days. Spill it, Bitch!"

"Well, we were together on Monday. He tied me to a table and made me cum so hard that I think I passed out. He has this uncanny ability to make me lose my mind. So then, he has me sit on a loveseat. He tied my arms and legs spread eagle with my ass nearly hanging off the edge so that he could whip me, fuck me violently, and not let me cum for the longest time. He choked me, too. I liked it; didn't think I would, but I do. He finally gave me permission to cum, but before I did, he pulled out of me."

"What a fucker!" Amy hisses.

I continue to tell the story while I count the streetlights passing overhead. "Oh yeah, I was pissed off. But he had other plans for me. You aren't going to believe this. He worked my pussy until his whole hand was inside of me. I've never hurt that wonderfully, in my whole life. He sucked and flicked my clit, while he gently fucked me with his hand until I was drowning in a state of euphoria. It was perfect."

"Fuck off! No shit?"

I smile and shake my head. "Then, he untied my arms and legs, pulled me off the sofa onto my knees, and fucked me with his cock while he held a vibrator to my clit. He really slammed me hard. Damn, that guy can fuck! When he was ready to cum, he yanked me back until I was lying on the floor. He likes to cum on my tits."

Amy is staring out the windshield with her mouth gaping, lost in my words. She is silent for the final five minutes it takes us to arrive in the bar's parking lot. She shuts off the car and turns to meet eyes with me, wearing an expression of wonderment. "I want him."

"You do?" I ask.

"No, I mean yeah, but no, not really. Or do I? I don't know what I want. That's not true, I just want something new. I need to feel like I'm desired – like I used to be. Lou is Lou, and not all that good with romance and flattery. I love him, never doubt that I do, but only for a nanosecond, I want to be wanted like Jake wants you. Sometimes I feel like I'm floating around in a dull haze with nothing in my life that is good for *me*. Everything I do is for everyone else. Do you know how long it's been since I was able to soak in a bubble bath with a glass of wine, without being interrupted by someone who wants to take a shit while they tell me some ridiculous story that I couldn't give a crap about? I just want to scream at the top of my lungs to let everyone, including myself, know that I'm still alive inside." Tears start to well up in her eyes.

I lean over and hug her, tightly. "Amy, if it's any comfort, I have a hard time picturing you as a wife and mother. You'll always be that wild chick from high school, who smoked a little Maryjane, drank beer and made out with Jeff Liniguish under the bleachers during a pep rally. To me, you will always be her."

"I remember that, fondly," she whispers.

I sigh and then present an offer. "I could try to set you up with Jake for a few hours. I'll cover for you. I don't mind sharing him. I'm sure he has the stamina to keep up with both of us."

Loudly, she laughs. "You are an amazing friend, but no, thank you. I love Lou and I'd never do that to him. Sometimes it's nice to dream of a more exciting life. One day when the kids are grown and not demanding so much of my energy, perhaps Lou and I will get back to being lovers who enjoy exploring one another's sex."

"Are you two still having sex?" I ask, hoping they are.

"Yes, we do, but it's usually quick enough that the kids won't walk in on us or because we're both so exhausted that we just want to get it over with and go to sleep," she tells me. "Okay, enough of this whining. Let's go in."

We are both feeling somewhat intoxicated after four beers and two shots of tequila. Two men who were playing a few games of eight ball, come over to ask if they can buy us a drink. Amy looks at them with her glossy eyes and alcohol-induced smile, and says, "You want to buy us a drink? Well, we've had lots of drinks already and do plan to have more. I should probably let you know right now that I am married, mostly happily, and have no intention of sleeping with either of you. My friend here, well, she's married too, and since she has two men rocking her world already, her body is way too tired to entertain you, or you. The likelihood of you guys getting to see her naked are very, very unlikely. So, do you still want to buy us that drink?"

I burst into ridiculous laughter and don't stop until the guys have scurried away. Amy doesn't laugh, she shrugs her shoulders and downs the rest of her beer. She holds it up toward the guys and points to it, offering them one more chance to buy her that drink. They shake their heads and go back to racking the pool balls, ignoring us, completely. This just adds to our amusement.

With intentions of heading to the bar for two more beers, I spin around and bump chest to chest into someone. I step back and look up to see his face but need a second for the drunken confusion to clear before it registers in my head who I've just smacked into.

He's looking at me with familiar, seductive blue eyes. His messy, sandy-brown hair hangs over his forehead.

"Jake!" I announce to everyone, with my arms spread wide. Other than Amy, nobody pays any attention to us. Without thinking, I press my lips to his while I reach around and grab onto his perfect ass. He doesn't kiss me back. He stands perfectly still with a stately expression. I step back, wondering why he isn't returning my gesture of affection. His eyes are locked onto mine, but I can't read his expression.

"Mrs. McDavid, are you drunk?"

I bite my bottom lip and squint while nodding my head. "Maybe a teeny, weeny bit."

"Perhaps I shouldn't have brought you a beer," he tells me while handing me a brown bottle. I still can't read his face. Is he upset with me or not? "You shouldn't be so familiar with me in public. Someone might recognize us."

Suddenly, I'm nervous as I scan the bar, looking to see if anyone is paying us any attention, but other than the two guys who tried to pick us up, nobody is. They are checking out Jake as if to size him up and see what he has that they don't. Jake is obviously younger than I am, so I'm sure they assume he's the one I'm sleeping with, other than my husband. I wish Amy hadn't said that, but it was hilarious at the time.

Jake hands my friend a bottle of beer, as well. "Hello, Amy. I don't think I've ever seen you in jeans before. Forgive me if I'm being too forward, but you have a great ass," Jake says with a naughty grin.

Amy's face immediately flushes, but she doesn't look away from his eyes. She swallows hard and then replies with her drunken wit, "And you, Sir, are masturbation material."

He smiles at her and then asks, "Do you masturbate often?"

"Whenever I get a moment alone, which isn't often enough. Do you?" she asks as she moves closer to him while gazing dreamily into his eyes. "What does someone like you fantasize about during masturbation? I'm curious. And, please don't be shy."

He leans in to put his mouth near her ear while he caresses her opposite cheek with the palm of his hand. I can't hear what he's whispering in her ear, but it must be good because Amy's eyes open wide. I can tell she's smelling him. His cologne must be loaded with pheromones because his scent is always intoxicating. When he backs away from her, she blinks several times while nodding, and then sips her beer quietly, with flushed cheeks and wide eyes.

She sets down her beer. "I'm going to go pee."

As Amy disappears into the crowd, I lean in and ask, "What did you say to her?"

He snickers, then sips his drink. "It's between her and me."

"You told me that if I ask you a question, you will always tell me the truth. Are you backing out on that?" Even drunk, I am quick-witted.

"Okay, okay. I told her that I close my eyes and imagine that I have a woman tightly bound in a position that allows me access to all of her entrances. I also said that I would spank her to get her ass red hot. I'd lick her from clit to asshole until she was ready to cum, but I wouldn't be so generous as to let her. First, she will need to let me sample all of her holes with my hard cock. Only then would I pleasure her repeatedly, until she couldn't possibly cum anymore because it's all about her, after all. I finished by suggesting that I might picture her ass when I'm naked, later tonight."

"You have no idea how happy you have made her. Trust me on this," I tell him before drinking a mouthful of beer.

"Too much?" he asks, and I shrug. "Should I have pulled it back a bit?"

"Nope, she knows about us and what you do to me. She's jealous in some ways, but happy for me. I think being a mom twenty-four-seven, is taking a toll on her. You said all the right things, especially that bit about her ass. Thank you," I say while rubbing his arm.

"She does have a great ass. I figured you had told her, based on the looks she was giving me. She never used to eye me up the way she just did." He smiles, shyly, which seems out of character for him.

I roll my eyes. "You must know that you are eye-candy to almost everyone who enjoys *the cock*. When I initially saw you, and you were looking at me the way you were, I wanted to fuck you right then and there. Hey, so what are you doing here, anyway?"

He points to a table of five people, three men and two women. "I'm meeting up with some of my college friends. We get together every other month, no matter how busy we are or where we're at. The man in the blue shirt flew here from British Columbia. He's been working there for two years now and always makes it back to see us. Kim, the woman in the dress, lives in Ohio so she drives here, spends the night in a hotel and drives back in the morning. I love these people. They are my closest friends. Come and meet them."

"Nooooo! I can't meet them. How will you introduce me? *This is my buddy's wife of whom I tie up, whip, spank, lick and fuck into oblivion about once a week*? I don't think so." I chug another few gulps of beer while I roll my eyes.

Jake smiles and then nods. "Yes, exactly like that."

"You wouldn't dare!" I taunt in my drunken state, not thinking he'll actually do that.

He takes my hand and nearly drags me over to the table. They glance up as we approach, each one smiling while standing up so they can greet him. They each take a turn hugging him, the girls kissing his lips while the guys peck his cheek or tousle his hair. I didn't think it was possible for him to look sexier with his hair even messier than usual.

"Everyone, this is my," he pauses while he looks at me with a half-smile, "my submissive, Beth."

They all seem completely cool with how he introduced me; it was as if he'd said that I was his brunette friend rather than his submissive. I wonder if they're all into that type of lifestyle. Each person introduces themselves as they shake my hand.

The last one to shake my hand is a gorgeous, dark-haired woman in a sexy blue dress. Her smile is beaming. "Hi, I'm Kim. It's nice to meet you. Jake must really like you. He's never introduced us to any of his submissives. Well, not since college anyway. How long have you two been together?"

"Um," I stutter, not sure how to answer her question, so I go with the truth, as Jake did when he introduced me. "We aren't together. I'm married to someone else. Jake and my husband are friends. My husband actually set us up."

"You have a great husband who must love you, a lot. You're a lucky lady. You should bring him along the next time we get together. I'm sure we'd all like to meet him." She pauses, a strange expression overcoming her face. She asks, "Are you okay? You look terrified." The woman moves in closer and puts her hand on my shoulder.

"I'm fine. You don't think our relationship is weird?" I ask her.

She shakes her head and then says, "No because I was his submissive for a few months, back in college. It didn't work out for us. We weren't sexually compatible, so we ended it and remained friends. I love Jake, just not enough to be committed to him. My career is everything to me and I have no desire for anything else at this stage in my life. Besides, he's more like a stepbrother to me than a past lover."

"I see nothing wrong with that. What do you do?" I ask her.

"Law. I'm in Corporate," she replies. "What do you do to fill your days, other than play with Jake?"

"I'm a writer... novels, mostly," I tell her but get interrupted when Jake pulls Amy between us to introduce her to his friends.

"Everyone, this is Amy. She's not my submissive, she's Beth's best friend. Say hello everyone," he announces. Amy looks confused, but she's smiling, anyway.

They all lift their glasses to toast her while smiling and greeting her with a very loud, "Cheers!" Amy laughs and lifts her bottle. The one man slides over in the booth, asking her and I to sit with them. Everyone squishes a little cosier while Jake and another man pull up two chairs.

The conversation is quite entertaining as they tell stories of the crazy adventures of their youth. I see Jake in a different light, now. He's a real person who has done silly things that seem out of character for the calm, cool and collected dominant I know him to be. If I stay, I'll start to like Jake and not just sexually.

I tap Amy's foot with mine to get her attention. After tipping my head, which is our signal to leave, she announces, "Well, it's getting late and we should get going. Sorry, everyone. This has been fun and I'm so happy to have met you all."

Groaning in disappointment, each of Jake's friends either shakes our hands or hug us as we slide out from the booth. Kim kisses me on the lips, and then smiles at me, as though we are members of the same sorority because we both slept with Jake. I return her smile, but secretly think it's bizarre.

I hug Jake before whispering to Amy that I want to use the washroom before we leave. She takes my hand and pulls me away from everyone while I wave. We make our way to the bathroom, and both go pee in silence. After washing our hands, she pulls out her phone to request a ride from the sober drivers who drive you and your vehicle safely back to your home.

I whisper, "That was fun, but I'm not sure I wanted to get to know him as a real person. I kind of liked the mystery of it all."

"Is that why you wanted to leave?" she asks. I nod, knowing she won't try to talk me into staying. If one of us wants to leave, we both leave, no questions asked.

As we exit the bathroom and make our way toward the main entrance, Jake is standing there with his back to us, scanning the crowd as if he's looking for someone. We walk up beside him and start scanning just like he is, copying his every move. Yes, we get silly when we're drinking.

He finally notices and says, "There you are! I was looking for you two. You're not driving, right?" We shake our heads. "Can I drive you both home?"

"You don't need to leave your friends. We have a ride coming," I tell him.

While showing him her phone app, Amy adds, "Yes, we have sober people coming who will drive my car and I home safely."

"That I am very happy about. Beth, let me drive you home," he asks convincingly.

I look at Amy, who is looking at us with a huge, toothy grin. "Are you two going to fuck tonight? Can I watch? I'm not perverted or anything, but you two are both beautiful people who have a very wild sex, from what Beth tells me. Who wouldn't want to watch you two do the nasty?"

"Amy, I should go home with you. We came together, so we should leave together, right?" I question.

Amy has had one too many beers. "Nope! If you want this delicious, tall drink of sexy man flesh to be all naked and sweaty, touching you with those strong hands and shoving his man meat into you, go ahead and get sweaty. Fuck like teenagers. Can I feel your hands?" She reaches out and grabs them before he can protest. He patiently allows her to examine them.

"Amy, his hands are big and strong, and you should give them back to him. What are you going to do with them, shove one down your pants?" I say while laughing like the silly drunk person I have become.

Her face lights up when she replies, "He could put one hand in your pants and one in mine. Maybe, if he's really good with them, he can make us both cum at the same time. That would be so hot! Are you righthanded or lefthanded? I want to know which side I should be standing on."

Jake is smiling as he listens to her go on and on about how she would justify him jerking her off as not being in the category of cheating since he would remain fully clothed. Somehow, he keeps his cool, not laughing at her even though she's being so obnoxiously forward, which would be completely out of character for her if she were sober.

I say, "Amy, we'll wait with you until the sober ride comes. I am not leaving you here alone."

She leans in and whispers, not all that quietly, "Take me with you."

I shake my head. "You know you can't come with me. Lou hasn't given his permission."

She scoffs. "Pfft, he never will. He is so singular when it comes to sexual adventures. Beth, I just want to watch what he does to you. I won't join in, I promise. You won't even know I'm there." Amy has started to beg.

I look at Jake, who looks away, leaving it in my hands to let her down easily. "You can't come with us, Amy. I have to get you home. If you were to come with me, and watch Jake do what he does to me, you know you'll regret it in the morning. Face it, you are a good girl."

"Come on! I just want to be really bad, for one night. What if I said that I won't regret it?" Amy is so desperate for excitement in her life that she almost has me convinced to let her watch us.

"You would," I tell her, as I hug her. "Come on, let's get out of here."

With my hand in hers, we stumble our way to the door, dancing and singing off-key to our thirtieth favourite song of the night. The bouncer opens the door for us. He's a big guy, very handsome with a tough biker look about him. His beard is long. Amy lets go of my hand to run her fingers through it. Her glossy, drunken eyes are locked on his mean-looking peepers and he doesn't seem at all impressed with her flirtatious touching.

While apologizing to the man, Jake takes her by the wrist and, much to her disappointment, pulls her from his beard. He puts his hand around her waist and escorts her out the door. She spins as if he's her ballroom dancing partner. Jake is smiling as he spins her around and then pulls her tightly against his body, so he can entertain her desire to dance with him. Their eyes are locked on one another as he guides her to his car while swaying his hips in perfect sync with hers. He's distracting her, hoping she won't protest leaving the bar.

As soon as we approach the car, he spins her toward me. I catch her when he releases her hand. Together, we laugh like schoolgirls. Amy snorts, which makes us laugh hysterically. Good thing we went pee just before we got out here.

Jake opens the door and lifts the seat, so one of us can hop in the back. I get in before she can, even though she tries to argue with me. He looks into her eyes, and with playful assertiveness, demands, "Get in the car, right now."

"Oh, yes Sir!" she replies with a wide grin. She plops into the seat while still locked in his gaze. He leans in, fastening her belt while she giggles, flirtatiously.

"Good girl," he whispers, with a wink.

CHAPTER TWENTY-TWO

The ride to Amy's house passes quickly, and before I know it, we are pulling into her driveway. Jake shuts the car off and opens his door. As the gentleman he is, he rounds the hood and opens Amy's door. In her drunken state, she forgets to unfasten her seatbelt before trying to get out. We both start laughing. Her, because her brain and body aren't working together. I'm laughing so hard, I'm snorting, because I'm going to be stuck I this backseat for all of eternity, if I don't get her out of this car.

I climb between the seats, fumbling like a clumsy, newborn giraffe, attempting to stand for the first time. My legs seem to have a mind of their own, not going where I need them to. Of course, our gut-busting laughter isn't helping the situation one bit. Jake leans in and undoes her belt, and then takes her hands, helping her to stand. She trips on the curb, nearly landing face down on the grass, but Jake manages to catch her before she does. He scoops her up in his arms and carries her up the walkway. She's swooning at the chivalry, but still laughing with me.

"I think I'm in love with you," I hear her say to Jake as he starts up the stairs toward her front door.

He rings the bell, setting her down on her feet when Lou opens the door. Lou looks shocked to see Jake steadying his wife, but shakes his head, and cracks a smile. I hear him say something, and then Jake shrugs his shoulders. Lou takes her hand. I crack up again when she starts dancing like an idiot in front of Jake while her husband watches on. Lou waves at me, and I wave back. The men talk to one another for a minute or so, before Lou reaches out, shaking hands with Jake.

Jake's face is flushed, and he's chuckling when he sits back behind the driver's wheel. By now, I've managed to situate myself in the passenger seat, but I can't seem to figure out the seatbelt. It seems to be stuck on something, and no matter how much I tug on it, the damn thing won't give. Jake leans over me to help out. He takes the strap in his strong hand and pulls. Funny, he has no problem with it. I no longer care about the stupid belt because his eyes are looking into mine. He's a bit blurry, but I can still see how handsome he is. My hand brushes his cheek, and he holds still.

I whisper, "I am so lucky to have these opportunities with you. I mean, look at you. You could have any woman you want. Why did you choose me?"

He kisses me very softly, just once, pulling back barely enough that we can see each other's eyes. "I am the lucky one. You are beautiful, smart, sexy and courageous. Henry should never let you forget how incredible you are. I haven't even thought about fucking another woman tonight. I want to fuck you—right now, right here."

The surrounding neighbourhood has completely faded away from relevance. It is only us and the sound of our breathing. I whisper, "I want you to fuck me."

"Take off your pants and panties." He sits back in his seat, unzipping and pulling his pants halfway down his thighs. A condom seems to appear out of nowhere. The man really is always prepared. I wonder if he was a boy scout? He's rolling it on while he watches me undress from the waist down. "Straddle me, Beth."

"Yes, Sir," I say as I do my best not to shuffle around in the same out-of-control manner as my adventure from the backseat, to the front. In my drunken stupor, I believe it goes smoothly, but it probably didn't.

I rest my right shin on the door's armrest while my left plants itself on the centre console. He grips my ass cheeks and squeezes until I wince. His smile is wickedly sexy as he watches the pain on my face. He is a sadist, without a doubt. Jake pulls my ass toward him, pushing my hips down until his thick, hard prick is sliding into me, filling me completely. My eyes shut, and I suck air between my clenched teeth, and without caring who hears, I moan loudly as the air seeps from my lungs. Fuck, his cock feels incredible when it pushes against my cervix!

When I try to rock my hips, he clenches my ass cheeks even tighter. My eyes pop open only to see him shaking his head. How does he expect me to remain still when it feels this damn good? And how can I fuck him if he won't let me lift my butt? I want his cock stroking my inner walls until they spasm around it, rocketing me into a glorious orgasm, just as he's done all those times before.

He lifts my shirt and bra, letting my tits fall from beneath it. His lips kiss my nipples with a warm softness that I adore, but when his teeth bite down, I squeal and grab his shoulders, hoping he'll release the little nib, and not bite it off. My clitoris twitches each time he nips at me.

Jake takes my wrists and pulls them behind me, switching them in his hands, crossing them one over the other and holding my fists against my ass. My tits jut toward his face. When he pulls me toward him, my hips rock, sliding his solid prick in and out of my heated pussy. His lips peck tiny kisses all over my breasts while he makes me fuck him.

"Don't cum until I tell you to," he demands. I simply nod, hoping I can comply after having had so much to drink. It isn't more than five minutes before his body is bucking up at me, and he's grunting with each deep insertion. "Cum, Beth."

"Thank you, Sir." My words come out louder than I had planned. His hand releases my wrist and grabs my neck, holding it tightly. I can't breathe, and my blood is being restricted from flowing to my brain. This action is increasing the power of my orgasm. I know I'm going to soak his lap. I try to calm myself but it's too late, I'm already well into a body-shaking climax, and I can't calm it down. Perhaps my intoxication is making it that much more intense.

Hot fluid flows from me. He releases my throat and I suck in a desperate breath. His hand slides to the back of my neck, pulling my face toward his and locking his lips to mine. My moans blend with his grunts, matching our thrusts as our lips mash together with so much passionate intensity. It's his turn to cum. We pant, huff and grunt until he holds silent, lost in the sensation of floating, as endorphins flood his bloodstream, granting him several seconds of utter euphoria. I watch his face tighten, and then quickly relax, his puffy lips parted just slightly.

All too quickly, we are recovering with our foreheads pressed together, our breath bouncing off one another's faces, as we battle to calm our racing hearts. He drops both of his hands to my thighs, stroking them with a gentle easiness that I find to be a bit too loving, especially the way his eyes are looking into mine.

Perhaps it's the alcohol blurring my mind, but I have to get off of him before my heart is tricked into caring for him. Why do I feel like I've just cheated on Henry? Maybe I did. Each time we've played in the past, I've asked his permission beforehand. This time, I neglected to do that. Was this wrong?

"Will you take me home to Henry now?" I ask, looking at his flushed cheeks, as the streetlight casts a slightly yellow hue to his eyes, making them look a pale green.

He furrows his brow and then says, "Yes, of course. Did I do something wrong?"

"No, you didn't. Just take me home now," I say, sliding off his lap and flopping back into the passenger's seat. While I try to figure out how to get my panties back on, I spin them this way and that, not sure when underwear became so damn complicated. Instead of continuing with this challenge, I simply stuff them into my pants pocket. I slip my legs into my jeans and wiggle my body until they are up. I fasten them and then exhale a heavy breath. That was a chore. I don't remember putting pants on in a car as being such a task. Perhaps that's because I was younger and nimbler, back then.

"Are you sure nothing is wrong?" he asks again, as he studies my face. I look over at him and try to smile convincingly, but it fades all too quickly. He frowns as he pulls off the condom, wrapping it in a tissue before lifting his hips so he can slide his pants up his thighs. As I'm fastening my seatbelt, which goes much more smoothly this time, Jake says, "You feel guilty because you didn't ask Henry's permission before you fucked me."

"How do you know that's what I'm thinking?"

"Just by the way you got off of me, so quickly. I hope you know that you have no reason to feel guilty," he says, as he zips his pants. "Henry told me that I can play with you any time I'd like, as long as I have your permission, unless it interferes with his plans with you. So, you see, no need for guilt."

"I know that; he told me the same thing. For some reason, this feels wrong," I say as my voice fades out.

Jake starts the car and pulls out. The drive seems to take a very long time, but I'm sure it isn't more than a few minutes. I know this route very well and it isn't a lengthy jaunt. When we pull into the driveway, I pop my seatbelt off before we've come to a stop. I open my door and prepare to step out, when he grabs my wrist, holding me back.

"Beth are you sure you're not angry with me?"

I shake my head with a low groan. "No, you did nothing wrong. I wanted you inside of me and you appeased me. We have permission to play, so…" My voice fades out, but then I look over at him and smile, shaking my head. "I drank too much tonight. Alcohol puts ideas in my head and makes me feel things that I normally wouldn't."

"Like what?" I hesitate to answer, wondering if I should tell him. "Beth, open honesty is a must."

I clear my throat before saying, "I wanted more of you than just your body. No, that's not true, exactly. For a moment, I imagined that Henry doesn't exist, and I am ten years younger, and maybe you and I could be something more. Please don't take that the wrong way."

"Is there a right way?"

"Well, Henry does exist, and I love him more than I could imagine ever loving another man. You are my sex partner and my friend, and that's how I want to keep it, but copious amounts of alcohol blurred my reasoning tonight. So, you see, I'm not angry with anything you did, or I did. I'm pissed off that my mind drifted there."

"I understand how that can happen. That reason alone is why I rarely have more than two drinks. I can't let myself feel anything for my submissives, other than desire and friendship. Being committed to anyone at this stage in my life is utterly terrifying to me," he says while chuckling, trying to lighten the topic of conversation.

"You wait; one day, you'll meet her – the one you're meant to be with – and those feelings will all change. What's worse is that you'll want them to," I tell him as I step out of the car. He follows me up to the door and waits while I find my keys to let myself in. I hold the door and wave him in. At first, he hesitates, but I grab his wrist and pull him inside, and then shut the door. Strangely, I feel a lot more sober than I did a half-hour ago.

"Henry are you home?" I yell, hearing it echo off the walls.

"Yes, I am," Henry replies from our bedroom.

I start walking toward his voice but turn to see Jake waiting at the door. "Follow me," I tell him.

"I think I should go. Henry might not approve of the sudden intrusion," he whispers.

"Wait here and don't leave. Promise you won't leave," I beg, not walking away until he nods. I'm not sure why I don't want him to go, I just don't.

When I enter the bedroom, Henry is lying across the bed, naked. He's watching porn on his computer. "Hi Sweetie," he says, smiling like a horny fool.

I notice his semi-erect cock and smile. "Um, I just fucked Jake in his car."

"You did?" he asks. "Was it good?"

"Um, yes and no. I only came once. It was nice of him to drive me home, and then drive it home," I say with a loud, ridiculous laugh.

He smiles and rolls his eyes. "That was nice of him. Is he still here?" he asks, sitting up while closing his laptop.

I smile and nod. "He is waiting at the front door."

"Waiting? Beth, would you like him to join us in our bed?"

I swallow before clearing my throat. "What would you think of me if I said *sure*?"

"I would tell you to go downstairs, and ask him if he'd like to join us," he replies with a sexy grin. Perhaps the porn has put some ideas in his head.

"Oh, someone's in a sexy mood tonight," I jest.

Jake is leaning against the wall with his arms crossed over his chest when I come around the corner. "Would you like to join us, in the bedroom?"

He licks his lips, lifting one corner of his mouth. "I would like, that very much."

I take his hand and lead him up the stairs to where my husband awaits us.

CHAPTER TWENTY-THREE

I stand before my husband while Jake observes us from just inside the bedroom doorway. Henry's cock is harder than it was when I left the room. He wants this. I wonder how long he's been fantasizing about him and Jake tag-teaming me. I'm nervous but thrilled. I've never been with two men at the same time, and I'm not sure what I'm supposed to do. What if I'm not able to keep up to them? I really hope I don't do something wrong and ruin Henry's fantasy.

Jake's deep voice breaks through the chaos of my thoughts. "Beth, take off your clothes." Good, he's going to give me instructions.

I look at Henry to judge his reaction. His deviant, crooked grin says it all, but to be sure, he whispers, "Babe, do what Jake tells you. He is your Master, after all."

Now I know that Henry is putting this in Jake's hands to choreograph our sexual dance, and it helps to calm my anxiety. I wonder if he is also unsure of what to do. I will follow Jake's instruction, to the word and without hesitation.

I remove all of my clothes as quickly as I can, leaving them in a heap on the floor at my feet. Henry stands when he looks past me in the direction of our guide. We stand silently, watching as Jake makes his way toward us, while slowly removing his shirt. Fuck! He's a sexy man! His eyes are locked on mine, but he wears no expression. My tummy flutters when he presses his slim lips just under my left ear.

"On your knees," Jake's order caresses my ear in a soft whisper of heated breath. I drop, looking up at him as he lets his pants fall to his ankles. "Take your husband's cock in your mouth and suck it as deep into your throat, as you can."

I shuffle my knees to face Henry and do as my Master ordered, taking the steel-hard prick all the way down my throat until my nose presses on his abdomen. Henry groans, as if he's been waiting for this all evening. My head bobs on his prick in a steady rhythmic motion, until I have to pull my mouth off to swallow the wad of saliva that's formed in my mouth. Jake is now naked and standing right beside Henry, so close that their arms are touching.

"Now take my cock and do the same." I lean in and do as he insisted, taking his thick shaft as far as possible without choking. "I think you can take both of us in your mouth. Try."

I gaze up at them as I fight to get both into my mouth, but my lips are stretching too much. Their members are just too thick. I reach up, grabbing both of their asses and guiding them until Henry's right hip is pressed against Jake's left, and they're turned in toward each other. Now their pricks are side by side and easier to get in my mouth. I cannot manage to squeeze any more than their heads beyond my overly stretched lips.

When I look up, I see Jake mouthing something to Henry who seems to understand, judging by his nod. Jake says to me, "That's enough, Beth. Stand up."

I raise to my feet with the help of his gracious hand. He weaves his fingers delicately through my hair, suddenly grabbing a wad of it and pulling my face to his. His tongue shoots into my mouth, exploring it while his hand slaps at the mound between my legs. Three slaps before he stops. He grips my pussy lips tightly and squeezing my outer labia together, pinching my clit between them. It feels good. Two of his fingers shove inside of me quickly, waving with lightning speed. It isn't more than a few seconds before I'm moaning over the sloshing sounds of my wet cunt being viciously fingered. It won't be long before he has me coming on his hand.

Jake yanks my head back, exposing my neck to his hot tongue. He licks up my throat and over my chin, his teeth nip at my bottom lip. With his sensually dangerous expression, he watches my face while I try to hold his gaze. Just before I'm ready to cum, he pulls his hand away.

"No! Please, don't stop!" My pleas fill the room.

It turns him on, watching me shift my weight from one leg to the other desperately hoping it'll grant me my release. He slaps my right breast, and then my left, soon alternating between them, until they are a lovely shade of bright pink, and my nipples are swollen and stinging. The burning hot sensation only increases the ache between my legs.

In his calm mannerism, he instructs, "Suck your husband's cock while I fuck you."

Henry has been patiently watching Jake work my body into a near frenzy. He's stretched out, on his back on the bed, stroking his erect prick. His other arm is resting under his head, helping to hold it up, just enough so he can see everything Jake is doing to me. I lean over and take his dick in my hand, feeling its girth. I drop my head down, sliding my lips up and down his beefy shaft, as my saliva coats its length. My mouth rides him, my fingers stroking its base while Henry softly moans and watches my Master touch me.

Jake rests his hand on my lower back while the other spanks my ass several times, harshly. I yelp when he shoves his thick manhood into me for the second time tonight. He holds still, probably waiting for me to breathe, or until I resume sucking Henry's very swollen man-meat. As soon as I begin, he starts gliding in and out of my eager cunt, slowly at first, but soon increases to a steady, but quick pace. He isn't trying to make me cum, he's gradually building me up. His goal seems to be to tease the hell out of me, get me right to the edge, only to pull me back. He seems to enjoy that type of torture.

Just as I thought he would, he stops before I cum, pulling out of me completely, refusing my release. I protest with several loud groans that are muffled by Henry's prick, which is filling my mouth. Jake isn't at all sympathetic to my hunger.

Cold liquid dribbles onto my asshole and then his finger pushes into it. The invasion adds fuel to the fire in my belly. I can feel my clitoris swelling; its way of urgently begging to be touched. Jake's voice breaks the silence, yanking my mind from its selfish thoughts—waking me to the realization that I had stopped sucking Henry's prick. "Lick his balls. Suck them into your mouth. Relax your ass because I'm going to fuck it."

With my concentration now focused on Henry's nuts, Jake is free to stretch my asshole with his fingers, little by little until he can easily invade me with his prick. He slowly slides in until he's buried deep and holding patiently, waiting for me to relax. I take my husband's very hard cock deep into my throat, pressing my face firmly, onto his belly. I want both ends of my body to feel filled completely. I wait until I gag before lifting my face. Henry moans appreciatively while running his fingers through my hair with his loving touch.

Jake's prick feels heavy as he fills my ass again and again. Both he and Henry are breathing heavily, their moans float softly on their breath as I take them both into my body. Their erotic sounds reveal their appreciation, boosting my confidence, knowing I can satisfy both men by just being present and allowing them to have my body as they please. Whatever happens next is up to them. If they want to fuck every one of my holes, they can, because I will let them. I want to experience everything these two hunky men have to offer.

Jake pulls out of my ass and then spanks me several times, once again waking me from my deepest, most erotic thoughts. "Straddle Henry and put his cock in your pussy. Fuck him, but I don't want either of you to cum. It will be worth the wait."

I do as he says, taking Henry's saliva-soaked manhood completely inside of me. We flash a quick smile at one another before our lips press together in a passionate expression of our love for one another. My hips rock over him, sliding him inside me. Our bodies shift when Jake climbs on the bed behind me.

The head of his hard prick presses into my ass. I immediately stop moving and kissing Henry. I don't know if I'm going to like this. I feel very uncomfortable, as if it's going to be too much. He's slowly pushing into me and I'm surprised that he fits alongside Henry, who's holding himself inside my twitching pussy. I'm whimpering, taking quick breaths, waiting for what seems like a very long time for his cock to be fully inside of me, and for my body to ease enough that I might enjoy this. Right now, It's overwhelming.

Everything pauses now that Jake and Henry are buried deeply. I'm barely breathing. They're waiting for my body to adjust to this level of fullness and accept this lusty violation. This sensation is more intense than anything I have felt before, including being fisted. I've been fucked in my pussy while having a butt plug in my ass, but this feels different. Now that I'm becoming accustomed, it's starting to feel so good.

I have two men inside of me at the same time. How fucking taboo is this? I'm a very lucky woman. I've seen pornos like this and always thought it would hurt like hell. Now that it's happening to me, I realize just how wrong I was. As soon as they begin slowly humping, the craving to orgasm is urgent. "Please, Sir, let me cum."

"No," Jake hisses, fucking me a bit quicker, purposely, to intensify my need for release. He grabs a wad of my hair, pulling my head back so he can kiss and tongue my mouth.

Henry is cupping my breasts and rolling my nipples while his hips lift and lower, matching Jake's tempo. He slips one of his fat fingers between my pussy lips. The last thing I need is anyone caressing my swollen clitoris. His lone digit has me squirming between them, in a desperate battle to hold back the heart-stopping orgasm that will surely stupefy me. My moans are loud and continuously being forced from my body by the relentless thrusts of the two rock-hard cocks. Jake releases my hair but grasps my throat before I can collapse forward onto Henry's chest. He's pulling back just slightly, making it even more difficult for me to breathe.

He presses his mouth next to my ear. With desperate urgency, he whispers, "Cum, Beth." He doesn't need to repeat himself. Both men launch into a bucking frenzy, pounding me hard and fast.

I scream, "Yes! Fuck me! Hard! Yes!" Jake tightens his grip on my throat until my instructions can no longer escape. My orgasm begins to reach its fullest intensity. When I try to breathe in, nothing happens. My mind starts to panic just slightly, but my body doesn't react. Instead, my muscles lock tightly in a frozen state of being, as I am granted a superb orgasm. It seems to linger until Jake releases my throat and I fall limply forward, onto Henry.

I gasp in several breaths, hearing the grunts from the two strong-bodied men and the sloshing sounds of Henry's cock fucking my saturated, cum-drenched hole. "Oh yes, fuck me! Make me cum again. I want to cum again. Please?" I beg in whimpers while looking into Henry's reddened face.

The scent of lust hangs heavily in the air as these two horny men sandwich me between them, taking me as their plaything. Ravishing me, as if I were only a thing for them to use in whatever way they want and not a living, breathing human.

Henry's wearing an expression I don't recognize. He's lost in his fantasy, watching me get ass fucked while he drills my pussy. For a quick second, I wonder how long he's had this yearning and why he never told me about it. All too quickly, that thought is stripped away, replaced by an even more unfathomably marvellous orgasm.

Henry's hips heave upward, his body jerking spastically as he is overtaken by his own mind-numbing climax. With each jolt of his body, loud grunts burst from the depths of his burning lungs. Soon, his prick will wither and slip from my body, leaving me with only one dick available to entertain me. I selfishly want to cum once more, just like the last two times, but it won't happen now that Henry has erupted. I'm disappointed, but grateful for the two they granted me.

Jake grabs my throat once again, pulling me up against him. With his other hand reaching around my waist, he leans back until I am sitting on his thighs and his ass is resting on his heels. His hand slides down so he can strum my clit like an expert guitarist. I bounce on his cock at the tempo I prefer, building myself slowly toward another climax, while Henry watches the action from beneath us.

I hear a familiar buzzing sound and I'm instantly elated. That is the sound of my favourite vibrator. Henry is sitting up with his legs pinned between ours. He pushes two fingers inside of my pussy while pressing the toy to my clitoris, holding it still while his fingers flutter gently in my depths. He takes my right nipple between his teeth, teasing it how he so expertly does.

Jake is still humping into my asshole, equalling my easy tempo, granting me some control over my own penetration. He pinches my other nipple between his thumb and forefinger, rolling it, awarding me with more pain. In my ear, he whispers, "Your husband is watching me fuck your ass. Tell him how grateful you are to have my cock."

"Thank you, Henry. I love you," I say with bated breath.

Jake demands, "Tell your husband how much you enjoy having my cock in your ass."

"I love Jake's cock in my ass. It feels so fucking good. He's so big. Oh, fuck! Henry, I love you!"

"I love you, Beth," Henry replies.

Jake's moans are low, yet they ring through my ear like the sweetest of songs. He whispers, "Do you want to cum? Ask your husband's permission."

"Henry, I want to cum."

Jake interrupts before he can answer, "Beg him!"

"Henry, please? May I cum? Please let me cum with Jake's cock fucking my ass," I beg.

Henry answers my pleas with a whisper, "Cum, Sweetie."

At this point, I think I would have erupted whether he'd given his permission or not. Jake doesn't squeeze my neck; he just holds it firmly to prevent me from toppling forward. My stomach muscles are stretched so viciously, and my back is bent. If he weren't holding me upright, I'd surely fall forward, pushing Henry back against the comforter.

Jake humps into me several more times before he also falls victim to his carnal needs. His hedonistic bellow floods the room. His prick swells inside my ass as he dumps his cum into the condom. His forehead comes to rest on my shoulder, his body holding still while his prick throbs and spasms. A heated lengthy exhale flows down my sweaty spine.

As soon as he can manage, he whispers in my ear, "Go shower."

Without questioning him, I stand on my trembling legs and stumble my way to the bathroom. I'm only in there long enough to clean myself. When I open the door and step back into the bedroom, I'm saddened to realize that Jake has left. I look around, half expecting him to still be getting dressed. How long was I in there?

"Where's Jake?" I ask Henry, who is sitting on the edge of the bed with a towel around his waist and a fully satisfied expression on his face.

"He asked me to say goodnight to you." Henry stands and walks to me, wrapping his arms around me in a tender embrace. "That was really fun."

"It was. Did you two plan that?"

He chuckles, releasing me from his embrace and making his way toward the bathroom. "No, this time there was no planning involved. Him stumbling upon you at the bar was a happy accident. He called when you and Amy were in the bathroom, getting ready to leave. He said he was driving you home, so I told him to come in and be with us. I am really glad you brought him home."

"Well, technically he was driving, so…" I joke with a shrug.

"Okay then, I'm glad you brought him to the house and asked him to wait so you could talk to me." He winks and then closes the bathroom door behind him.

I shimmy into a slip and pull the covers back from the bed before I get in. Even though my body is truly exhausted, I am hungry and need something to eat. I think a sandwich and a glass of milk are just what I need before I drift off to sleep. When I return, Henry is snoring in bed. I slide in and cuddle up against him. I quickly drift into a deep sleep of my own.

CHAPTER TWENTY-FOUR

It's been a week and a half since that very memorable night with Henry and Jake. Having them share me was an experience I would love to revisit. I'm sure it will repeat many times throughout the years if Henry has anything to say about it. Since that night, he's had a persistently raging erection that never seems to be satiated, for very long. I'm not complaining, mind you.

We have arranged for the four of us to play in Jake's sex room, tonight. I want to see how Jenna dominates Henry. Of course, he is curious about how Jake is with me when he has all of his equipment at hand. I've tried to describe the furniture, bindings and the painful, yet pleasurable toys, but he's anxious to see them for himself. He says that it will help him to visualize our playdates when we're lying in bed afterwards, and I'm describing everything in great detail.

Maybe one day Henry will allow me to be his Mistress, or perhaps he will be dominant with me. I don't know if I have it in me to be bossy enough to please him, but if it's something he is interested in trying, I'll do my best. First, however, I would need to take instruction from Jenna. The last thing I'd want would be to make a fool of myself, or worse yet, cause him injury.

I'm just getting out of the shower when Henry comes home. After yelling to announce his arrival, Henry makes his way to his office to put his briefcase on his desk, as he does every day. The third stair on the staircase creaks as he climbs. He's been working long hours lately, engrossed in a very important case. Today though, he's home earlier. I'm sure he's excited about our play date.

He and Jake have been working side by side for over a week now. If only I could be a fly on the wall to listen in on their private conversations. How thrilling would that be?

"I'm in the bathroom," I call out.

Henry walks in and slides his hand down my back as he leans in for a kiss. "Hello, Sweetie."

"How was work?" I ask as I carefully run a wide-toothed, bamboo comb through my hair.

"Oh, it's coming along, but I don't want to talk shop." Our eyes meet in our reflection on the mirror. "Are you ready for tonight?"

My wide, toothy smile takes over my face and I nod. "I am very ready, or at least I will be once I get myself all dolled up for you and Jake."

"And Jenna. Don't forget about Jenna," he adds.

"I know she's going to be there, but she'll be entertaining you, not me."

He leans on the doorframe and crosses his arms over his chest. The expression he wears tells me that he knows something I should. I look at his reflection and tilt my head just a bit.

Henry starts chuckling. "Sweetie, she is a bisexual."

Terror sweeps through me. What if she wants to have sex with me? I suppose if she wants to touch or lick me, I'm okay with that, but what if she wants me to reciprocate? Can I do it? Will I do it? I have never been with a woman and I'm not sure I would know what to do.

"She didn't tell me she's into women, too. Um, did she say that she's interested in me?" I ask, suddenly overwhelmed with nausea. I turn to meet his eyes. "Are you fucking with me?"

"She might have; I don't remember. Look, whatever happens tonight, just go with it. It's not like any of us will ever judge you for anything that is done to you, or that you're told to do. If there is something that makes you uncomfortable, just tell the person asking you to do it. I'm sure they aren't going to force you to eat her pussy if she happens to tell you to. Although, I'd like to see that."

"You would?"

"Absolutely! I'm not sure if you know this or not, but it's not uncommon for men to have a fantasy involving two women pleasuring each other," Henry explains with a hint of sarcasm.

"Yes, I didn't know you were among that group of men." I ponder the idea of testing those waters, and then an unlikely thought comes to me. "What if Jake tells you to suck his cock? Will you do it?"

Henry is quiet for a few seconds and then replies, "I think I would."

I'm shocked and my expression proves it. "You would? I didn't think you'd be interested in cock. And, you work with him, so don't you think that'll make for a bit of awkwardness at the office?"

"No, I don't. Jenna works with me as well and I've had sex with her. When we're at the office, we are business associates and not sexual partners. We keep the two separated; otherwise, it wouldn't work. We'd be so preoccupied with sensual thoughts that we would never get any work done. So, do I think the office will still flow smoothly if Jake and I have sex? Yes, I do," Henry says as he strips off his suit piece by piece, hanging them up as he does. His shirt, socks and boxer briefs are tossed into the hamper.

"I can't picture you sucking Jake's prick. Perhaps I'll get the visual tonight," I say just to watch the nervousness splash across Henry's face. I glance at him while the image runs through his mind. His eyes are wide as he runs the scenario through his mind. I giggle while lining my eyes with the kohl coloured eye pencil.

Henry showers quickly and then heads downstairs, still wearing his towel. When he returns, I'm just finishing my hair. He hands me a glass of white wine and taps my glass with his, toasting to new experiences.

I decide to put on a red dress with spaghetti straps but wear no bra or panties underneath. I slip my feet into the shoes Jake had me wear the second time we were together. If I do say so myself, my legs look great in them.

As I'm walking down the stairs, Henry is ascending at a jog. He stops in front of me, looking me up and down, slowly nodding his approval. He's still in his towel, which falls off when he crouches to lift my dress. He seems pleasantly surprised that I chose to remain bare. His finger slides between my labia and begins to caress tiny circles over my clitoris.

"Do you want me to make you cum before we go?" he asks, his eyes focused on mine with a dreamy look to them.

"Yes, please," I reply.

Henry drops to his knees and buries his mouth between my thighs. I bend my knees open and shuffle my feet to widen my thighs, so he can enjoy all of my pussy. His tongue shoots over my clitoris as his lips suck and kiss it. He sucks gently while whipping his tongue over my swelling nub. I grasp the railing. My eyes close. I don't want any visual distractions.

Henry's mouth is suckling and slurping at my pussy, quickly bringing me closer to my goal of a rushed orgasm that should temporarily satisfy me, until Jake gets hold of me, of course. Strangely enough, the thought of Jake's fingers entwined in Henry's hair as he forces his prick deeper into his throat, excites me. I picture Henry bent over and getting reamed in the ass by Jenna's fake cock that's attached to her by a leather harness. He has told me how much he enjoys himself when she penetrates him. I have yet to do that for him.

I imagine Henry sucking off Jake while getting fucked by Jenna and it's enough to blast me into a screeching orgasm. Henry slurps at my slit before removing his glistening mouth from my twitching pussy. My legs are shaking so much that I have to sit before they quit on me. I'd hate to fall forward onto Henry, having both of us tumbling down the stairs to our death. Okay, we probably wouldn't die, but you can never know for sure, so why risk it.

"You should hurry, we don't want to be late," I tell him with a grin, while still trying to catch my breath.

He kisses my lips softly, before rushing up the stairs to the bedroom. "No, late is never good. I don't want to be punished any harsher than she's already done to me. That woman can be wicked when she wants to be."

"Yeah, but she's sweet otherwise," I say with a snicker.

"You wait, if she has her way with you, you'll see her dangerous bitch come out." Henry disappears into the bedroom.

I gradually make my way down the rest of the stairs and into the kitchen. I pour a little more wine in my empty glass and suck back a big mouthful. My excitement is rising with each sip I take. The four of us are going to play in the same room. What will happen? The possibilities are endless. When Henry calls my name, I startle, suddenly realizing that I was lost in a sexy fantasy of what might actually come true, within the hour. It's almost time to go and Henry was one hundred per cent right in stating that we do not want to be late.

After getting out of the car, Henry takes my hand and escorts me up Jake's driveway to his front door. He taps lightly, before opening it and ushering me in. I'm surprised to see both Jenna and Jake sitting at the bar, looking at us, as we enter.

Jenna smiles wide as she approaches us, wrapping her arms around me to give me a hug and then pressing her lips to mine. She holds my biceps while her mouth kisses mine, her tongue slowly slithering its way between my lips. I notice how much softer her skin and lips are in comparison to every man I've ever kissed. She is more sensual than men, as well. I like this very much.

She pulls back, winking at me before she exchanges my mouth for Henry's. Jake's fingers weave into my hair, pulling my mouth to his. He has a strength in his kiss that screams dominance, even when he isn't playing rough. It might be that his pheromones quickly drive my mind into a heightened state of arousal whenever he's near. When he releases me, I half expect him to kiss Henry, just as Jenna kissed me, but he doesn't. He shakes his hand as they gaze into one another's eyes for an uncomfortable length of time. Perhaps they're having a silent discussion or sizing each other up. I don't know.

"Come, sit and have a drink with us," Jenna interrupts their moment of silence. "What can I get you, Beth?"

"White wine would be perfect, thank you."

"Excellent. Henry?" she asks, as she's taking a wine glass from the shelf behind her.

"Same for me," he replies after clearing his throat, nervously.

Jake stands behind the bar with Jenna while Henry and I sit on black barstools. We are quiet for a moment while Jenna fills our glasses halfway and then hands them to us. The wine is smooth and crisp with a pleasant aftertaste that I can't quite place. I will have to find out what this wine is called, but right now, they look like they have something to discuss with us.

"How are you both, tonight?" Jake asks.

Based on our smiles and my blushing cheeks, it's obvious we are both excited and nervous.

I sip my wine, and then call out the elephant in the room, "Is there something you want to ask us?"

Jenna answers me, first. "Yes, there is. I want to know if you would be willing to experience being with a female dominant. What I'm asking is if you'd be willing to pleasure me if I tell you to?"

"I would give it a shot. It's not something I've ever done, so I can't say I'll be any good at it, or that I'll enjoy it," I reply shyly.

"Just do to me what you would want done to you, pay attention to my reactions, and alter your movements to get the best response from me. Don't worry Beth, I'll direct you if I don't think you're doing it how I like it. I'm good like that." She winks with a friendly grin.

"Well, I suppose if you're going to direct me, I can't really get it wrong then, can I?" I say with a shy smile followed by an unusual giggle that I don't recognize to be a sound I've ever made.

She takes a small swig from her glass of whiskey on the rocks. "I am happy to hear that you're open to trying new things. Now, for Henry. Jake, do you want to take the podium?"

He smiles at her and replies, "Yes, of course." He turns his attention to Henry. "Judging by what Jenna asked Beth, I'm sure you can figure out what my question to you will be."

Henry scratches his chin and raises his eyebrows when he glances at me, probably for moral support. He looks back at Jake and clears his throat. "Are you asking if I want to suck your cock?"

"Yes, Henry, I'm asking if you want to suck my cock."

"Will you suck mine too?"

"No," Jake replies matter-of-factly.

"I suppose it doesn't really matter. You're the dominant, so if you just want me to suck on you, it's okay, I suppose. I'll do it, but I'd like you to make it seem like I don't have a choice in the matter. I think if I'm believing the choice has been taken from me, I will be able to just give in to it and not let my thoughts overwhelm me."

"I'm curious to know what thoughts you want to drown out," Jenna says in a soft tone.

"It's ridiculous, but I think if I have the choice to do it or not to, and I say I will, I'll be so busy worrying whether I'm gay, that it'll interfere with my performance. Especially, if I happen to really enjoy taking you in my mouth. Is that wrong of me? I have nothing against gay people. I really don't." Henry seems to be quite worried about how they'll judge his fears.

"Henry, just because you enjoy the fantasy of a man forcing you to suck his cock, it doesn't mean you're gay. At most, you could be bi-sexual. My guess is that you simply enjoy being ultimately submissive. Play rape is also known as consensual, non-consent. I don't often use the term rape because the submissive holds all the power and has the right to stop everything, at any time. Rape victims don't have that option, unfortunately." Henry and I nod. "Henry, I'm not gay but I have used a man's mouth, on occasion. I enjoy the dominance of the situation, especially if it involves a man with power. I could never see myself being in a committed, long-term relationship with a man. I simply prefer the scent of a woman, so to speak. It's my personal preference."

Henry looks worried. He struggles to ask, "Are... are you going to... going to... fuck my, um... my ass?"

"Would you like me to? Jenna has told me that you really enjoy getting a dick shoved deep into your rectum. Was she wrong?" Jake asks him.

"No, I love it! I suppose if you want to fuck my ass, it's okay with me. Again, make it seem like I don't have a choice. I just think it'll be easier for me, for my first time with a guy." Henry seems more relaxed talking about it, now.

The three of them discuss the case they're working on while we finish our drinks. The shift in conversation seems to calm our nerves. I welcome the chat, even though I have no idea which case they're talking about. They are including me in the conversation as best they can, which I appreciate, but it isn't necessary. I'm enjoying watching how well they play off each other, knowing what each of their roles entail, in the case. What one person doesn't know, another does. It's fascinating.

"Well," Jenna interrupts, "I don't think I can wait much longer. You two need to be naked and under our control. Both of you can go downstairs and take off your clothes. Henry, I assume you'll instruct Beth on how I would like you both to be positioned to wait for me."

"Yes, Mistress," he replies as if he's said that phrase a million times before. I like how he instantly switched roles from boss to *pet*.

Henry stands, putting his hand out for me to take. Together we make our way to the lower level while Jenna and Jake follow. We both begin taking off our clothing outside of the room as the two of them watch us without saying a word. I feel subconscious about taking my clothes off in front of such a beautiful, young woman. I doubt she'll judge me, but I am my own worst critic.

I walk into the playroom with Henry right behind me. He gasps when he sees how incredibly intimidating this room can seem, at first. I take his hand in mine to get his attention.

"It's just a room and trust me, you're going to love it in here. Now, tell me what Jenna wants us to do."

"First off, you cannot call her that. You have to call her Mistress. Don't forget! She doesn't like it when you forget. Now, come kneel beside me next to the door and rest your ass on your heels." Henry guides me until we are both in a position to please her.

"You cannot call him Jake, in here. He is Sir or Master," I tell Henry and then tease him. "Don't forget."

"Got it. Are you ready for this?" he whispers.

"Fuck, I hope so. I'm thrilled, actually."

"Put your hands on your knees and look straight ahead," Henry tells me just as Jake and Jenna are walking through the doorway.

CHAPTER TWENTY-FIVE

Jake follows Jenna into the room. My eyes are focused on the lengths of rope that are braided and hanging on the opposite wall. I especially like the red ones. Jenna's heals are clacking on the floor as she walks around the room, picking things up as she goes. I don't know what she's gathering because I don't dare shift my eyes in her direction, even though I'm sure she wouldn't notice. Rules are set and not to be broken.

Jake's feet make a stomping sound as his heavy boots carry him toward the ropes I've been admiring. I watch him as he ponders which he prefers to use today. Much to my disappointment, he finally chooses the black one. He lifts it from the hook and then walks over to me, putting his hand out for me to take.

I come to my feet and go where he leads me. He has me stand off to the left side of the room with my hands down at my sides. Knowing I am now in Jake's care, he likes it when I look at his eyes. In fact, he insists on it. He stands before me, our gazes locked. Doing this with him is very difficult for me. He intimidates the hell out of me, so it's a battle not to cast my eyes down, in defeat. He winks, lifting the corner of his mouth ever so slightly, letting me know that he's not such a hard-ass and that I should try to relax. But he is a hard-ass, I know this firsthand.

Master finds the centre of the rope and bends it. This I now know to be called a bight. He begins behind me by pulling my forearms together, my hands holding near the opposite elbow. He binds them together in the centre of my forearms and then walks around me as he ties knots here and there. It isn't long before I understand that my arms will be held behind me for longer than what will be comfortable. This excites me, probably more than it would most people. I know my muscles will ache, but I'm not worried that I can't take the pain because I know I can. I have before, and I will again.

Meanwhile, whenever Jake is behind me, I'm free to watch what Jenna is doing to my husband. She has him lying on his back with his feet, thighs, waist, chest and head bound to the table with leather belts. His hands are also cuffed and attached to the outer edges of the straps that are securing him at his waist. Needless to say, he is rendered motionless.

Jake walks in front of me and stops working my binding which captures my attention. "Is there something you're more interested in than me?"

"No, Master. I apologize," I reply, making sure my eyes lock onto his, even when he looks down at the rope he's looping around other parts of the fancy binding.

When he makes his way behind me again, I take the opportunity to catch another glance at Jenna and Henry. She is doing something to his genitals, but I can't see what. She's standing in the way, blocking my view. I don't mind because she is wearing black thigh-high stockings, very high-heeled shoes, a black, lacy, thong panty and a matching push-up bra. She must have been wearing this outfit under her clothing and I hadn't noticed.

Her hair is pulled up into a high ponytail that seems to fountain over the sides of her head. I had noticed that her make-up was applied heavily, as it was when I watched her leave our house, after playing with Henry. She looks damn good and I'm sure Henry isn't disappointed. I wonder if Jake is getting excited from seeing how sexy Jenna looks. Then I wonder if he's ever seen her dressed this way, before today.

Jenna hops up onto the table, straddling Henry's waist, facing his crotch. She guides a rope through a metal loop dangling from a chain that is attached to the ceiling. She watches his genitals lift and stretch while pulling the rope taut. Henry groans under his breath, not loud enough to seem like he's complaining, but I can tell it is uncomfortable for him, judging by his tone.

Now is when I can see just what she's done to his penis and scrotum. The rope has been wrapped around his cock and between his testicles, pushing them apart by a twisted line of rope. It looks horribly painful to me, but then again, I don't have a penis, so I suppose I'll never know from personal experience. Henry told me he liked it the last time she did it and he doesn't seem to mind now. In fact, his prick is hard and thick. The ropes might have something to do with that though.

Jake comes before me, again. This time I'm sure to look at his eyes, hoping he'll look up and acknowledge that I'm behaving myself and honouring him with my full attention. He doesn't. Instead, he's admiring his handiwork, touching each knot delicately, his fingertips brushing across my skin from time to time. I want him to grab me and take me, make me feel something other than an occasional gentle tickle from a casual touch.

In a flash, his calm demeanour shifts. He grabs a knot on my chest and yanks me forward. I would have stumbled, had I not been expecting him to do something sudden like that. I'm getting to know his ways. He sits onto a stool, pulling me onto his thighs belly first. His hands grasp the bindings and jerk me into a more balanced position, ensuring I won't topple off his knees and onto the floor.

Before I can right my thoughts, his hand slaps down onto my butt cheek with a loud crack. My back arches, raising my shoulders in an attempt to flee from this pain. This is when I realize how tightly bound my upper body is, both at my chest and my back. I cry out, but it's useless, he has no sympathy.

Again, he slaps down, this time onto the other cheek. I yelp loudly, flopping my chest back down, expecting I will receive at least two more on each cheek before he is satisfied. I despise the initial pain of the first few spanks, but a few seconds after the sharpness ebbs, a hot sensitivity will set in that makes my pussy tingle from arousal. In total, I am granted eight hard spanks.

Master stands me up while keeping a secure hold on me, in case I am off balance. He kicks apart my feet and then squats down, attaching ankle cuffs to me.

I watch Jenna slap Henry's cock, making his whole-body jerk and his chest rise and fall rapidly as he fights to slow his breathing, making every attempt not to scream. I want to yell at her to stop because I was always taught to never hit a man's groin unless I am under threat of serious injury, by him. But Henry isn't screaming. Even while having the ball gag in his mouth, I know he can make some type of screaming noise should he feel a need. He isn't, he's quietly accepting Jenna's torture. His prick is bigger than what is typical for him. I wonder if it's the rope bindings or the painful slaps that are the root cause.

My attention is instantly redirected by an openhanded slap to my vagina that sends pain shooting straight up inside of me ending only once it reaches my belly button. It buckles me forward, nearly bringing tears to my eyes. I look down at my Master to see him glaring at me, very disappointed that I'm not giving him my undivided attention. How can he expect this of me? Henry is being tortured and I want to watch. Isn't this why we decided to play together, in the first place?

He applies two clamps to either labia and then attaches thin chains to each. This must look incredibly sexy, but the clamps are quite tight and really hurt, causing me to whimper pathetically. To ease my complaining, Sir runs a finger over my clitoris and slips it inside of my pussy. He drags it back and forth until I am no longer concerned about the pain his slap caused. He stands quickly, slapping both breasts, simultaneously.

He has me straddle a rectangular stool but keeps me standing while he ties my ankles to the base of the legs. The chains hanging from my labia clamps drape over either side of the short bench. He lifts them when he has me sit with my knees pointing out to the sides as much as possible.

Master leaves me to collect something so I take these few seconds to watch Jenna and Henry interact. She is sitting on his face while she alternates between light touching, slapping and stroking his bound cock and balls. Henry is squirming, and his hands are balled into fists. She lifts slightly, allowing him to take in several breaths before sitting back on his face and rubbing her crotch back and forth.

Jake returns, my eyes darting to his so that I won't be punished for being disrespectful. He's carrying weights and they look heavier than anything he's attached to my body, before. He squats down, clipping one to the end of each chain and slowly letting them hang to prevent them from swinging. My labia are being pulled apart, viscously. Surprisingly so, it's turning me on. I can feel my clitoris heating up and swelling against the cooled air that surrounds it.

Next, he attaches what I'm later to understand are called clover clamps, to my nipples. The pain is outrageous at first, but somehow, and I don't know how I manage to contain my agony. Judging by the level of pinch, I assume the same clips are on my labia, but they don't hurt as much down there. To make it that much worse, he hangs weights from my nipple clamps which pull my breasts downward. I try my best not to breathe too quickly because that makes them swing, and it's nearly unbearable when they do.

He smiles, relishing my expression. "You look beautiful when you're in pain. You're stronger than those clamps are. Don't quit on me. I'm going to step back and let you watch Jenna abuse your husband."

My eyes follow him as he walks out of the room momentarily, returning with a bottle of water. He takes a sip and then offers me some. I gladly accept. As he tips the bottle, the icy water pours into my mouth, but he purposely splashes some off my chin and down my body. The cold shock has me gasping, making the weights on my nipples bounce as I breathe quickly. He enjoyed that. I should have refused the drink.

Henry is moaning from behind the ball gag. She is leaning forward, her bottom no longer pressing down on his face. My eyes scan down his body to his genitals and see that she is fucking his cock with something. I blink, hoping I didn't just see what I think I saw. But when I strain to get a better look, I'm quick to realize that I had seen correctly. She has a metal rod that she's fucking his pee-hole with. She isn't moving quickly, but he is reacting with lengthy moans and groans as if she were. His abdominal muscles remain flexed, but his ass muscles are tensing to keep up with the tempo of the penile penetration. I can't believe what I'm seeing.

She pushes its length in until only the wide end remains exposed. Henry seems to be calming down by the time she's climbing off of him. Now is when I see how red his face is. She was either sitting firmly, or he's having a lot of anxiety, perhaps both.

Jenna hooks wires up to the steel bar in his shaft and then plugs them into a small control box. She is watching his face while she increases the intensity of the electric shock. When his mouth is opened wider than the ball inside of it and emitting a bizarre sound; a pain and pleasure combination—she sets it down on his belly. I watch her clip clamps identical to mine, onto his nipple. For a moment, I pity him, but it's fleeting when I hear him moan as though he's pleased with the agony they're creating for him.

Jenna removes the ball gag from his mouth and then climbs back on the table, straddling his face once again, only this time, she's turned around and able to look down at his eyes.

"Stick out your tongue and lick my cunt." She suddenly jerks her pussy off his face, slapping his cheek hard. "I said lick, not suck! You're a fucking pathetic little pansy who can't follow instruction. Are you worthy of tasting me? Do you think you'd like to try again? Can you do it the way I told you to?"

"Yes, Mistress," Henry replies.

"Stick it out, Pet!"

She is obviously enjoying his tongue, judging by how she's starting to moan and rock her hips. She reaches back grasping the chain that links the two nipple clamps and gives them a tug. Henry cries out while his body tenses in protest. His ass is flexing as he humps the air. He's moaning louder and breathing much heavier than only a moment ago.

Mistress lowers herself off the table. She pulls the nipple chain and asks, "Do you think you've earned the right to cum?"

"Yes, Mistress."

"Beg me to let you cum. Convince me."

"Please Mistress, if it pleases you, may I be allowed to cum?" His moans are getting louder and sounding more pathetic and desperate.

She turns the dial, increasing either the tempo or intensity of the electricity flowing through the urethral sound. He immediately begs loudly, "Mistress, please! May I cum?"

"You may cum," she replies with a softly spoken voice.

Her hand covers his mouth and nose, blocking his ability to breathe, while she pulls the chain connecting his nipples, stretching them. I cringe at the thought of how much that must hurt. Mine are throbbing. His body tries to buck, but the restraints are holding steady. I watch his muscles flex and ripple as he battles to free himself. Mistress lifts her hand, allowing him three fast breaths before restricting his airflow once again.

I watch Henry's entire body tense and jerk repeatedly until he is locked in a hard flex that stems from his forehead to his toes. Mistress releases his mouth and the chain, and then turns off the unit, before removing the metal rod. As soon as it's pulled out, shot after shot of thick semen launches from his pulsing prick, splashing onto his chest. His loud primal wail fills the room, vibrating my chest.

Henry seems to give in to the restraints, as though his muscles are simply too exhausted to continue resisting them. His chest expands and contracts quickly, as he strives to consume enough oxygen to ease his heart back to its original pace. He appears to be totally spent.

Mistress begins unbinding his withering manhood, as Master weaves his fingers through my hair, grasping a wad of it and pulling my head back. His lips press to mine firmly, while his tongue juts into my mouth filling it, completely.

Sheer agony tears through my left breast as the clover clamp is slowly released. I scream into his mouth, but he pays it no attention. It burns hot as the blood begins to flow back into my flattened nipple. The anticipation of the same horror that will soon engulf my right breast has me shaking with adrenaline. It isn't long before I'm screeching once again.

He releases my hair as he positions himself behind me. He reaches around my shoulders grasping my nipples between his thumbs and forefingers, pinching them roughly while spinning them gently. A loud bellow blasts from deep inside my chest. It's pure torture. My body bends forward as if trying to escape this evil torment, but he refuses to release my tender little buds.

"That's right, Beth, scream for me," he insists.

Master finally frees them, much to my relief. He slowly walks around me until his crotch is directly in front of my face. He lowers his zipper and reaches in, pulling out his thick erection. He grabs the back of my head and pulls it toward him. "Suck my cock, you little slut."

I open wide, taking him between my lips. I lick the head to make him slick. He pushes deeper and deeper until he is buried into my throat. It's hard not to gag because I wasn't yet prepared to take this much of him just yet. In this position, I can't bend well enough. When I move, the vaginal clamps are unbearably painful at this point. Each time I lean in, they shift, making it more and more difficult not to yell out the safe word. I think he knows I can't, with his prick so far down my throat.

He fucks my face, giving me only a few seconds to breathe after five long, deep humps. I'm catching onto his rhythm, so it is easier to stay calm, decreasing my gag reflex. In my peripheral view, I can see that Henry is sitting up on the table, watching us. I can't see Mistress though. Maybe Jake is blocking her with his strong body.

He yanks his prick from my mouth, remaining connected to me by a long string of saliva. I catch my breath while he unclamps my labia, erupting sharp screams each time one is released. Before I can recover, they are pinched back on, further back on my labia. I cry out before holding my breath until the pain eases and I can open my eyes. This is when I see Mistress lounging on the loveseat. She waves her finger at Henry. He immediately slides off the table and kneels next to her like an obedient dog awaiting the next command.

Master grabs the spider web patterned weave of rope on my back, bringing me to my feet. He walks me toward the mistress who is now sitting at the edge of the cushion with her legs spread wide, elbows on her thighs. I am pushed to my knees between her legs. I don't meet eyes with her. Somehow in all of this, I remember that Henry had instructed me not to.

"Little whore, you're going to lick and suck my cunt. Hopefully, you'll do a better job than your worthless, piece of shit husband did." She leans back, pulling her panties to the side, exposing a very pretty pussy. For some reason, I had expected to be grossed out from being this close to another woman's vagina, but strangely, I'm not. Hers is actually quite pleasant looking.

Master weaves his fingers into my hair and guides my mouth to her heated vagina. I'm surprised at how soft it feels against my lips and tongue, as I begin to explore her. She tastes sweet with a slight tanginess. It's pleasing. Her scent is mild and seducing. My eyes close as my tongue roams through her folds, tasting all of her. I hear her exhale heavily, something I am quite familiar with because I do it when Henry's mouth first begins to pleasure me.

My pussy twitches as I suck her labia gently, darting my tongue all around her opening. I suck her clit into my mouth. The vacuum pressure I'm using has her moaning softly with each released breath. My tongue softens as I rub up and down her swelling nub, continuing with the harshest sucking I can manage. I know that I love it when Henry does this to me. Mistress is quite enjoying it, as well.

I had no idea how much of a turn-on it is to pleasure a woman with my mouth. She tastes so good, and the sounds she's making have me yearning to satisfy her. It's purely selfish on my part, wanting her to cum. In the back of my mind, I know the guys are watching us, but it's irrelevant. Pleasing her is all about me, and I don't care if the guys are here or not. This is something I want to do for her, again and again.

"You're a good little girl. That's right; keep sucking my clit. You're so much better at this than your useless, pansy spouse. Do not fucking stop!" she hisses.

A hand slips between my thighs and slaps side to side, silently instructing me to spread my knees. I open them as wide as I can, not skipping a beat with my mouth. Pain rips through my pussy as the clamps are removed, simultaneously. I whimper, momentarily halting my mouth's actions. Mistress grabs my hair, yanking my face upward. She slaps my cheek, hard, and it stings worse than an ass spanking.

"I told you not to fucking stop! Apologize, selfish whore!"

"I'm sorry, Mistress. Please, forgive me."

"You're forgiven." She pulls my head back against her pussy. I immediately begin sucking on her clit. I'm startled by a slap to my pussy from something flat and hard. The lingering pain from the clamp removal burns hotter after that slap. Again, I am swatted on my excited cunt. This time, the sharp contact ignites my clitoris causing it to swell with anticipation for the next shock, but it doesn't come.

Mistress is breathing heavily. I'm sure she'll cum soon. The thought that my actions are bringing her to climax is beyond arousing for me. The thought that she'll make me stop, shortly after it comes to an end, has me wishing I wasn't quite so good at this.

My ass cheeks receive a brutal punishing spanking by my master's open palm. I can feel the heat intensifying under my flesh after each blow. This makes me suck her even harder and flick more feverishly, at her bloated clit. Her hips are rocking on the sofa, causing her clit to pull forward and back from the steady intensity of my mouth's grip.

"Yes, suck my cunt, Pet," she whispers through panting breaths.

Her hand holds my hair, keeping my head in place. I don't let up, even though my ass cheeks are on fire from their abuser. This whole scene is so fucking sexy. If he touches my cunt, I will erupt into such an intense orgasm that I'm sure I will forget that I am to keep pleasuring Mistress.

She grabs my head with both hands, pulling my mouth so tightly against her that I can barely manage to suck and lick. Her hips are bucking against my lips, crushing them between her pelvic bone and my teeth. I open my eyes just in time to see her head tip back with her mouth wide open, eyes squeezed tightly shut. Her chest is ballooning from a deeply inhaled breath. Her body freezes in position, locked in the mindless euphoria of a clitoral orgasm. Suddenly, the air blasts from her lungs with a lengthy moan until she has nothing left inside. Her body crumples listlessly against the cushions, twitching and shaking as her eyes slowly open.

Mistress looks at my eyes, which shamelessly stare up into hers. "You can stop now, good girl." I lift my face, thoroughly pleased with myself. That was so exciting! I can't wait to do it again. "Stand up and let me untie you while your Master toys with your man," she says as she rises to her feet and helps me to mine. I want to look for the guys, to see what is happening.

She positions me so that I can see what Master is doing to Henry. He has my husband's hands bound behind his back and attached to a hanging rope, which is pulling them up, awkwardly. He is bent at a near ninety-degree angle and his feet are being forced apart with the aid of a spreader bar. It looks like an uncomfortable position for his shoulders, but he isn't fussing. The only sounds he's making are protesting grunts each time the heavy flogger comes down on his ass. His butt is a brilliant red, very likely matching the shade of mine.

Mistress circles me as she painstakingly unties each knot with her small fingers. She is a beautiful woman, especially now with her slightly flushed cheeks and glistening skin. Her eyes seem brighter as well. The gentleness she exudes at this moment has me wondering if the cruelness I know she is capable of, is simply a figment of my imagination and in no way a reality.

As soon as she circles behind me, I look over at my husband who now has my master's cock buried deep in his throat. I'm startled at how belittling this action looks, but then I'm awoken to the reality that he is extremely aroused. His penis is thick and rigid once again. A string of pre-cum dangles from the tip of his prick as it bobs between his legs.

Master pulls his prick from Henry's mouth just long enough for him to take in a few breaths. During this time, he swings the flogger with a stretched arm, cracking it down on Henry's glowing red ass cheeks. He jams his prick back into his mouth while he grips his hair firmly, holding his head in a position to best allow him to fuck his face, rapidly. When he yanks his dick from his mouth, he releases his hair. Henry lets his head hang while he catches his breath.

Mistress is almost finished freeing me. I wonder what she'll have me do now. I'd rather keep my attention on the men. Master applies clover clamps to Henry's nipples and then hangs weights to them, stretching his teeny nubs. They are going to be bruised tomorrow. The only way I can be sure they're hurting him is by his pained facial expressions. He is remaining silent, something his mistress must expect of him. Jake likes it when I scream.

Master pulls something metal and shiny from a drawer and fiddles with it as he approaches Henry's backside. He squats down and then reaches forward, grasping his testicles with his left hand.

I was so distracted that I hadn't noticed Mistress has bound my wrists together behind my back. She pushes me forward to make me walk, stopping me only a few feet from Henry. My wrists are being pulled up in the same fashion as my husband's until I am bent forward just as he is. She cautiously kicks my ankles to get me to spread my feet, allowing her to apply the ankle cuffs and spreader bar, so I will completely mirror my husband's position.

When Master stands, I can see that Henry's testicles are being stretched by a weighted metal ring that was affixed between them and his body. When Henry moves, it swings. To me, it looks painful, but he is licking his plump lips as low moans escape from between them.

Mistress slips one of her small fingers into my asshole and begins pulling and stretching it until it's open enough to allow a second and then a third. She gently pushes a cold and smooth ball against my rectum. It feels very large and heavy, much larger than what is comfortable, but once it's inside me, I quite enjoy its size and weight. I can't see what she's doing, but I can feel this object moving and tugging at my behind. Soon, it's pulling upward, forcing me to arch my back.

"You look sensational with a hook in your ass," she tells me just before applying clamps onto my nipples. Likely, they're the same ones from earlier. The fucking pain has me whining loudly and shaking my head in protest.

She slaps my ass. "Shut up."

I bite my lips between my teeth and try to absorb the pain instead of fighting against it. This seems to help, but I am not enjoying this, at all. The painful memory of them being removed has tears welling up in my eyes. That was so damn excruciating and I'm not looking forward to experiencing it, again.

Master has his cock buried down my husband's throat, again. Each time he humps forward, Henry's body moves, making his balls swing. His prick is huge and dripping a long string of pre-cum that is almost touching the floor.

Seeing my big, strong husband bound and at the mercy of a very dominant man, being manhandled in ways I would never have imagined him submitting to, is surreal. Will I ever get accustomed to watching Jake fuck his throat until his body lurches from gagging? I quite enjoy that Henry is excited by this, but I wonder if he had fantasies involving other men, and for how long. Why has he kept all of his urges hidden from me? Did he think I wouldn't accept them?

Master pulls his prick from his mouth and quickly walks toward me, taking my hair in his grasp and lifting my head. "Open your mouth."

I do as he instructs. Without hesitation, he pushes his prick deep into my throat and begins fucking my mouth. He humps me several times before allowing me the privilege of breathing.

Before I can get in two full breaths, he's pushing back in. A harsh gag lurches my body as my throat desperately tries to get him out. Instead, he holds still until I gag a second time. When he pulls out, a long line of gooey saliva follows.

I'm still gasping when he makes his way behind me, ramming his cock roughly into my drenched cunt. My breath stills in my lungs while my body compensates his size. The invasion is a welcomed one, but I wish he had entered me a bit slower. Without a moment's grace, he begins hammering into me, relentlessly. My breath is forced from my body in bursts. Oh yes! Fuck me hard! I can't get enough. He's holding my hips and pulling me back each time he slams forward, filling me to max capacity.

It doesn't take more than thirty seconds of this hard fucking before I'm coming so wildly that my legs are shaking, ready to quit on me. Master doesn't slow his pace until I've climaxed three times in a row. Why hasn't he punished me for coming without asking permission?

He pulls out of me and then reaches down to remove the clamps from my aching nipples. This time, it doesn't seem to pain me nearly as much as last time. Perhaps they've gone numb from all the abuse. When he squeezes them with his fingers, I quickly realize that they definitely are not numb. Pain shoots through my chest and straight to my pulsing cunt.

I peek up after Master walks away. Mistress is wearing a strap-on and fucking Henry's asshole—hard. He has a ball gag on with a trail of spit matching the pre-cum that's seeping from his swollen prick. He seems to be lost in his own body, an expression I have never seen on him, other than those few seconds during his orgasms. I will have to buy one of those and please him the way she is.

She is talking to him, saying degrading things that would make a person profoundly upset in any conventional situation. He is trying to reply to her questions, but the gag in his mouth is preventing a clear response. I know how he feels. She doesn't seem to pay it any attention, she's too focused on filling his ass with her fake cock.

Master gently removes the ball end of the hook from my rectum and then dribbles lube over my stretched hole. With much more care than he took with my pussy, he inserts his thick shaft into my butt. He's slowly gliding deeper and deeper into me until his pelvis is pressing against mine. He holds his position, allowing me a moment to adjust to his thickness.

My clitoris is twitching, aching to be touched. It's so swollen that I can feel it jiggle each time he humps me. My shoulders are in so much pain. I'm trying to arch my back to relieve some stress, but it's no use. Master is fucking my ass in a slow easy manner that is seductively redirecting my thoughts back to the pleasure zones on my body. Each time my clit bounces, it sends tiny arousing shock waves toward my bellybutton. *Please touch it*!

As if he were reading my thoughts, Master has compassion. He presses something cool against it. The moment he turns on the vibrator, my orgasm begins. Just before my body reaches peak climax where it can't be pulled back, he removes the vibrator. I scream and wildly buck my whole body, in protest. He is snickering behind me. Why is he punishing me?

He replaces the vibrator, increasing its speed. I remember to beg, "Please, please!"

His prick humps me, quicker. I'm almost there. Yes! Almost! He pulls the vibrator away again, halting the orgasm for the second time. He continues to fuck my ass, while thoroughly enjoying my protesting whimpers. He waits until I have quieted, when he knows I'm no longer teetering at the threshold of ecstasy. He replaces the vibrator. While he hammers me, the speed of the vibration is at its highest intensity. It only takes the count of five for me to be right back to the edge of the virtual orgasmic cliff I've been dangling over. If he withdraws again, I might mistakenly yell out the safe word.

Just when I think he's going to be generous, he proves me wrong, removing the wand for a third time. My clitoris feels like it's filled with molten lava and ready to erupt into a burning blaze.

"Fuck you! Fuck you! I fucking hate you! Asshole! Goddammit!" My screams fill the room as I battle against my bindings, with so much force that I fear I may injure my shoulders. I'm so full of rage right now that I don't feel the pain. He needs to know my level of frustration.

What angers me more is the humiliating and persistent laughter coming from Master and Mistress. I fight the need to call her a fucking cunt, something that a submissive should never direct at her dom. Although, I did just call Master an asshole. I'm surprised I didn't get punished for it. Perhaps he deems this as being enough punishment.

The vibrator is pressed to my painfully throbbing clitoris for the fourth time. I no longer want to get myself to the point of near climax, fearing he'll only torture me, yet again. I have no choice in the matter, my body is once again defying me. I writhe with a need for release. He taps the vibrator against me, not holding it steady. This is prolonging the build-up, slowing my ascent into euphoric bliss.

Mistress pushes her fingers into my drenched, eager pussy. It isn't more than a few seconds before she has me filled completely and she's twisting. I think her entire tiny hand is inside of me. The thought is so erotic.

The both of them fuck me at different paces. Master is fucking me quickly, while Mistress spins side to side, gently fucking me. He must have given her control over the vibrator because both of his big hands are hanging onto the rope attached to my waist, using it to help balance and give him better leverage to pound into me, relentlessly.

That's it, I'm over the top. My orgasm is holding at the apex of its climax, not releasing me from the delirium of this ecstasy. My mind and body are held captive in the exhilaration of the highest reward. I am floating in a sea of bliss, as they ravish my body. Nothing, and I mean nothing, can ever top this!

My mind slowly sinks back to reality. My body is void of penetration and vibration and I'm happy about that. I can't take any more. I am utterly spent.

Master is putting on a fresh condom. Is he going to fuck Henry's ass? He whispers something to my husband, who nods in response. He positions himself behind him and then eases his prick into Henry's tight butt. The moans coming from my husband escape him, effortlessly. Watching how slowly and sensually he is being penetrated is spellbindingly beautiful.

My wrists and ankles are released from their prisons by Mistress. She walks me on my shaking legs to the sofa and tells me to sit. From here, I have a perfect view of everything that's transpiring between the men. I can see the expressions on their faces. Both men are captivated by the pleasure their bodies are granting each other.

Mistress reaches her hand beneath Henry, taking his penis in her grasp. She strokes him slowly, squeezing his shaft as she does. Meanwhile, she releases the buckle holding the ball gag in his mouth and then removes it from behind his teeth. This leaves him free to moan in appreciation for the pleasure they are so graciously allowing him.

Master is speeding up the rhythm of his thrusting. Mistress jerks Henry's prick faster. Both men are grunting behind clenched teeth as their orgasms build to a near eruption. Henry's wail comes first as his climax comes to a head. Master roars from deep in his body, sounding like something primal and no longer human.

He yanks his cock from Henry's ass, tearing off the condom and gripping his throbbing shaft. He pounds his meat with incredible speed until his mouth opens wide and his head tilts back. Both men are at the peak of climax, jism spewing from their pricks in great volume, emptying their pleasure onto the floor. They seem to deflate as their muscles twitch, proving their gratification.

Mistress quickly unties Henry while he catches his breath and Master removes the metal testicular weight. Within minutes, Mistress and I are sitting on the sofa while the men are propped up on the table that she had Henry bound on.

"Mistress, thank you," I whisper.

"Beth, we aren't playing right now, so you can call me Jenna." She smiles at me and takes my hand in hers. "And, you're very welcome."

"This was better than I thought it would be. I had no idea that I would get excited by going down on a woman. It's very sensual," I confess.

"It can be, for sure. I'm happy that you enjoyed yourself. You have a natural talent. Most women are remarkably good at cunnilingus because they know what feels good to them."

"Ladies, should we shower quickly and then head upstairs for a drink?" Jake asks.

We all stand and make our way to the bathroom. Jake takes me in the shower and lets me get wet first. As I'm soaping, he's wetting his body. I rinse while he soaps. After I rinse, I step out while he stands under the water. As he steps out, Henry and Jenna step in.

Jake and I are dressed and upstairs before the other two are even out of the shower. We pour some more drinks and take them onto the patio. We sit opposite one another and sip our beverages.

"Did you enjoy yourself?" he asks, wearing a devilish grin.

"You are an asshole!" I say while chuckling. "Seriously, you are. If you had held me off once more, I would have called it quits."

"I know, that's why I let you cum. Tell me, did you cum hard?"

"You know I did," I reply with a sheepish grin.

"Then wasn't it worth it?" he asks. I nod while rolling my eyes defiantly. "So, how do you feel after seeing me fuck your husband's mouth and ass?"

I can feel my face flushing, which is absurd at this stage of events. "I quite liked it, I think. It's strange to watch the person you've always seen as being strong, powerful and..." the words aren't coming to me.

"Dominant in your marital relationship?" he suggests a suitable ending for my sentence.

"I suppose. It's just strange to see him being taken by another dominant person. At first, it took me by surprise to see how he allowed Jenna full control over him. I've never seen or thought of Henry as being weak."

"Allowing yourself to be dominated is quite the opposite of weakness, as you know. You have to be a very strong person to trust your welfare completely, to someone else. It's not easy to give yourself up like that. Besides the fact that a submissive has to endure so much punishment just to earn pleasure. To allow a dominant permission to do what they want to do takes a lot of strength."

"I suppose you're right."

"Did you enjoy seeing Henry under my reign?" he asks before sipping his drink.

I nod and reply, "Yes, I absolutely did. I watched your faces, which is very sexy, by the way. You were really enjoying each other. It was more than just fucking, at least, that's how I viewed it."

"Well, we are friends first," he assures me, tipping his glass in my direction, as a toast to their friendship.

When Jenna and Henry join us, we discuss the things we enjoyed, didn't care for and how we can improve for the next time.

Although the four of us do plan on playing together from time to time, we all agree that Jenna and Henry will still have their private rendezvous, as will Jake and I. Having solo playdates with just two people, a dominant and a submissive, as opposed to it always being the four of us together, makes what we do alone, feel so much more illicit. Henry only wants to be intimate with Jake when the four of us play and not alone, so we've set a rule that only a man and woman shall play together unless we are a foursome.

CHAPTER TWENTY-SIX

It's been nearly a year since Henry and I opened our lives to our new friends. Our friendship with them is strong and unbreakable. We do many interesting things as a group, other than having sex together. We've even taken a two-week vacation to Australia as two couples; Jake and I as one, and Jenna and Henry as the other.

Jake and Jenna started dating each other a few months ago. They seem to be a great match and have worked out their need for sexual dominance by taking it out on us, which we love. Alone with each other, they are neither submissive nor dominant.

We've never had friends like them before. Lou and Amy have always been our best friends, but they don't know us as intimately as Jake and Jenna do, and they never will. They understand the close bond we have with our sexual partners and have never shown an ounce of jealousy; curiosity definitely, but never jealousy. Even still, we do our best to spend an equal amount of time with Lou and Amy and Jake and Jenna.

Will this adventure ever end? Maybe, maybe not. Nobody knows the future, but as of right now, life is going quite well for all of us, and we're trying to live in each moment as best we can.

As for my writing, I have an extremely popular BDSM series based on our playtimes. I have claimed them to be fictional tales because nobody needs to know the truth. After all, I have an unending source for new material to use in my books. What can be better than that?

The End

About the Author

Pebbles Lacasse is a contemporary romance and erotica author. She leans toward writing bad boys desiring women who didn't know they have a kinky side. However, she's also known for her women with a dominant nature, and a secret yearning to be loved. Her books and short stories often take her readers into the BDSM lifestyle while revolving around real-life issues, and there's always a happy ending. The captivating stories of romance, love, and tender moments keep her readers coming back for more.

As someone living with Porphyria, Pebbles stays indoors to avoid UV light which gives her plenty of time to write. That's not to say she doesn't love "glamping," fishing, kayaking, and swimming, she just has to do it with protective clothing. If there's something she wants to do, she'll find a way to make it happen.

Pebbles is very family oriented. She and her husband of 30+ years raised their children in southern Ontario where she was born, and remains to this day. A 150+ lbs Mastiff takes up a lot of room in their home and in their hearts. His best friends are the two rescue cats that think they rule the home. The chickens couldn't care less about the dog until he chases them when they come too close to his outdoor toys.

Discover more about Pebbles on her website
https://www.pebbleslacasse.com

Keep swiping for more books you may enjoy!

You May Also Enjoy:

Full Novel Series

The Complete My JoeSmith Collection contains:
My JoeSmith: Anonymity, Book One
My JoeSmith: Anonymity, Book Two
My JoeSmith: Nurture, Book Three
My JoeSmith: Unity, Book Four

The Coaching Rayna Boxed Set contains:
Coaching Rayna, Book One
Coaching Rayna: Bound Hearts, Book Two

The Naughty Goldie Series contains:
Goldilocks & The Three Bear Brothers, Book One
Goldilocks & The Three Bear Brothers: Trifecta, Book Two
Goldilocks & The Three Bear Brothers: Overture, Book Three
Goldilocks & The Three Bear Brothers: Liberated, Book Four

Full Novel Standalones

My Wife and Master Jake
Broken Charm

Short Stories

Little Miss Muffet
Hello Officer
Mistress Rabbit
A Run with Charley
Carter's Mistress
Still Waters Burn Deep
Dominatrix for Hire

Anthologies

Quarantined: A Boxed Set of Pandemic Proportions – Still Waters Burn Deep

To read teasers and see book cover photoshoot photos by Pebbles, visit
https://www.PebblesLacasse.com

Connect with Pebbles

Facebook
https://www.facebook.com/PebblesLacasseEroticRomanceWriter/

Facebook Group
www.facebook.com/groups/pebbleslacasseandfriendsgroup/

Newsletter sign-up
https://BookHip.com/BQLKDCM

Website
https://www.pebbleslacasse.com

Instagram
https://www.instagram.com/pebbleslacasse/

Twitter
https://twitter.com/pebbleslacasse

Goodreads
http://bit.ly/Goodreads_2y5xJji

Bookbub
https://www.bookbub.com/profile/pebbles-lacasse

Youtube
https://www.youtube.com/channel/UC3Jb8ofSw0m3TFn4cMWu5dw

Subscribe

Sign up to receive Pebbles Lacasse's newsletter and receive a free short story to welcome you. Be among the first to read teasers from the books she's writing, learn what Pebbles does to keep her busy when she isn't writing her steamy novels, discover the captivating authors she's reading, be led to books with similar genres grouped together just for readers like you, and other crazy antics.

https://bookhip.com/VVNPMJP

Join Pebbles' Team

Would you like to be a valued member of my ARC team? Advanced Readers receive copies of my soon-to-be published novels to read with the promise to leave reviews by the date set by Pebbles.

You'll get my books for FREE forever as long as you leave reviews! Sound like a good deal?

https://forms.gle/gseo39XRubENVWjA9

www.ingramcontent.com/pod-product-compliance
Lightning Source LLC
Chambersburg PA
CBHW031943010726
47493CB00007B/2058